This book is a work of fiction. Names, characters, businesses, organizations, places, events and incidents are either a product of the author's imagination or are used fictitiously. Any resemblance to actual persons, living or dead, or locales is entirely coincidental.

Published by Griffyn Ink

www.griffynink.com

For ordering information or special discounts for bulk purchases, please contact Griffyn Ink at Mail@GriffynInk.com.

TOUCH OF MAGIC | BOOK ONE

WISHCRAFT

SAVANNAH KADE

CHAPTER 1

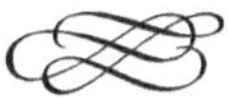

The olive told Delilah *no*. It went counterclockwise, and that clearly meant *no*.

Tonight, the olive had turned down every single man she had asked about. Maybe Gin's was serving her past-their-expiration-date olives in their martinis.

Surely someone in this crowd was suitable, but the olive wasn't telling. Delilah ate the little green liar and signaled the bartender for another drink. Her third. At this rate she was merely going to get drunk, by herself, and have to walk home all alone. Because the olives kept saying *no*.

Short, buffed nails graced the ends of the long fingers she used to push her empty martini glass to the back of the bar. She grabbed the new drink by the stem and gave it a swirl. In her mind she could see the man coming up behind her at the bar. Good-looking and full of himself—if the way he walked was any indicator—he was perfect for her.

The toothpick and olive swirled counterclockwise again.

Delilah sighed.

His elbow entered her field of vision as he leaned against the bar next to her. "Can I get you another martini?"

Yes, he was definitely full of himself. He was about as subtle as a dog scenting for a female in heat. But she wasn't his girl.

Well, maybe.

Delilah gave him one more chance and gently shook the stem of the martini glass again. The liquid almost sloshed out, telling her she wasn't as gentle or as sober as she thought.

The olive went counterclockwise again.

"No, thank you." She sighed even as she spoke it. "I don't need another martini." *I need a man who can make my olive go the other direction.* She let her chin find her palm and she sat, propped up and discouraged, ignoring him until he took the hint.

He didn't.

"Maybe you need something else . . ." He let the words and the innuendo trail off.

"No. Thank you." Delilah may have wanted to go home with someone tonight, but she had learned a long time ago not to argue with the answers. People, even witches, could ask whatever they wanted, but you really had to take the answers you got. The universe was always right—even when the messenger was an ornery, little, pimento-stuffed, pickled fruit.

She sipped at the martini, but still Mr. I'm-your-dream didn't leave. "I know I can make you scream."

She closed her eyes and fought the urge to show him right there in the bar that, yes, he could make her scream. But not the way he wanted. Big, bad trouble always happened when you went against the powers that be.

Instead of screaming, she sighed again. He wasn't just full of himself, he was a total ass. Already the olive had been proven correct. He was a definite *no*. What had she been thinking? So she said it again. "No, thank you."

"I'm extra nice to blondes." He leaned even closer, his mouth quirking at the corner as though the two of them shared a secret.

Delilah fought the urge to yank a hair from his head right there at the bar and show all the drunk patrons exactly what she could do. But casting spells in public was a bad idea. And casting while drinking was a *really* bad idea.

Before she could form words to express her revulsion, he reached up for her hair, trailing his fingers through the curls she'd liked so much just a few hours ago.

"Don't touch me." Her voice was low, and she was mad enough to work a little mojo into the glare she gave him. Delilah did not want him to have a piece of her. She had already given him her time and her voice, and they were far more than he deserved. She knew what could be accomplished with a single strand of hair even if this idiot didn't. She wasn't about to let him get one, so she added a little red into her eyes and some depth into her voice, and made certain that only he could see and hear it. She repeated her words. "Don't. Touch. Me."

His eyes widened and his brain was clearly fighting for comprehension through the mild beer haze he was in. At least no one would believe him if he told anyone what he saw. Finally, he backed off.

Delilah breathed out her relief. Seriously, the night had been a bust. No men. Not a single one had made it past the olive. Usually, her internal radar was in much better alignment with the universe. She could spot a liar across the room. Almost as though he had it tattooed across his forehead. She'd warned more than one friend away from a bad egg, and avoided becoming the topic of gossip or the paramour of an ass herself when men weren't as honest as her instinct. It was simply that she'd been sure tonight was a good night to go out. Something had told her to just come here. To walk the four blocks to the bar, even though she was by herself. Even though she had to be at work at three a.m.

Her instinct told her to be here. It was supposed to be good. So why was she here with Mr. I'm-so-hot coming back again?

He slipped in next to her barstool and seemed to get comfortable. This was going to be bad.

"Are you a lesbian?"

Her mouth fell open. Delilah only managed a squeak instead of a comeback. Was he going to offer to let everyone know that she wasn't if she would sleep with him? She hadn't heard that one since high school.

She was about to tell him just that, when a masculine hand fell on his shoulder and a voice came from the other side of Mr. Slick.

"If you don't leave the lady alone, she might have to become a lesbian out of self-defense."

She must have been tipsier than she thought, because she had to start laughing at that.

The voice was soothing and determined at the same time. "Richard, really, you must leave this kind woman alone. I would never have ordered that last round if I had known it would come to this. Now, back to the table."

With that, Mr. Hot-and-bothersome was gone.

And so was the man attached to the voice.

Bummer.

Well, she hadn't seen him anyway. Who knew what he was?

She decided to sip at the martini, and maybe enjoy half of what she had paid for. Delilah took a few deep breaths between each taste and rubbed her finger in a small circle on the bar as she did it. The sobering spell was an old one, and she'd practiced it enough this last year that she could perform it accurately even when drunk.

She was taking her last sip when the voice came again to her right. "Three more drafts, please." She recognized the hand as well when he held up three fingers to be sure the bartender had understood above the cacophony that was the usual music in Gin's.

Her mouth got ahead of her brain, and she spoke before she

even looked at him. "It's bad enough that you're friends with him. You're giving him more beer?"

"He's not a friend. Just a buyer that didn't pan out." He turned to look at her, green eyes making contact with her own, and she read the sincerity there. She also read the straight nose, full mouth, and molasses hair that was cut just long enough to bear a full curl. His voice brought her wayward thoughts of him back around. "And yet, here I am buying him the beer. I'm really sorry about him. I regret unleashing him on a bar that I used to be welcome in."

She laughed a little at that, then reached for her martini as he turned back to the bartender.

Delilah blinked.

She didn't remember bumping her glass. But she must have.

The olive was swishing in the half-drunk liquid.

Clockwise.

Before Mr. Green-eyes could reach for the mugs of draft in front of him, she stuck out her hand. "I'm Delilah."

The lush smile banked by a pair of dimples hit her full in the gut. "Brandon." His fingers curled warm around her own, just the right amount of pressure, his palm slipping flush against hers.

Delilah pulled her hand back at the small sizzle that hit her with the touch. She usually avoided palm-to-palm contact as it tended to let her see and know things she was better off not knowing. But the handshake was intended to set the evening off as less formal, almost like a business agreement.

In the moment it took her to register what she had learned from the contact—he was unattached, just looking for a good time, he worked with something involving computers, and loved grapes—his attention turned back to the bartender. He slid bills across the smooth wood and grabbed the handles of the three frosty mugs. "It was great to meet you . . . Delilah."

With that, Mr. Clockwise-olive disappeared.

She wanted to scream. How much more frustrating could this night get? Maybe aliens could abduct her right from the barstool. Or a llama could appear and spit on her. There just weren't that many ways for this night to get worse.

She figured she'd polish off the martini because it clearly didn't matter if she was drunk or sober. She lived only a few short blocks from Gin's, and it wasn't like anyone was going to take advantage of her anyway.

Delilah held the toothpick with the lone olive out of the way while she drained the glass. Then she fixed her gaze on the last of the green liars and gave it a good stare down before she popped it into her mouth and chewed it to a pulp so it could never give another bad answer again.

Funny, it tasted just like any other olive.

It was so rare for a night to go awry like this that she just got horribly frustrated when it did. Usually there was a man. One who just wanted to get laid. One who would happily go away in the morning. But tonight was not going to be her night. Now it was late and she had to get some sleep, because she did have to get to work at three a.m.

Placing both her hands flat on the bar, Delilah gave up. She pushed away and turned to leave, not reacting fast enough to avoid the green button front shirt that was apparently hiding a granite sculpture behind it.

"Umph." The sound she involuntarily made was muffled against the fabric and her nose started that low throb of anger at being banged.

One hand grabbed her arm to steady her and, before she could look up to see who she had literally run into, she recognized the voice. "I'm so sorry. And I was coming over here to apologize for releasing Richard on you."

Her fingers found her nose and quickly she made the pain disappear. "Really I'm fine, and that was my fault. I had a little more than I intended."

With the haze of pain having vanished, she could see him looking at her, searching her face. "Were you leaving?"

Okay, maybe the night wasn't going to be such a bust after all.

Before she could respond, he spoke again. "Because I just left my partner back at the table with Richard so I could come . . . beg forgiveness from you."

Her mouth spoke without warning, nice and loud over the din in the bar. "Are you gay?"

He frowned. "No. Are you?"

"No." Delilah shook her head. How had it all gotten so tangled up? It had made total sense when she thought it in her brain. She pointed back to the other man sitting in the booth with Richard-the-far-too-brave. "You called him your 'partner'."

Brandon laughed out loud. Even teeth showed through the wide grin, and his eyes crinkled above cut cheekbones. It was a good thing he wasn't gay.

Within a moment, he led her to a table that had miraculously cleared out. Delilah blinked. She hadn't done that. *Had he?* But she found herself seated and ordering a soda and watching his eyes while he spoke. "Dan is my business partner. And Richard spent the day taking up a lot of our time only to back out on the deal at the last minute."

Maybe that sobering spell hadn't quite done the trick. Her brain twisted itself up at that. "So you took him out and bought him beer? Did you think he'd sign on if he was drunk?"

"No." Brandon drained the beer that had been in his hand and ordered a soda from a passing waitress. "He's a lot better at talking people into things when he's sober. And he does know a lot of people who might like to get on board. So we thought we could use his contacts. We'll see."

Delilah nodded. On the one hand, she didn't need all the chit-chat. On the other hand, she didn't want to alienate the only man that the universe deemed suitable tonight. "So what do you do?"

"We build video games."

She had absolutely no way to respond to that. She didn't think she'd ever thought about what went into a video game. Didn't own any. Couldn't remember the last time she'd even played one. So she smiled, and shook her head. "I can hardly hear what you're saying. But I live four blocks up. Do you want to go?"

A few minutes later they were out the door, the night air just a little chilly against her skin. It had been hotter than Hades when she'd walked down, so she hadn't brought a jacket.

"Are you cold?" Brandon watched her rub at her arms as she started down Hollywood Boulevard. People passed by on either side of them, not really observing any kind of traffic pattern.

"It was warmer when I came in." She shrugged. But he was out of his button-down shirt before she really even managed a protest. The move revealed a t-shirt underneath that looked expensive, soft, and slightly frayed as he draped the green cotton shirt around her shoulders.

Delilah grabbed at it to pull it closer. As she did, her palms brushed against the material and she felt the lingering traces of information he'd left on it: he didn't wear it very often. She should have finished the sobering spell before she left the bar. She shouldn't have shot the last of that martini. Because the universe was always right. So here she was, catching images that she usually avoided.

"Up here." She pointed up Poinsettia Street and made the turn. In a block they were beyond the buildings and the businesses that made up the main drag. Condos and apartment complexes marched up the Hollywood Hills, crowding each other for space and straining to see over the adjacent rooftops.

As the two of them climbed the steep sidewalk, Brandon turned, commenting that he thought he might be able to see his own roof from her place. Delilah smiled and nodded politely, but didn't care. She wouldn't be going to his place, so she didn't need to know where it was.

Inside her building, she fitted her key into the lock and pushed the door open.

He frowned down at her hand. "You really should do the deadbolt, too, you know. You should lock up better than that."

She fought the urge to laugh. Just because there was only one lock on the door didn't mean the place wasn't protected. Instead, she grabbed the front of his t-shirt in her fist and invited him in by tugging on the fabric.

He didn't need a second nudge and his mouth descended on hers, blocking out all thoughts of locks and bolts.

Delilah disengaged long enough to shed his shirt from her shoulders and leave it on the floor in the entryway before taking his hand and leading him down the hall to her bedroom.

Because this was the only way she got involved these days, and because it only happened when she let it, she was prepared. When Mr. Green-eyes peeled his t-shirt, she was waiting with a condom she had pulled from her bedside drawer.

Quickly, they stripped away their clothes and the bedcovers. Delilah was only a little surprised that he fought her for dominance. She should have been a little more firm about how it was going to go. But later, lying there, sated, she realized she hadn't thought that far ahead.

Brandon stood, naked, and looked down at the woman dozing on the fine cotton sheets. Her fingers curled in against her palms and her hands were pulled in next to her body. She looked peaceful and docile and nothing like the hellcat who'd just wrung him out.

Wandering down her hallway, he touched his head. He still felt drunk, although the physical activity he'd just completed should have sobered him right up. Also, he'd only had beer, and not that many of them, at the bar earlier. It seemed much longer than . . . two hours? since she'd offered to bring him back here.

Brandon glanced down at his watch, the only item of clothing that he still had on after that crazy round of sex. He searched the fridge, finding a glass and a pitcher of cold water. The chill hit him as he drank it while making his way back over the soft carpet to her bedroom. For a brief moment he wondered if she had a roommate or someone he should worry about while he was walking naked through her apartment. But he dismissed the thought as quickly as it came.

A strange light flickered in the doorway of her bedroom, and that combined with the cold water brought him fully alert. As he stepped into the opening, he was surprised to find her awake. She was sitting, facing away from him, on the side of the bed. Moreover, he was relieved that the odd light was nothing more than the glow of a candle she was lighting.

Her blonde hair was almost platinum in the amber glow, and it brushed the middle of her back in loose curls that had previously been near-perfect ringlets. Now it was a near-perfect mess, and knowing that he was the one who'd messed it was sexy as hell.

She turned to smile at him, pink lips reminding him what she'd done and where she'd done it. Her eyes were liquid and fathoms deep in the candlelight. She picked up a sprig of something and held it into the flame. Soft, gray smoke curled upward and disappeared.

Brandon didn't think anything of it until the awful smell hit him. His nose wrinkled against his will and without thought he dove across the sheets toward her. "Don't please. I'm . . . allergic to a lot of incense."

That wasn't true at all. But that stuff *stank*.

He grabbed it from her hand and blew out the glowing ends

on the small blooms, sloshing a little of his water on the sheets as he did.

He figured he should apologize, but now that he was lying across the bed he felt the turning sensation in his brain again—like he was drunk. He closed his eyes and the world felt like a boat rocking beneath him. For a moment, he wondered if he'd been slipped something more powerful than alcohol at the bar. He'd thought only women really had to worry about that. He was getting ready to ask her if she'd noticed anything, when he realized he couldn't remember her name.

She was leaning over him, reaching for the half-ashed stem in his fingers. She took it away and asked him what it was that he wanted.

But that was a stupid question. She had just leaned over him, naked, making him forget all about her stinky incense. The world had stopped spinning as the ends of those mussed curls tickled across his bare chest. The sheets were still tangled from the best no-holds-barred sex he could remember. And she asked him what he wanted.

So he reached out for her soft skin and showed her.

Delilah gazed at the man beside her, watching his chest rise and fall in rapid waves, much like her own was doing. She let out a breath.

The universe was right. Tonight had been her night. The olives had not deserved the way she'd cursed them.

It was midnight. Perfect timing. If she got him out of here and then passed out within twenty minutes, she could catch a neat two hours of sleep before she had to get up to go to work.

As her breathing and his slowed to a more normal rate, she moved into action. Delilah kissed her fingertips, imbuing her touch with an extra nudge, leading him to agree with her.

"Thank you. That was fantastic." She caressed his upper arm with a sweet stroke, intending him to absorb both the compliment and the suggestion a little more deeply. "But I need to get some sleep now. I have to get to work at three."

He rolled to look at her, his eyes showing that he'd been affected by the simple magick. He smiled. "I should get some sleep, too."

However, instead of standing, he reached for the covers, pulling them all the way up and over both of them before she could get her bearings. She tried again.

"No," She kept her voice soft but steady and firm, "I need to sleep alone. You should go."

His laugh rumbled low in his bare chest; he was still not agreeing. "You don't need to sleep alone, and I'm too tired to move." His arm came up and around her, pulling her closer and alarming her more.

Surely he wasn't immune to her magick.

That would mean that he was stronger than her. She would have sensed that right from the start.

Again she pushed a little extra power into her touch and shoved against his chest, still barely budging him. "I have to go to work at three. That's just a few hours."

Delilah hadn't even added a kick to her words. She was a little panicked by his nonchalance, which was enough to make her forget the magick that should be second nature. She was functioning on pure logic.

Unfortunately, logic didn't work on him either.

"You shouldn't have invited me home if you have to work that early. The room is spinning like I'm drunk, so I can't drive. And I don't think you really go to work in a few hours anyway. Who starts work at three a.m.?"

He snuggled in a little deeper under the white fluffy comforter and let his eyelids drift shut.

Fine, if he wanted to sleep, he could just sleep through the forgetting.

As his face relaxed, Delilah rolled herself up to sit on the side of the bed, relaxing now that she had a Plan B. With a deep breath to re-focus herself, she lit the white beeswax candle again and pulled out a fresh stick of lavender, lighting the tips of the small white blossoms.

She woke him to hand him the smoking sprig figuring she would just push him out the door while he forgot.

But he didn't go.

Brandon sat up, coming awake with the burning lavender in his fingers. He frowned at it, crinkled his nose and blew it out. "That smells bad. Stop doing that."

He handed her back the burnt blossoms and rolled over, tucking the covers under his chin.

What was wrong with him?

Delilah sniffed the lavender for herself. It didn't stink. It wasn't beautiful, but it didn't produce a smell worthy of the faces he made.

She was startled from her wonderings of what the hell she might have done wrong by a soft snore.

The damn man was out like a light.

She should never have indulged in that second round with him. She'd worn him out and now what was she going to do?

Her shoulders slumped. She could burn the lavender and cast the spell on him. He'd forget about her and what they'd done. But he'd still be in her bed, so that was just fruitless.

After nudging and shaking him more times than she could count, Delilah gave up.

Fine, he'd believe she had to be at work at three a.m. when she woke his sleepy ass up at two fifteen.

CHAPTER 2

The harsh, incessant beeping of the alarm woke her just like it did every night she worked.

This time it also woke the sleeping man beside her. Which never happened.

He groaned and held his head. Then moaned, "Turn that off."

"I have to go to work." Delilah gave him a good shove, pleased to see that she had finally roused him. It hadn't even taken any magick, just a nasty sounding alarm.

"Seriously?"

She sighed back at him as she stood up. "Yes. I told you that. Now get your ass out of bed and get dressed."

He didn't.

By now that didn't surprise her. She had a plan now; she could work around it. He sat there, the covers pooling at his waist, looking like just the thing she'd had in mind when she'd blown some of her hard earned money on the very expensive sheets. She simply hadn't planned on him still being here in her sheets afterward.

"Just what kind of work do you do at three a.m.?"

He was trying to catch her in a lie, but she wasn't lying. Still she wasn't quite up to the whole story. "It doesn't matter."

"Sure it does." He sat there, making no moves to get out of her bed, her apartment, her life. "I don't owe money, do I?"

All she could do was gasp an outraged *"ah!"* in response to that. His raised eyebrows and the grin that signaled the start of a laugh only made her more upset.

This time she went for Plan C. It made little difference what she told him. Once she got his hand around that lavender long enough to say the word, he wouldn't remember any of this. "I'm a pastry chef."

"At three in the morning?"

"I'm done by eleven when the restaurant opens." She opened her closet to reveal a row of black and white checked chef pants beside pressed white jackets. Grabbing one of each, she started getting dressed. Let him watch. He'd already seen her naked. And he wouldn't remember it anyway.

But when she turned, Brandon was climbing into his own previously pressed pants and stretching his t-shirt over his head.

Excellent.

As he disappeared into the bathroom, she lit the candle for a third time.

He must have only ducked in to wash his face or something, because he never closed the door and he was out before she had the first blossom burned.

"Oh God, please. Not the incense again." His handsome face twisted at the smell and his hands came up in front of him as though he could ward off the smoke. "Burn something else, I beg you."

Crap.

There was no way she was going to be able to hand this man a sprig of burning lavender. Not that he'd remember later, but if she couldn't get it into his hands now . . .

"Then go into the living room. I want to burn it."

"Fine." He made a face and shoved his hands in his pockets.

Delilah sat for a few minutes of her precious morning time and watched the lavender turn to smoky ash. Would it matter if he just went out the door now? He wouldn't forget, but he might go.

Or he might come back.

He just couldn't come back. She couldn't afford to see anyone. Maybe later when she was steadier on her feet, but not now. Not when she'd bungled the last time so badly. Not when she'd been so off her alignment earlier that night.

She caught the falling ashes on a tissue and carefully wrapped them before tucking them into the wide pocket of her pants. Best to be prepared.

Draping the chef jacket over one arm, she went out into the living room to find Brandon sitting there on the couch waiting for her. With a smile, she led him out of the apartment into the dark of night. Twice in the hallway and again in the elevator, she tried to slip the lavender ashes into his pocket. Since they'd accidentally left the bottle-green button down shirt where it had been kicked the night before, she was stuck trying to get the tissue into his pants pocket. Not an easy feat for someone with absolutely no sleight-of-hand skills.

He evaded each attempt without even realizing it. So when he tugged at the door handle on the passenger side of her car, Delilah didn't try to stop him. She'd slip the lavender to him—somehow—and let him off back at Gin's. He could drive himself home from there.

Unfortunately, having her hands on the wheel made it remarkably hard to stuff a tissue into his pocket. Especially when he was sitting on the only pockets he had. So she pulled up at Gin's having made no headway whatsoever. "Here you go."

She'd kiss him and stuff it into his back pocket under the pretense of feeling him up.

"Where are we?" He looked puzzled.

Oh dear Goddess. "We're at Gin's. Isn't your car here?"

Bad move. How was she going to sneak in a passionate, stuff-ashes-in-your-pocket kiss after that snotty remark?

"My car isn't here. I'll bet Dan drove it home." His hand went to his head and he grinned. "I swear I'm still drunk. Did you slip me something?"

Not in his drink.

Delilah sucked in a breath. Was he half-spelled? Had all the partially burned lavender she'd handed him had an effect?

She laughed as though, no, of course she hadn't done any such thing. Then topped it off by rolling her eyes at him for being so silly.

He grinned back, dimples emerging again as the humor spread across his face and into his eyes. "You know, you're gorgeous when you think I'm being ridiculous."

She faked a laugh again. This was not good. Somewhere too deep down to remember, her heart gave a small tug. Even though she knew for a fact that he was snookered on lavender smoke and he didn't mean a bit of it.

To combat the melting around her heart, Delilah put an extra edge to her words. "Can't you just call a cab?"

"Sure." Still he made no move to get out of her car.

Delilah waited. For her efforts she was rewarded with, "I'll call from your work. Can you feed me?"

"You have got to be kidding me!" She blew. That was it. He wanted to be fed?

All he had to do was hold the damn lavender while it burned. There wasn't even a flame! Every other guy had thought the lavender was cute, or sweet, or interesting, or *something,* and they'd each gone out the door saying goodnight until she'd told them to forget. She'd made certain that it worked. Every time, she watched out the window, seeing them wander out the front of the apartment onto the sidewalk and take a confused look around. After a moment, they seemed to get their bearings and they'd walk off with no memory of her. Why couldn't he?

Why couldn't he be serious? He could *not* come to work with her. Could *not.*

As he broke into her mental rant, his voice was melodious and low, as though he were telling a lover a secret. "You made me work up an appetite. And I want to see where you work. I've never seen a pastry chef cook before. I'll bet you're fantastic."

"I'll bet you're high!" She retorted.

He shrugged. "Sure sounds like it."

Her shoulders slumped. It was her fault he was high. Half cast spells were unpredictable and therefore dangerous. They weren't always merely half as effective. There were often weird side effects. Clearly, Brandon was getting firsthand experience of that now.

Delilah put the car in gear and thanked her stars that no one worked her shift with her. Of course, that was by design, but certainly not because she expected to be driving hot, hungry, half-spelled men into work with her. She couldn't unleash him on society like this—middle of the night, high, left alone in the heart of Hollywood. Who knew what he'd do?

She pulled up at the back entry to the restaurant without saying another word to him. She didn't need to talk to him, she had a whole bitch session going in her head. Stepping out of the car, she finally spoke two words. "Come on."

Like a puppy—make that a large, tipsy, male puppy—he followed her into the kitchen. Paying attention to him out of the corner of her eye, Delilah grabbed her old-fashioned time card that she secretly loved and punched in five minutes before three. Deep night converged beyond the windows blocking all sense of the world outside the brushed steel walls.

Brandon watched as she slipped her arms into the chef's jacket and buttoned the white cord frogs across the front. She pulled her hair clip from her pocket, only briefly noting that she'd tucked the red one there before hanging it in her closet.

He tilted his head. "Very fifties."

She smiled and slipped her ponytail into the matching hair net sewn into the huge red bow. "It was either this or those nylon things. I love to cook, and I like my hair long."

His eyes hinted that he was interested in more. And maybe that his brain still wasn't quite screwed in straight. "It's kinda sexy."

No, it was the only non-cafeteria-lady way around something that was necessary. But he took that thought out of her head as he braced his hands on the counter behind him and prepared to hop up.

"Don't!" She reached out to pull him away.

Startled, he let her.

He was probably a smart man. He'd seemed so before she'd messed with his head. It was all her fault that his decision making skills were shot. She explained. "You can't put your butt on the counter, I cook people's food there."

It was time to end this. She pulled the tissue with the ashes from her pocket, then frowned. He was a little loopy, not stupid. He wouldn't just take the ashes from her. He'd want to know what it was. While she was strong enough to nudge him, only the very best could make a creature act against its nature. Jules had been able to, but not Delilah. There was no way she could completely override his strong dislike of the stuff.

When she looked up, he was gone.

Her breath sucked in and her heart fluttered with panic. Her soon-to-be-ex lover was a little drunk and now lost at her job.

But he reappeared from the office with her boss's chair, which he promptly plopped into the open space beside her and then he plopped his sweet ass into it. His eyes twinkled and he grinned the same grin that had made her take him home in the first place. "So, what do you do first?"

She sighed. First, she thought, I solve all my problems. On to Plan D.

There was a note that the pile of small pumpkins in the corner was overstock from a cancelled wedding. The groom had left with his old flame and the restaurant was left with an overabundance of shrimp, asparagus, halibut, dark chocolate, and pumpkins.

While she couldn't go back and convince the bride that getting married was a bad idea, she could solve the pumpkins and chocolate problem, that was for sure. Turning to Brandon, she motioned with her fingers. "If you want to eat, wash your hands. You'll have to earn it."

"I thought I already did." He protested, but his body belied his words, already eagerly getting to his feet.

Delilah thought better of handing him a large knife. She didn't think he should be wielding it, especially if he ever realized she was to blame for the fact that the room was still spinning around him just a little. So she gave him a big metal spoon instead.

She capped the first pumpkin and set Brandon to scraping the insides clean and washing out the seeds. She chopped large cubes of the orange squash and had him feed them into the industrial strength food processor. When the pumpkin was thoroughly pulverized, Delilah picked up a tongue depressor from a steel canister and tasted it before expertly tossing the taster stick into the trash.

Handing him a new large spoon, she told him to move the mixture into a steel bowl and laughed when he mimicked her motions, picking up a wooden stick and licking off the orange mash. He made the worst face. "That doesn't taste right. Isn't it supposed to be sweeter?"

"No, silly, it's squash. We have to add sugar and cream and spices."

Together they poured in huge quantities of vanilla, molasses, brown sugar and sorghum honey. She had him grate nutmeg into the mix, which he agreed to only after he had examined the acorn-looking nuts thoroughly. Most people had never seen nutmeg except as a pulverized powder from a can, and Mr. Video-games was no exception.

When the batter was ready, she began ladling it into individual ceramic baking dishes and popping them into the oven. Brandon, with nothing to keep him busy, placed his hands on either side of his hips, where he leaned against the counter. Something about the way he stood there, the way he commanded the space around him, made her wish she had another night with him. But wasn't that the whole point? She couldn't handle another night. Certainly not with a man who'd had his tongue loosened and yet was still polite and sweet and occasionally shooting her those wicked grins.

Delilah had no idea how the half-spell would change his normal behavior, but she did know that she hadn't done anything strong enough to make him cluck like a chicken or do anything he wouldn't normally do. She couldn't make a complete ass into Prince Charming. Aside from being a little pushy, he was fun and funny and sweet and a little silly. There was no way she'd survive another night without getting attached, and she knew from experience that would be bad. So she had to get him out of here. Even if she was having fun.

She reminded herself that she'd likely be fired if she were caught.

Turning, she gave him a new set of instructions. "Get down that big pot, and pull out that bin of sugar."

Like a kid, he eagerly went about each task. Even when she taught him to weigh the sugar, he did the work carefully. She made him do it in small batches, keeping him busy measuring and dumping it into the pot.

It didn't matter how much sugar was in the pot at all. Only that he didn't see as she added a little extra honey and the lavender ashes to the last dish of pumpkin. She pushed it to the front corner of the oven before shutting the door.

She then wet the sugar in the pot and had him stir it while it heated into goo. When it hit thread stage she pulled the pot off the flame and attempted to teach him how to make doodads.

"What?" He leaned a little too close for her sanity and she tried to take a step back.

"Doodads. Those crispy sugar-art things that come on your dessert." She couldn't help it. She wound up grinning. Then laughing full out, when he was forced to eat the vast majority of the designs he had poured simply to hide the evidence. He shoved three of them in her mouth after she insulted their looks.

She smelled the pumpkin cakes hitting their peak and pulled them from the oven, showing him how they had each risen to the point just before the surface cracked, then slapped at his hand as he made a motion to grab one. "We aren't done."

She made him watch while she whisked eggs and cooked heavy cream into pastry custard. She added a shot of Kahlua and handed him a taster stick. When it hit his tongue, he moaned, much as he had only five hours before. She tried to ignore his look of ecstasy as his green eyes rolled back before he tossed the stick into the trash and reached for another.

Delilah made him hold the pastry bag while she filled it. She fitted it with a needle-like tip and amazed him as she injected the cream into the center of each cake, taking advantage of the holes that had formed while it baked. At last she handed him the needle to hold, and he made her laugh again as he mimicked injecting the cream directly into his veins. She formed her hands around his, showing him how to inject the cream. She let him do two of the cakes, one of which was his with the lavender baked in.

She whipped fresh cream and piped it on top of one of the cakes, grating more nutmeg shavings across the top and sticking a doodad in to finish it off. Carefully she added two apple shavings and three raspberries to a plate and set the whole concoction on a pedestal that she then covered with a glass dome.

"Noooo!" Brandon wailed. "It's for display?"

He drooled at the pretty little cake behind the glass, and Delilah couldn't help the chuckle that surfaced. "That one is so the staff knows how to present it. They add all the whipped cream and garnish when it's ordered." She used a black china marker on the glass dome to label the parts.

Still Brandon looked bereft. Good.

She smiled at him, even though it made her feel a little hollow inside. Maybe he didn't deserve this, but she was committed.

Here goes nothing. "You want one?"

"You have to ask?"

So she made two, hers and the lavender cake. She dolled them up with toppings and added the last survivors of his mutant doodad collection. Then she handed him a spoon.

While she carefully ate her cake and licked whipped cream off the spoon, she watched as he savored each bite. If he tasted the lavender, then he didn't realize it wasn't supposed to be there. Baked in, with all that sugar like it was, he probably couldn't tell. Which was just as good.

He ate each last bite, before he looked out the window to see the sun start to lighten the sky. Then he cocked his head at her as though he wanted to ask a question but it had slipped his mind.

"Come on." She took his hand and led him out the back door. Pressing a quick kiss to his lips, she whispered *"forget"*.

CHAPTER 3

Light streamed in through the windows at an odd angle, startling him from a very deep sleep. His head was muzzy and his vision was strangely sideways. Odd noises, like digital bird sounds, flitted beyond the edge of his grasp. It took a few moments to gather the off-kilter sensations together into a full picture.

Brandon realized he was lying on his couch—poorly. One leg hung off the side, and his head was resting on the arm, his neck at an odd and painful angle. He was still in yesterday's clothes. He didn't remember yesterday ending, only that he and Dan had taken the very smooth-talking Richard Cain out for beers.

So it had to be the next day.

Something about the light still bothered him, until he looked over his shoulder to the microwave display in his kitchen, one of the few clocks he had in his house. 12:14.

Holy Crap! He sprung up. It was noon. That explained why the light was so bright. Why the angle seemed so odd. It was hours past when he should have been up. Past when he should have been at work.

The chirping sound called his attention back to the sleek black and silver state-of-the-art phone. Caller ID showed it was his partner calling—probably wondering where the hell he was. Pushing the 'talk' button, Brandon sank down on the sofa in a seated position—the way the makers had intended it to be used.

"Hi, Dan." He croaked from beneath the hand he was rubbing across his face. He could hear the sounds of the office in the background.

Dan just laughed. "I didn't expect you to be in early, but seriously, bud, we have to head out of here in an hour. I called twice already and was about to come peel your sorry ass off the floor."

Brandon groaned. "You waited until noon?"

Another laugh came across the line. "Well, you left with that blonde last night. I figured you might need a while to recuperate."

"*Hmph*. Try 'resuscitate'." His throat felt like he'd swallowed his t-shirt. Dirty.

"That good?" No chuckle this time.

Brandon groaned soul-deep in his chest. "I wouldn't know. I don't remember any of it."

"Really?" There was no more laughter from Dan. That alone told Brandon that the situation was possibly more serious than he'd thought.

He took stock and started talking. "I don't feel hung-over. Not like I did when I drank too much in college. No headache, no upset stomach. But I'm not right."

Dan's voice was suddenly louder and the background noise disappeared—he'd taken off the speaker phone. "And you don't remember? I mean, she was hot, and she walked you right out of that bar."

Brandon searched the corners of his brain. He remembered telling Richard to back off from someone. He remembered going to the bar for more beer. "The three of us sat in a booth together. I ordered more beer . . . . After that, I'm pulling a blank."

"You're obviously at your place, since I called on the landline." Brandon could hear the thoughts churning through Dan's mind. "I'm guessing you would have noticed if your kidneys were missing."

That opened his eyes. Just for safe measure, and because he did feel odd, Brandon checked. Then breathed a little easier. "No, I didn't wake up in a tub of ice."

"Did you check your wallet?"

"Crap!"

Brandon dropped the phone to the wood floor for once not caring if he marred it. He'd been had. He knew it.

But his fingers found his wallet in his back pocket. Quickly he thumbed through it—his driver's license and credit cards were exactly where they were supposed to be. With a sigh, he scooped the phone off the floor. "It's all here."

"All of it?"

For the next five minutes he and Dan discussed the contents of his wallet and decided that he had to call all his cards and make sure she hadn't copied the numbers and used them over the phone or something. He didn't carry his social security card in his wallet, thankfully.

Eventually, Dan sighed. "Is there anything else you can remember? Anything weird? Some clue?"

Brandon thought for a moment, then sniffed the air. "I smell pumpkin."

"You're shitting me."

"No. I smell pumpkin." He walked around the small house sniffing. First the kitchen, although he didn't—*couldn't*—cook so that wasn't really logical, then his bedroom. It took a few more tries before he found the source. "It's me. My clothes smell like pie."

Dan groaned. "Don't call your credit cards. You weren't robbed. You probably have a brain tumor."

Finally, Brandon found some humor in the situation. He replied in his best Arnold Schwarzenegger voice, "It's not a tumor."

Dan didn't laugh. "Look, you shouldn't drive. Just get dressed. I'll come get you for the meeting."

There was a click on the line as Dan hung up.

Gently setting the receiver back in the cradle, Brandon set about gathering all the cards and money he'd spilled from his wallet. The lingering scent of pumpkin pie followed him until he peeled his clothes and climbed into the shower.

CHAPTER 4

Delilah stripped the bed a little more furiously than necessary. She was tired as hell.

Well, duh, she thought, she'd hardly slept last night. And when she had, there'd been a man in her bed. It turned out that just having a warm male body beside her brought back all sorts of unhappy memories. During the day she recalled flashes of bad dreams she'd had the night before.

So, no bar prowling tonight. She arrived home just after eleven and decided it was time for a good night's sleep. Only, when she climbed under the covers, her eyes refused to close and her brain churned.

Still early in the day, the light was pouring in through the cracks around the blinds. Faint noises came from the apartment just on the other side of her wall. Scents of Brandon and sex had lingered in the fine weave of the cotton. When she finally started to drift off, she got hot and bothered. And that just bothered her. The man wasn't even here, and he was still getting to her. That wasn't good.

After an hour of suffering, she gave up. She peeled the bed

linens and walked down the hallway to the laundry room to wash him away.

Forty minutes after that, she decided that she should have just thrown the bedclothes in the hamper and put on her old sheets. It was her stubbornness that had led her to want to sleep on the Egyptian cotton with only the smell of fabric softener. And that was the problem with the community laundry room: once you started, you were committed.

So she sat in her living room waiting on the washing machine and pondering her ability to cast a 'forget' spell on herself. Eventually she decided against it, realizing that she'd likely just forget her laundry and lose her expensive sheets to a greedy neighbor. Also, if anything went wrong she'd never remember what she'd done, so she'd have no clue how to fix it.

Bummer.

She walked down the hall and transferred the sheets to the dryer and dried them on 'low.' It was kindest to the cotton, but today the extra time was unkind to her. She wound up watching infomercials to stay awake and before she knew it she had spent some of her savings and a Showtime Rotisserie was on its way to her doorstep. She almost called back and cancelled the order, but that would be too much trouble. It wasn't about the money, she had backup money. She had no intention of ever touching it, but it was there.

Later, she finally got the fresh sheets on her bed and fell into a deep and blissful sleep, only to have her alarm go off in the middle of the night, yanking her from some seriously wicked dreams involving pumpkin cakes and pastry cream and, of course, Brandon.

Delilah fought the urge to call in sick—which was really just cruel when she considered that the executive chef/owner had likely only gone to bed about two hours earlier. When she hired on, they'd asked if she called in sick a lot. In two and a half years she hadn't once. So she wasn't going to start now. Certainly not over a man she knew for a fact wouldn't recognize her on the street.

Pulling on her checked pants, she thought about how he had blinked his eyes just outside the door to the restaurant. He'd looked confused for a moment, then pulled out a tiny, fancy cell phone and called a cab. She'd heard the car pull up and peeked out the window to see Brandon glancing at the buildings all around him. From the alley, in the dark, the place looked deserted. He had to have wondered what the hell he was doing there. But he wouldn't even remember that later. He wouldn't be able to trace a path back to her.

Determined to wash him from her brain, Delilah pulled the hair tie from her pocket. The blue rose. She stuffed them there when the jackets came back from the dry cleaners. One time, early on, she'd showed up to work without a hair net.

Once.

Now she had a spare in her tiny cubby in the office and one stuffed into the pocket of each clean chef jacket in her closet. Concentrating on her reflection, she pulled up the blonde loops of her hair, brushing it back, over and over until the ponytail was smooth.

Her husband had always raved about her hair. And she'd loved that he loved it. He'd commented on it. Stroked it. Admired it. Right up until the day he'd died.

Delilah didn't think so much of it anymore. Her long hair was just something frivolous and probably not as beautiful as he'd said. Now it was just something to tuck out of the way into the pretty little net attached to the large turquoise fabric rose.

With her jacket draped over her arm, she headed down the hall to the garage and pulled out into the still of night.

Street lamps spilled light across the sidewalks, illuminating the pinkish stars set into the concrete. People walked down

Hollywood Boulevard or lingered under the lights, even at this hour. Still, you could tell it was two-thirty in the morning, because there were less of them, and more of the people who were there were in pairs or were trying to be.

In the dark, it was easier to see that the streets actually did sparkle. Leave it to Hollywood to sprinkle their asphalt with glitter. But she liked it. It was exactly what she needed. Exactly where she fit in. All show and magick, with little requirement for substance.

Her work was only eight blocks away, but she always drove. Things might look tame on the main streets, but you didn't want to walk down LA's back roads in the middle of the night. All of the city was like that, the neighborhood could change drastically from one block to the next. The section where she worked was only one street off a bad neighborhood, but here the front of the trendy restaurant matched the surroundings, glass and chrome melded into art that cared only just slightly for function. The bright sign was left on all night, the waste of electricity justified as an advertising cost.

The alley was a different story, cinderblock and brick that bore stains. The pavement did not glitter back here. Not that Delilah felt threatened in any way, but the alley was definitely the 'back lot.' In several hours, the delivery bay would welcome trucks bearing common fish with exotic names, fresh produce from the farms just beyond the city's borders, and once a week huge bags of flours and grains.

Delilah pulled into a spot that wouldn't hinder the trucks from either getting into the alley or backing up to the loading bay. That meant that she was behind the salon next door, which was often as far as her tired feet could make it by the end of a shift. Setting the parking break, she climbed out, shut the door, and clocked in. This morning's note asked her to test her ability against a delivery of puff pastry and blackberries.

Her mouth watered just thinking about it.

With nimble fingers, she closed up the front of her jacket and got to work. Finally pushing the green eyes and quick, wide smile all the way to the back of her mind. She had blackberries to tend.

CHAPTER 5

Brandon fought his way through the week. He'd felt out of whack since that night he'd gone out with Dan and Richard Cain. He hoped that a good lunch would put him back on the right track. Although why he thought that was unclear, it wasn't like anything else this week had straightened him out.

Dan still swore Brandon left the bar with some hot blonde, and Brandon believed him. It wasn't like Dan would lie about that, nor did Brandon have any memories to contradict his friend. Still . . .

He looked up at the server, "I'll take whatever you have on draft."

While Dan's eyebrows shot up, the server merely nodded and walked off to fill the drink order.

Dan leaned across the table. "What's that about?"

Shrugging was the best he could do. "Hell if I know. Maybe it *is* a tumor. I just figure that drinking got me into this, maybe another beer will snap me out of it."

After a moment of silence between the two friends, the server showed up again placing a pilsner with a perfect head on it in front of Brandon. The perfect lunch beer. Even though he'd decided that drinking during work hours was a no-no when he'd discovered his first shred of responsibility in his early twenties, he took a sip.

It didn't solve anything.

He didn't really want the beer. He didn't want the fish he'd ordered. He shouldn't have been out drinking during the week last Thursday either, but slick old Richard had talked them into it, and he'd gone right along.

He hadn't been sleeping well either. Not that he could make out what was bothering him. The dreams were all vague and lingered only at the fuzzy edges of his consciousness when he woke. He figured they were about his missing night, but figuring that part out didn't seem to help him find any clarity or get beyond the nagging sense that he was missing something important.

"If I don't get over this by next week, I'm going to go see a doctor."

Dan shook his head. "Not that it makes me any expert, but I tried to find your symptoms online and I got jack squat."

Brandon picked at his fish. How in the hell had Dan quantified what was going through him? "What'd you search?"

"Memory loss. Cravings for pumpkin pie and pastries. Not eating them."

That was accurate if not complete. "So, no miracle internet diagnosis, huh?"

"Oh, the net diagnosed you, all right."

Brandon leaned forward, wondering what his friend was withholding. Dan rocked back in his seat and stared his partner right in the eye. "You're pregnant."

If it wouldn't have landed him face down in his fish, Brandon would have collapsed right there. He wasn't sure of he should laugh it off or seriously consider a good momentary mental breakdown.

Not that most of what he was suffering was that bad, it just wasn't him. He wanted sweets—constantly. He rarely ate desserts, but he'd bought no less than ten in the past four days and hadn't finished a single one. None of them was 'right.'

He stayed silent and sipped the beer while Dan scarfed down the burger he'd ordered. There was nothing with pumpkin on the dessert menu, so Brandon pushed the pretty laminated pictures away and forced himself to not order anything, even though the crème brulee looked really good. He never ate crème brulee.

They walked back to the office, just like they had once or twice a week since they'd moved in a year ago. But Brandon still wanted . . . *something*. They passed a coffee place he'd been in only once, but some odd fact about it pecked at his memory.

"What?" Dan called out as Brandon disappeared from the sidewalk, ducking into the shop and scanning the rows of bagels and sandwiches until he found the cakes. It didn't take him long to find the desserts perched under their glass domes. He didn't question why that seemed right to him.

There it was, a pumpkin cupcake with cream cheese filling and a cute little fluff of white on the top.

He ordered it.

Smiling and waiting until they hit the sidewalk, Brandon shook the pristine little cake at his friend before he took the first bite. "This is it."

Dan stayed stable. Far more stable than he felt. "This is what?"

"The right cake."

Dan eyed him, but he didn't care. Brandon peeled back the wrapper and bit off half of it in one bite. He grinned.

Then grimaced. "Ohmph."

He couldn't chew. "Eehch."

He tossed the remaining half in a trash can as they passed. Then went back to spit out the other half as politely as he could at two in the afternoon on the Sunset strip with people pressing by all around him. "Blech."

Dan waited patiently. "Still not the right cake?"

Brandon gave him a dirty stare. The cake had been way too dry, but he didn't voice that. He shook his head.

Dan spoke straight ahead as they continued down the street. The words were dryer than the cake had been and did nothing to erase the bad taste in his mouth. "Call a doctor when we get back in, okay?"

Brandon nodded and stayed silent the rest of the way back.

But when they got in, he started puttering around his desk, doing things to occupy his brain and he didn't make the call.

He let himself get busy with work, and Dan didn't nag him, so he just let it slip. He finished very late in the day, not going home until well after everyone else had left the building. He ate noodles for dinner over his sink and decided he was doing better.

Until he'd woken up in the dead dark of night and hauled his sorry ass down the block to the 24-hour grocery store to buy an individual pumpkin pie from the bakery case.

He microwaved it when he got back in the door, then ate it with a fork right out of the plastic container as he stood at his counter and watched the sky start to lighten in a premonition of dawn.

He forced himself to finish the whole thing this time, but he could only wonder what had happened to him in his missing hours, and why the hell it still wasn't the right pie.

CHAPTER 6

Delilah was in the kitchen when she felt her brother's presence on the other side of the door. It was more Tristan's gift of getting her attention than any psychic bent on her part. She'd honed what little gift she had in that department over the years, mostly by casting 'sight' spells on herself. She made a mental note to work another of those when she cast her circle on Saturday night. Lately, she had let the spellwork slide in that area, and her skills had dwindled to only the odd glimpse of trivia here and there.

Except for Tristan, who came in loud and clear in her head. She not only knew he was there, but she could hear his thoughts from beyond the apartment wall.

Are you serious, Delilah?

Since she had no idea what he was asking about, she sighed and walked across the lush carpet to her door. He stood on the other side, a large white box held easily in his thick arms.

Holding the door wide for him, she asked, "How the hell do I know what that is?"

"Ah-hem." He gave her a questioning look as he stepped by

and set the box carefully on her dining table before turning it to face her.

The Ronco Showtime Rotisserie stared back at her in all its glory.

Truly, she had no response. So, whisk still in hand, she ignored the rotisserie and her older brother and went back to the eggs she was scrambling. With her back to him, she managed to add the half-and-half and a small glob of homemade mayonnaise before he spoke.

His voice was deep and serious, fairly unusual for him. "Li, have you been hitting the cooking sherry again?"

"Uh!" Outraged, she spun to face him, the eggs running off the whisk and onto her hand. "That only happened twice! And both times were with good cause!"

"No argument there. But this worries me." He sat back in one of her stiff wooden chairs, long arms and legs taking up space, and he fixed her with one of those big-brother stares.

She would have been mad, except he'd always been there for her. Even against Jules. So she rinsed the whisk, and went back to fluffing the eggs. "It's only a rotisserie. I couldn't sleep and the infomercial was on. No big deal."

He didn't respond, not even just inside her head, and the silence was too loud for her. She had to finally speak the words. "I swear, I wasn't drinking anything but water."

"But this is weird." He chuckled, then frowned at her mockingly. "Are you really my sister? When's the next new moon?"

"Friday."

"What's your star sign?"

She rolled her eyes at him before turning on the gas burner under the eggs. "Virgo on the cusp of Libra. Seriously, it's just a roaster."

Tristan came up behind her, towering over her like always. He sniffed at the egg mixture, taking in the diced tomatoes and spinach, sautéed mushrooms, and shredded cheese. He closed his eyes, inhaled, and smiled. But then he spoke. "How much did that whisk cost?"

Agh! He was after something and she didn't know what. But she was certain that she didn't want to give anything away. She hedged. "I don't know. It was part of a set."

"How much was the set?"

"One hundred and thirty dollars." She watched as the eggs fluffed, wondering why she cooked for him.

"For . . .?"

"Three whisks! What is your point!?" She turned to face him, more pissed to find that he looked like he was concerned rather than messing with her.

"The point is: you are a kitchen snob. You wouldn't have cable if it wasn't for the cooking channel. That . . . thingy" he pointed to the omelet pan, "costs more than your rent, and there's an *infomercial* rotisserie on your table. I'd be stupid not to worry."

She turned the eggs, letting the raw yolks run under the cooked part. "I hear it makes perfect chicken."

"What's going on, Li?"

She deftly ignored him. Grabbing a long serrated knife, that did in fact cost more than her rent, she pulled out the loaf of fresh French bread. Over the ready cutting board, she sliced it on the bias, popping the neat pieces into a waiting basket lined with a cloth napkin. Delilah turned the eggs again and reached into the fridge. She pulled out a small ceramic pot filled with boursin that she had made up from some cream cheese and butter and spices the night before and a bottle of frizzante champagne.

She held the bottle up to him, her mild irritation plain across her face. "Would you like to open this? Or would you rather I not drink at all?"

"Li." He took the bottle and thankfully went after the cork.

He popped it, then set it on the table before picking up the rotisserie box and asking her where she wanted it.

"Over there." She pointed to the corner of the kitchen with her spatula. Of course, she didn't want the thing at all now that she'd been raked over the coals for it. She'd bought it on a whim, nothing more. It cost her some of her savings and now the third degree. It better make some damn good chicken.

He watched her while she added the mushrooms and tomatoes, cooking them into the fluff. But he just poured himself some of the champagne and didn't let up. Not yet.

"You still sleeping around?"

"Christ, Tristan." She almost burned herself on the edge of the pan, although she didn't know why. It wasn't unusual for him to be that forward. "Do you want all the details?"

"Lord, no." He held up his hands as though he could ward her off.

After a moment, she took pity on him. "The answer is 'yes'."

"Li." The sigh in his voice was too much to bear.

"Come on, Tristan. You really want me to meet a nice man and get married. But why in hell would I want to do that? Do you really want that for me again?"

"No." He didn't say it out loud but it was there: *not after what you went through*.

"If it's any consolation, it's way less than last year. I've lost some of my angry edge."

He nodded. "That's good news, at least." Then he let the subject drop, and only occasionally eyed her as though he was worried. They sat down to eat, talking about Blessed Be and how he was handling it. Their mother had willed the magicks shop to all three kids, but after her death Tristan had been the only one around to run it. With his instinct and business sense, he'd changed it from their mother's break-even hobby into a real thriving store. But then again, a quality shop catering to those in all levels of the craft was a good bet. It didn't hurt that he could cast spells to see what should and shouldn't be stocked, what should be added or removed. Or that the store was in the heart of Hollywood.

And he was close enough to Delilah that he often turned up on her doorstep for lunch. Although, he usually didn't find infomercial kitchen products waiting for him.

"You should come back tomorrow. I'll make you chicken in that thing." Delilah pointed her fork toward the unassuming white box in the corner.

Tristan just laughed, the last of his concern for her finally slipping behind the gold flecks in his observant hazel eyes. He ran a masculine hand through his chocolate colored hair and looked at his watch. "Crap. Yasmin's going to start her class in twenty minutes."

"The beginners' class?"

He nodded, quickly standing to clear his plates and pop them into her dishwasher. He had to get back with enough time to cast his own protection spells to keep the shop safe before Yasmin set the beginners to their candles and incense. Yasmin had come late to the craft, she hadn't grown up with it the way they had. She was also blessed with a gift for the magick, and another for real common sense. What she lacked was the knowledge that not everyone had common sense. So Tristan was in constant battles with her about what she could teach the beginners and what was safe.

"I'll be back tomorrow for that chicken. About one o-clock again?"

Still seated at the table, she nodded to him and accepted the kiss he dropped on her head.

"Good Luck!" She spoke it to the air after he left. Then she decided that he could use some real help. Standing, she took her dishes to the sink before pulling out her candles and lining them up along her altar. She lit an assortment of colors, the tall tapers looking like a haphazard rainbow across the wooden surface.

She blew short and hard on the end of a thin maple stick, starting a small blue flame that quickly took hold and turned orange. One by one she used it to light each candle, wished Tristan luck, and then snuffed the twig lighter with two well placed fingers. She left the remaining candles to burn and work their magic.

Tristan was a good brother. He had every right to be concerned, there had been some tough times. And the two of them were all that was left of a once thriving family.

Later, as she snuffed the last candle, his voice popped into her head. *Thank you!*

CHAPTER 7

Delilah hugged Tristan and kissed him good-bye. Sitting on the barstool, she watched him weave his way out Gin's front door, leaving her alone in the crowd.

Gin's was a good place. They had good margaritas and martinis. The bartenders were friendly, and most knew her face if not her name. Usually it wasn't too loud to hear yourself think, and tonight it was even relatively quiet. Still Tristan had wanted to get up and check his books before the store opened in the morning.

She looked up at the glass coming her way and frowned. The new bartender was hot and most of the girls at the bar were throwing themselves at him. Just not Delilah. She looked around but didn't spot anyone who would be the likely source of the drink.

The bartender cleared it up. "It's on the house."

"Thanks." Her voice must have conveyed that she was confused.

"Your boyfriend just got up and walked out. And it really isn't my place, but he was seriously eyeing other women while you were here."

Her smile grew, but he kept going. "You shouldn't let him get away with that. Pretty girl like yourself, you could do a lot better." His blue eyes held sympathy and maybe something else, but she wasn't going to think about that. She wasn't out trolling for men tonight. Just thinking.

"No, I can't do any better than him." She held her hand up when the bartender started to protest, even while he poured a round of beers for the waitress standing next to her. "Tristan is the very best *brother* in the whole world." She pushed the unidentified concoction across the bar toward him. "Do you want your pity drink back?"

"No." He pushed the tall glass back at her and smiled. That smile. The one that said he was glad the other man wasn't her boyfriend. The smile that let you know he scented available female.

"Then you must tell me what it is." She frowned at the suspicious looking drink. Crushed green strips of what looked to be chopped leaves floated up and down in the clear liquid. Gin's always squeezed the lime into the drinks before they served them, and the crushed fruit slice added to her overall concern for the beverage. It looked like a spell gone horribly awry.

"You've never had a mojito before?"

"That's what it is? I've heard of those. What's in them?"

He smiled. "I'll tell you later."

With that, he disappeared to perform some necessary bartender task, and she was alone with the mojito, which turned out to be wonderful, despite lacking an olive for spellwork.

Tristan hadn't made it back for the chicken until dinner tonight. He always left work when the shop got too busy—said he couldn't get anything done. He had missed his rotisserie appointment from arguing with Yasmin about the beginner spells, which he said had taken the better part of two days to repair. Yasmin countered by pointing out that they had at least six new, dedicated customers.

He'd finally given up and tapped out when the Friday evening crush came in. Friday evenings and Saturday mornings were probably a third to half the weekly business. Most of the clientele was Wiccan like themselves, and that was when they geared up for their Saturday midnight spells. This week had been a little slow because of the new moon.

At least she and Tristan finally had a good dinner together, and the rotisserie had impressed him. He said the chicken was perfect and didn't ask her again if she'd been drinking the cooking wine.

Delilah sipped at the mojito, figuring she'd head back home when she was finished. Her hair was down, and she made the fatal mistake of sweeping it behind her ear to keep it out of the drink. From the corner of her eye she caught a movement and turned to see what had grabbed her attention.

None other than Brandon and his business partner. For a moment, her heart rolled over. But it was nothing. She could afford to be seen. She didn't think his business partner had gotten a good look at her the other night and Brandon wouldn't remember her face. It had happened before that she ran into men she had spelled and none of them ever recognized her. Even when she looked them straight in the face.

Last year, she'd been hell bent on getting over her husband's death, and she'd been through a good handful of men. One of them had even been introduced to her by a mutual acquaintance a month later at a party, and he didn't have a clue.

So Brandon caught her looking as she tried to reel her bouncing heart back in. That had been a crazy night. She almost hadn't pulled it off. Due to that near debacle, she hadn't been out again. Still, since he wouldn't recognize her, it was okay to look and maybe offer a polite half smile. He smiled, then tipped his head to the side, as though he had a question.

Quickly she turned away, afraid that if she stared at him he might remember something. But a moment later when she peeked, he was wound up in conversation with his friend.

Her breath let out.

It had been silly to hold it in the first place. He wouldn't remember.

She sipped at the mojito, enjoying the taste and the fact that she had no schedule tonight. She was off from the restaurant, and it was a new moon, so it wasn't a good time to cast anyway. She'd probably watch whatever was on The Food Network and curl into her soft sheets.

There was a faint smile on her lips by the time she got up from the stool. Thanking the new bartender, she passed over a generous tip and made her way out the front door.

Her arms naturally came up around her when she felt the air. She didn't carry a purse into bars, and her hands had nothing better to do than express that it was noticeably cooler than when she and Tristan had come in.

"It was chilly last Thursday, too."

The voice stopped her dead in her tracks. She knew that voice. She'd heard it moan and laugh and muse. And now she knew what he sounded like deadly angry.

Slowly she turned, her eyes round with confusion. How was he speaking to her about last Thursday night?

His eyes were a hard jade as he stared at her but didn't move. "I had a green button-down shirt when I left the bar with you. Where is it?"

At the bottom of a pile of laundry, so I didn't have to decide yet if I should keep it.

Instead she made her voice as even as possible and said, "I don't know what you're talking about."

He took a step closer to her. A couple came by on the sidewalk, too wrapped up in their own conversation to pay any attention to her.

His voice stayed hard. "My friend recognized you. I left with you. What did you give me?"

She shook her head, confused that he remembered anything. And she lied. "I didn't give you anything." Then she realized she had come very close to admitting she'd been with him. So she added, "I couldn't have, I don't know you."

That last part, at least, was true. She didn't know him. Well, in the biblical sense she did, but she didn't really *know* him.

He stepped closer again, this time grabbing her arm. He held her firmly, not hurting her as long as she didn't try to pull away. Which, of course, she kept trying to do.

"Did you take my wallet? Copy my credit card numbers? What?"

"No!" All she'd taken was a good time and his memory of it.

"Did you get suggestive photos, thinking you could blackmail me?"

"God, No!" How could he think such a thing? They'd had fun. She'd had fun. End of story. Or it was supposed to be.

Luckily they were right in front of the bar, and the doorman stepped out just then. "Everything all right?"

No! But she couldn't very well say that.

He did let go of her arm. But he got closer to her and whispered. "I can report you to the cops."

"For what?!" But she'd blurted it out before she thought better of it. The more she said, the more she could be construed as confirming that there was actually a connection between the two of them. So she put on her meanest face and threatened back. Even added a nudge of belief to her words, hoping this spell would stick to him. As maybe the other hadn't. "You have me confused with someone else. I'm leaving, and if you follow me, *I'll* call the police. Good night."

With that she turned and stormed off in the wrong direction.

Delilah stomped a full block over, fuming for help from the

universe. She was another block south before she ran into a cab that she flagged down and took back to her building. Paying the driver out of the folded bills in her back pocket, she told him to keep the change and bolted up to her apartment.

The whole while she'd been in the cab, Delilah had frantically searched for a reason, a way the spell had gone awry. Honestly, it was just easier that they all forgot her. No awkward moments, no explaining, no thoughts or ideas of something further, for them or her. Truly practical magick.

But as she reached the top floor, having foregone the elevator for speed, she realized that the 'why' didn't matter. What mattered was that he *did* remember. And he was pissed.

Too late, she understood the complete wrongness of what she'd been doing. Never mind that she'd had her own memories altered once and it had ruined her life. Never mind that what she had done was petty in comparison, and what she had taken was something none of these men would likely ever miss. It still wasn't right.

Brandon had a right to be mad, she'd messed with his thoughts.

So now she had to fix it.

She knew two wrongs didn't make a right. She believed that. Most of the time. However, right now the best thing for everyone was if Brandon forgot. Really forgot.

Fumbling the key several times, she finally got it into the lock. She could cast a 'forget' from a distance. It wouldn't be as strong. But it didn't have to be. He admitted that he still didn't remember everything. Or even much of anything. He only knew that he didn't remember.

Had she been smart, she would have yanked a hair from his head as she left. It would have made the whole thing easier. She could have snapped a photo on her cell phone and printed it. She could have . . . but she hadn't.

Right now, she needed something with a connection to

Brandon to make the spell as strong as possible. The sheets would have worked, had she not washed them. Had it been closer to the time he had slept on them.

Her thoughts whirled around her, frantic and unsettled. She could only be grateful that Tristan had left earlier or he would have picked up her broadcasting thoughts loud and clear.

Scattering her keys and remaining cash across the table as she passed by, Delilah went to get the one thing she had with the best connection to Brandon.

His shirt.

She turned over the pile of laundry and pulled the green cotton free, shamelessly sniffing it and pleased beyond words that it still held his scent. She ran back into the small living area and cleared her square coffee table of all the trivial pieces she displayed there, leaving only the wooden surface behind. From the bookshelf she pulled her four candles in red, green, yellow and blue, placing them in their proper North, South, East, and West alignments.

She grabbed the box of salt and the lighter, hastily poured a dish of water, and folded the shirt. She peeled off her jewelry and her clothing with metal pieces, which left her in a t-shirt and undies, standing before her makeshift altar.

Taking a deep breath, Delilah centered herself. She was more powerful than most, both gifted and practiced, but that didn't matter much if she couldn't find the focus for the spell.

A few moments later, she found the calm she had desired, and she began casting.

Only it didn't work.

She poured the salt, she lit the flames, she repeated the rituals. She could feel it . . . *not* working. It was like something was blocking the flow of magick in the universe tonight.

She glanced out the window and lost whatever cool she'd found.

She was working against the new moon.

CHAPTER 8

Brandon stood outside the club feeling the tiny doors in his brain opening. From the moment Dan pointed her out, sitting there at the bar, small memories had started to trickle in.

Her name, or so she'd said, was Delilah. He counted himself grateful to have woken up the next day with his hair intact, but he wondered what—besides his memory—she'd taken. Surely, Delilah wasn't even her real name. You wouldn't use anything that could be traced when running a scam.

Her reactions out on the sidewalk had been telling. She'd looked at him like she recognized him, like she'd been caught. And several times she looked like she was lying. Why he thought he could distinguish that was beyond him. But, truth be told, there was no knowing just what he knew.

When she finally made real eye contact, he'd seen the first flashes of Thursday night: her face when she was sitting at the bar, when he apologized for Richard. The grin when he agreed to go home with her.

All those remembered reactions seemed very genuine, which only made things more confusing. Then again, who knew how much he could trust his obviously faulty brain?

He stood there alone on the sidewalk, willing more of his memory to return. It didn't. His trigger had left, stalking off into the night, taking with her his chances to reclaim what was his.

Upset and determined to get more information, Brandon started after her. She'd stomped off heading east and he traced the angry path she'd tread.

At the end of the block he stopped, somehow knowing that he wasn't headed the right way. None of the options before him looked right and none would lead him to her. Not that he knew how or why he knew that. He just did—a fact that made him even angrier.

Giving up, he lowered his head and trudged back to the bar, his mood darkening as he went. Only when he reached the front entrance did he look up. Facing west on the street, he saw the path to Delilah. Another door opened in his memory and he knew she had led him this way last Thursday night. It was better than nothing, and he decided to see where it would lead.

His hand reached into his pocket and he hit the speed dial for Dan, who was still sitting inside the bar. Brandon didn't want to go inside, even for a moment. He didn't dare lose sight of this piece of the puzzle.

As usual, they didn't waste time on useless pleasantries. Dan merely asked, "What'd she say?"

"That she doesn't know me, but she's clearly lying." As he looked down Hollywood Boulevard, he knew he needed to turn north at the next block. "I remember a few things. I'm going to follow it as far as I can. I'll see you tomorrow."

His thumb started to reach for the 'end' button, but the voice of reason stopped him. "She could be dangerous. Or be in with people who are. You want me to come out?"

From the sounds over the phone, Dan was already headed his way. The last thing Brandon wanted was a buddy. For some reason that he didn't question, he wanted to do this alone. "No.

Stay put. I promise not to do anything stupid. Besides, it's likely going to lead me nowhere anyway."

He said good-bye and hung up before his friend could protest. His feet started down the walkway and he made the right-hand turn before Dan could get out Gin's front door and follow him.

When he faced Poinsettia Street, he was again flooded with memories. 'Delilah' smiling at him, and tugging him along, her hand small and warm in his. He remembered passing through her apartment door with the black C15 in the middle and kissing her just inside the entryway. Heat flooded him at the memory. Anger followed quickly as he realized just how thoroughly he'd been played.

He trudged up the street, stopping and looking again for his rooftop, knowing he had done the same last week. Last week there had been a large sliver of moon, but tonight all the light came from the city lamps. Again, when he looked up the street, the vision triggered a memory of which place was hers. Or, which place she had taken him to. The building she'd *said* was hers.

Upset and overheated by his own memories, he trudged up the hill. He'd slept with her! He remembered soft sheets and wide smiles. Feeling goofy and smitten. Now he just felt used. She'd gone a long way for a handful of credit card numbers. Not that anyone had used them. He'd put alerts on every account he had, and no one had tried anything.

Maybe she'd just used him for sex. Dan would have asked why he was upset about that, but he was. He'd have given it willingly. But this . . . this felt vaguely creepy. Still mad, he climbed the front steps and yanked at the building door. Only to be thwarted by the security system.

Crap.

Of course the door was locked. In his memory he could see her hand, fishing a ring with two keys out of her back pocket.

One fit her apartment door, and the other this security door to the building.

It was the end of the road.

This was where she had taken him. But now he couldn't get in. Even though the flimsy buzzer system could likely be snipped, cut, or short-circuited by the cheapest of thieves, Brandon had no such skills. For a moment he paced, not yet ready to give up.

His brain started to fuzz as he stood there. As though he'd had too much to drink, as though someone were slipping him a drug right then. His thoughts were harder to grasp, and he fought the sudden urge to just call it a loss and walk away. Certain he was more than a little nuts, and trying to act against the feeling that his head was starting to swim, he grabbed the door and tugged it again. Still it didn't budge.

His eyes read the entire list of names on the directory, but he couldn't find hers. Either he hadn't ever known her last name or she wasn't listed.

Fighting against the spinning sensation in his brain, Brandon pushed one of the buttons on the directory at random. After a few tinny rings, a female voice said, "Hello?"

It wasn't *her* voice. Brandon hit the button to hang up. He tried another. A man. Again he hung up. Two more answered their intercoms, obviously not expecting anyone. Two just rang and rang. The seventh button rang once, and the door began to buzz.

A surge of triumph shot through him, and he lunged for the door, yanking it open.

He took the elevator, as they had that night. She'd smiled up at him, chatting aimlessly about nothing at all. While the elevator made its slow crawl upward, he searched through the jittery new memories blooming in his head. He examined them for artifice on her part.

And found none.

There hadn't been anything that night to tip him off. To make him think he'd been drugged.

The ding of the elevator brought him out of last week and into the present. He'd promised Dan he wouldn't do anything stupid, yet here he was doing just that. Still, that knowledge wasn't enough to stop him from walking the hallway until he hit the door marked C15.

For a moment, he stood there fighting the waves of rolling sensation that hit him. They'd seemed to get stronger as he approached her unit. He tried to savor the color and the letters on her door. The exact size and shape of his memory, they vindicated his crazy flight from the bar.

Another round of dizziness hit him and anger surged at what she had done to him. Somehow it still had an effect on him here.

Enough was enough.

Without thought, his hand reached out and clenched the knob. For a split second he was surprised that it opened, and in that moment he remembered chiding her sweetly about not using a proper bolt.

The door swung wide, right into the tiny living space of the apartment.

'Delilah' stood before him, wearing only a white t-shirt and tiny flowered underwear. Big blue eyes stared at him in surprise, startled by him bursting in or shocked that he had found her. Brandon couldn't figure out which.

His missing green shirt hung from her loose fingers and a row of candles was lit on the coffee table, casting her lithe form in dancing gold. Her blonde curls caught shades of red from the flames, making it look as though fire cascaded around her shoulders.

Her mouth opened in a tiny 'o' and her chest heaved as she stared.

It occurred to him that he should laugh. *She* actually looked frightened of *him*.

But he couldn't laugh. He couldn't think. Nothing penetrated beyond the image of her standing in front of him holding his shirt and the sudden knowledge that all the spinning in his head had stopped.

He was finally at the center of the storm, and she was the cause of it.

His own mouth was open as he stared at her. All of it came gushing back in a great flood. Rolling in her white sheets with her. Feeling drunk and making her take him with her to work. The heavenly little cream-topped pumpkin cakes that made everything he'd eaten all week just not 'right.' Her eyes, wide and luminous, when she'd been sighing underneath him. The feel of her skin under his lips, and the feel of his skin under hers. The look and sound of her lush mouth curling when she laughed. The noise she made when he entered her.

How had he forgotten all that?

He wanted to remember.

Brandon didn't feel the door shut behind him, he merely heard the *click* as the catch slid into place. He didn't know or care if he'd shut the door or if it had been moved by some force of the cosmos. He took a single step forward, leaving the eye of the hurricane. He was assaulted anew, this time by a fire that caught deep in the base of him and swept upward. An unseen force pulled him to her as she stood motionless awaiting him.

His arms slipped around her, anchoring her in place as his mouth fused to hers. His shirt dropped soundlessly from her fingers, again forgotten on her living room carpet. Easily lifting her, he followed the pull in his belly to her bedroom, shedding his shoes as he went.

Her fingers hooked the hem of his cotton shirt and lifted it over his head. She discarded it, his breath rushing out when her touch found his skin again.

This, he remembered.

Only now as her hands re-learned the planes of his chest, her sweet mouth followed their trail. His breath sucked in as she plucked the snap on his old jeans and slid the zipper open. She pushed his clothing down his legs until he was naked under her ministrations, her fingers and tongue tracing mystical shapes on every part of him.

His hands sought her hair, nudging her to slide her body up along his, her soft skin brushing against him, sparking wildfires at every point of contact.

He couldn't touch her enough. Driven by some unseen force, he acted upon his every urge, stroking and tasting her until they both writhed in need. Her breathy gasps for relief penetrated his mindless want. Pressed fully along her, he slid between her open legs and buried himself to the hilt.

Their voices mingled in the nonsense of want as they moved together, reaching for release. Harder and harder he pushed into her, driven by the sounds she made. Twice she spoke his name, trapping him in the filmy haze of desire and something deeper.

At last, the movement of her body beneath him pushed him over the edge. Her own cries echoed in his ears, as her body, hot and wet, clenched him while he spilled into her.

Forever he fell, his body pumping mindlessly as he came.

For some unknown time after, he lay against her, her skin a swath of carnal heat amidst the cool sheets. He breathed deeply and evenly, slowly resetting his internal axis. Her breath came, soft and warm against his neck, a sweet reminder of the woman beneath him.

A woman he didn't know.

Slowly, his brain managed to shake off some of the lethargy that had stolen over him, even if his body didn't. She hadn't taken his wallet, or anything else, for that matter. Maybe he'd lost his memory of the night some other way.

But a drug was the only thing that made any sense.

Maybe she hadn't been responsible for it. That was what he wanted to believe. That this creature curled up soft and quiet against him couldn't be responsible for it.

Unfortunately, her innocence didn't add up either. While she might not have hopped right up and thrown herself at him when she spotted him at the bar, she wouldn't have pretended she didn't know him either. Unless she knew he wasn't supposed to remember.

She'd been involved in some way. That much was certain.

Slowly he gathered the power to lift his head and ask her about it. Even as he did, he pondered the wisdom of asking such a question while he was still intimately joined to her.

That brought another question, as important as the first. How was it that she made him lose all reason? He'd had plenty of sex, but he couldn't recall it being as mindless right from the first kiss as this had been. He took a little dose of honesty and admitted he had been lost pretty much from the first second he'd seen her standing there in her underwear holding his shirt. Had she been waiting for him?

There were simply too many questions. And he wasn't about to ask them from on top of her, naked. So he found what little remained of his strength and pushed himself away the few inches required to separate them. As his mouth opened to ask her the most pressing of the questions, her voice came to him soft and firm.

"I have to go to work."

When he rolled to look at the clock he was almost startled to see that it was after two a.m. He wondered where the hours had gone, if maybe they'd fallen into sleep or an alternate realm.

"All right." It was the only thing he could say. He didn't know what to ask first, or how to ask it. And there clearly wasn't enough time anyway.

She pushed herself upright, her naked body lithe in the dark of night. As she disappeared into the bathroom, the click of the door closing and the sound of running water signified an end to the interlude.

Blinking several times to himself, Brandon wondered what the hell had just happened. Then he resigned himself to the fact that he might never find out. As he pulled on his pants and shirt, he wondered if he'd even remember this later. Or if this night, too, would just slip his memory, leaving another blank in his mind.

When he was dressed, she came out of the bathroom, with a robe on, tied tightly at the waist. No admittance. Brandon stood next to the bed, the four to five feet of space between them simply too large to breach.

Her voice was solid even if the image of her in his mind wasn't. "Good night, Brandon."

It had the ring of good-bye in it.

"'Night, Delilah."

She smiled softly, and he figured it was her real name.

Without looking back, he let himself out of her apartment, this time remembering to scoop the button-down shirt off the living room floor as he passed.

CHAPTER 9

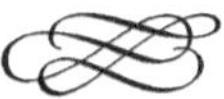

Delilah heard the door click. The sound released the tight lock she had on her knees. Her legs buckled under her and she sank soundlessly to the floor, too weak and too far away to get to the bed.

With great gulping breaths, she curled herself into a small ball and cried.

Tears poured down her face. Her chest heaved in deep sobs. It didn't seem there was anything she could do to stop it. All of it was too much.

She was lucky that anger was his only retribution for what she'd done. She deserved far worse. Instead he had kissed her, fierce and swift, and reminded her why it had been so important that he forget last week.

She couldn't handle him. That was certain. She'd get attached, and she simply couldn't survive another betrayal. The last had broken her. She was only just now getting on her feet. Only just now not waking up every day feeling angry and guilty and resentful. Judging by the force of the simple wrong she'd done to Brandon, that was not a safe combination in a witch.

It was clear now that she had to stop. At least Tristan would be happy about that.

She hiccupped a small smile at that thought, but it brought on another wave of hurt. This one swamping her with its force, and she began crying in earnest again.

She cried for all the past that had gotten her here. She cried for the Jules she had lost. A missing piece of her heart she only rarely let herself feel between months of hate. She cried in anger over the Jules who had wounded her so savagely and seemed to think it was no big deal. Nothing that couldn't be cleaned up with a little magick.

She wailed that she couldn't actually have Brandon. Not now, after how she had abused him. And not now, after she'd been so abused. He seemed like the kind of man who would one day decide he wanted a wife and family after all, and he would simply get them. The universe had smiled on Brandon, until she entered his life.

Then again, the universe had smiled on her, until she had learned the truth.

Tears came again, even more savagely this time. Then a small voice broke into her thoughts.

Li?

It was three a.m. and Tristan was awake. She was broadcasting her misery to any and every receptor in the area.

I'm fine, Tristan. Just getting the last of it out.

With that thought she mentally closed the door on him. It was easy enough to keep Tristan out, but like so many things, she had to remember to do it.

Tears came fresher this time. Not the old, wrung-out tears of misery that should have passed, but fresh guilty tears.

She hadn't really flat-out lied to Brandon.

Not before tonight.

When she'd told him last week that she worked at three a.m. he hadn't believed her. He'd demanded proof. But this time, he accepted it, when she was lying through her teeth to get him out of her apartment. She couldn't handle the questions she saw forming in his eyes. Didn't want to admit to what she'd done.

Worse, she had even contemplated casting another 'forget' on him after he left. She did the right thing and left him alone. Only partly because it was the right thing to do. Ultimately, she decided not to cast on him because she had bungled it so badly the two times she'd tried.

The first hadn't stuck, and she still had no idea why. It had been good, solid magick. She'd felt it working. Maybe it was because of the half-spells when he'd interrupted her. But she'd *felt* it. She was one of those witches: she felt her magick.

Tonight he'd caught her in the middle of trying it again.

His shirt had been in her fingers over the flames. She'd been fighting the low power of the new moon. Still, she'd felt it starting to catch. This one would have done the trick. The wrong trick, but he would have forgotten everything.

Then he'd thrown open the door that she'd forgotten to lock because she'd lost all sense when he started accusing her of things he shouldn't remember. And she hadn't expected him to show up *here* of all places. He'd looked so angry, she had been certain he was going to kill her.

Instead he'd kissed her.

The spell had gone horribly awry from that point.

Ready to feed his shirt into the smoke and make him forget, she'd stood in the midst of all that power—now focused only on the feel of his kiss.

No wonder they'd gone off like a rocket.

And now, like every time she'd cast a strong spell, she was wrung out and empty.

Still on the floor in only her bathrobe, with her knees tucked up under her chin, she finally cried herself to sleep.

CHAPTER 10

The sun was coming in the windows, forming squares around her on the carpet where she lay. Her muscles creaked as she made the first move in hours to get herself off the floor. When she tried to look up at the clock, it came to her in blurry red letters and her eyelids hurt just from looking at it.

She'd cried herself to sleep on the floor and it was time to pay.

Dragging herself into the kitchen, she pulled a cucumber from her vegetable drawer and cut two thick round slices. Still sniffling after last night's downpour, she shuffled back to her room and laid herself out on top of the comforter. She pushed the cucumbers against her eyelids and spent a moment focused on coming awake. She pictured her face as she was used to it—eyelids not puffy, smooth complexion with no little pink blotches, her nose a normal skin tone rather than red. Then she put some power behind the picture.

Still she lay there, as comfortable as she could be given the aches and cricks in every bone and joint. The bed was soft and warm from the light that fell across it in the late morning. And her mind wandered off out of her control.

She'd gotten the job as pastry chef the same day she'd chosen the apartment. She'd just spent two weeks planning funerals and packing boxes and had been in no shape to make major life decisions. But they'd needed to be made. Delilah had completely not cared where she wound up but forced herself to see no less than five different apartment buildings.

When she walked into this bedroom, something had spoken to her—she didn't know or care what. She only knew that the universe was always right. So she'd taken it.

During the next week, as she started work and tried to establish a routine, she realized that the sun came in through the big windows only by mid-morning, warming the bed and waking her softly. Or creating a soft distant glow when she pulled the shades and fell asleep after a long night baking. Now, it was a godsend, the light comforting her when she needed it.

Slowly she drifted into a state of non-being. Open of mind and free of her own concerns, she lay there only half awake. The bed cradled her like a lover's arms and she sank into it. The heat of the sun warmed her soft robe like breath against her skin. The sheets gave off the comforting smell of man. Delilah rolled over, burying her nose in the scent, as though she could reclaim the sensation of Brandon wrapped around her.

With a jolt, she sat up.

She did not need to be rolling in her sheets that, once again, smelled of that man. The cucumbers fell from her eyes and so did her illusions.

Swinging her legs over the side of the bed, she sought another way to free herself from last night. Dressing quickly in jeans and a t-shirt, she pulled her hair up into an easy ponytail, wrapping the elastic around it several times to hold tight. Then she went off to practice her own brand of magick.

Tristan's magick was simple yet effective. He didn't own or use ninety-nine percent of the pieces he sold in their mother's store. He considered them puff and show. Juliet's magick had come from somewhere powerful inside her, a natural gift that needed no conjuring. It seemed Juliet had only to wish something and it came to be. And Delilah was the chef.

She had an instinct for the colors and smells and textures to create the outcome she wanted, whether it was a spell or a pie. Food was an excellent delivery system for magick, and their grandmother always said that cooking was a kind of sorcery in itself.

Tristan would likely appear in about half an hour. The eternal bachelor, he showed up on her doorstep when he was hungry and she was home. Never mind that she fed him out of guilt, too. The colossal explosion of herself and Jules and David had put him off finding his own relationship. If she didn't feed him, who would?

She stepped up to the counter and enjoyed the satisfaction of knowing what she was doing. It was a welcome change from the tears of last night and the truth of this morning.

Delilah reached for flour and baking powder and finely ground salt. She used skim milk and a dash of rum and five minutes later peeled the first crepe off the griddle and threw it into the trash. With an economy of motion she turned out a large pile of the perfect thin pancakes, which she stacked under a cloth and stowed in the warm oven.

Next she sautéed thin strips of chicken, then reached for pears and deftly peeled them. Using her mandolin slicer, she reduced them to a pile of precise slivers, then popped them into the pan she'd used for the chicken, adding chardonnay and molasses.

Li? The key turned in the door, and slowly it opened, giving her the chance to shout out a warning if it were necessary.

When she'd first moved here, Tristan used to just turn the key and barge right in, never considering that he should check first, that his widowed little sister might not be alone. But one Saturday morning she'd been in the back and he'd opened the door on a half-naked man who put up a fight. Her overnight guest had figured she'd lied. Since the man coming through the door possessed both a key and an easy familiarity with the woman in the house, it was likely an easy assumption that he was her husband. It was also wrong. Nevertheless, the man had taken a swing or two at Tristan before Delilah could close his fist around the lavender and send him off.

Tristan had stumbled backward into the hallway, too shocked to conjure any answers or even simple questions as Delilah's guest passed by. Only later did he ask about her new boyfriend. Unwilling to lie to him, she wound up explaining about the 'forget' spells and the fact that it hadn't been the first time.

Her brother had worried about her ever since. Probably rightfully.

Now he came up behind where she worked and sniffed at the pears bubbling in thick juice on the stove. "Mmmmmm."

She smiled, sliding the chicken back into the pan and sprinkling raisins throughout the mixture.

She wiped her fingers on the half-apron tied around her waist, and turned off the heat. She pulled down plates and didn't need to speak. Tristan let himself into her fridge and got out a large bottle of sparkling water, pouring it into two glasses and setting the table.

She loved this, having him here. He was an anchor for her as she still tossed about in a torment that should have been long gone. He was the only one who seemed to really understand. Rolling the mixture into the crepes, she made two plates, his much larger than hers and turned to carry them to the table.

"Delilah?" The sound was accompanied by sharp concern.

He was looking at her face. Her still-a-little-puffy, still-a-little-blotchy face, because she'd cried herself to sleep and then couldn't lay on her bed long enough to fix it because the bed smelled like the man who'd burst through her door and made love to her then left.

She sighed. There was nothing she could do now. And she just wanted her crepes. She offered up a sad smile and tried eating.

Before the first forkful hit her mouth, Tristan had the question out. Only it wasn't the one she'd been expecting. "Does this have anything to do with the rotisserie?"

Finding no point in lying, she said, "Yes."

Again he didn't say what she expected. Didn't ask what kind of trouble she was having, didn't ask about the man. Instead he went straight to the point. "I thought you were doing better. Why is it all coming up now?"

She shrugged. "Don't know."

She had no clue why her spells were going awry. Why Brandon had been able to come back. Why she'd been so scared last night when she saw the questions forming behind his eyes.

Finally, she got the fork into her mouth and ate the first bite of the crepe. Letting it melt on her tongue, she stayed quiet and enjoyed the simple peace of eating.

CHAPTER 11

Brandon's week went much better than the previous one had. He still had no idea why he'd been drugged or what role Delilah had played in it. But at least now he remembered all of it. Seeing her, walking up her street, making love to her, had all triggered memories. He got his missing night back.

And he got a new night, too. Although he wasn't sure what he should make of that.

At times he wished she hadn't been involved in whatever had gone wrong. Otherwise he would have definitely liked to keep seeing her. Even if she'd only wanted it for the sex. But a man had to have his standards. He couldn't risk getting his memory ripped out again. And there was more than a decent possibility that she was more than a little nuts. What kind of woman drugged a guy for no real purpose? He would have counted her more sane if she had taken his money. That at least would have made sense.

It also would have made it a little harder to want to see her again. Or easier to let her go. It all depended on how he looked at it.

He still craved desserts and pumpkin pie, but now that he

knew where the desire came from he could manage it. Plus, most of the stuff he could buy, even in nice restaurants, wasn't as good as hers. So he wasn't stuffing his face anymore on the quest for the perfect cake.

Dan had assaulted him the next morning, calling him at the house and asking how it had gone. Brandon had lied through his teeth, saying that he hadn't found her. He'd just gotten lost. Then he'd had to lie again when Dan said he'd called to check in several times the night before.

Sure enough, the cell phone call log showed exactly that. Right during the time he'd been in Delilah's bed again. He told Dan that he must have bumped the phone off since it was in his pocket.

He had no idea if Dan believed him or not, but his friend hadn't pushed the issue.

At one point Brandon wandered out for groceries, walking the two blocks to the store and returning with three bags of frozen foods. His mouth watered for fresh cooked dinners and he thought about a certain chef, but he quickly turned it off and stuffed it to the back of his brain. He wasn't the kind of guy to go after the wrong woman. Lust was certainly something that he could take control over. So he'd eat his tasteless frozen food and be glad that he could remember every bite of it.

By Thursday, he and Dan fielded calls from four people who said they had money to invest, and that Richard Cain referred them. Brandon could not have been more shocked. Who knew Richard would turn out to be decent in his business deals? He'd been such a schmuck to Delilah.

They lined up investors to come in and tour the offices and get a presentation on four different days the next week. Dan thought they should go out to celebrate and didn't say anything, or even raise an eyebrow, when Brandon suggested Gin's.

It wasn't like he really thought he'd run into Delilah there. He'd gone to the bar over the weekend to meet an old friend from school who was in town. Delilah hadn't been there, so he couldn't say he was going because he was *expecting* to see her. He didn't question it any further than that. Gin's had all kinds of great beer on draft. That was enough for Dan.

They pushed through the swinging door at the front, letting the noise and smells assault their senses. It always took just a moment to assimilate the atmosphere inside a bar, and Gin's was no different.

Brandon took a quick visual sweep of the place, assuring himself that Delilah wasn't there, before he and Dan settled into one of the last few open booths. Certainly it wasn't a small pang of disappointment that he felt as he slid into the cushy seat.

They ordered beers and relaxed. Dan hit on the waitress as he always did, and the two of them got into the same argument they always did. Dan saying that flirting was a part of the job requirement in any establishment where the waitresses were outfitted in tight jeans and belly-baring tops. Brandon argued that the individual flirting with the customers was only a job requirement for strippers, though he did figure there was better money in it. Maybe it meant 'look but don't talk.'

They discussed strategies for the different investors next week. They talked about tweaking the presentation to suit the various demands. They ordered another round and tried to guess what those biases might be, what each investor might most be looking for. Then Dan suggested they write off the evening's whole beer tab since they *were* working.

A half hour later they had hashed out most of it when Dan abandoned him to talk to some woman he knew at the bar. Brandon was about ready to call it quits, not wanting to sit there by himself, when Dan reappeared.

Brandon raised his eyebrows.

"Bust." Dan shook his head and shrugged before taking a drink of his freshly ordered beer. His finger was up, signaling for Brandon to wait, before he finished swallowing. "However, I believe I might have seen your little druggie girl in a booth on the other side."

"What?" Brandon shook his head. *Druggie girl?*

"The one you lost the other night. The one you went home with two Thursdays ago, that we don't know yet what she took. That one."

"Are you sure?" The words were out of his mouth before he could question the wisdom of them. He'd never caught Dan up to speed on the fact that he had found her or that he stayed part of the night with her. Only that his memory was gradually coming back. But he'd already decided he was done with her. Enough was enough.

"I can't say for sure. I never did get a really good look at her face that first night. But I think so."

Brandon squirmed, trying to make the right decision. Trying not to care.

"She's sitting over there with some guy. Looks like a date."

Why that pissed him off, he didn't know.

"You could just go to the men's room and see if it's her."

Brandon nodded as though doing something so juvenile actually made sense. But it did. All he needed to do was just go see if it was her. It probably wasn't anyway. Then, when he sauntered by oh-so-casually, it *was* her and he felt like a real moron. At least he really did have to pee, so the whole trip to the bathroom wasn't a total sham. But, really. He wasn't going to talk to her or anything.

He double-checked on the way back from the bathroom, all the while making sure she didn't see him. Then he walked off, embarrassed and irritated with his own behavior. He really thought he'd left junior high behind him. Couldn't remember the last time he'd snuck around trying to get furtive glances at a girl. He hadn't ever even gone the 'grown-up' route of that mess —his house had a view of a good portion of the city and he didn't even own a pair of binoculars.

Slinking back to the table, he prepared to cry off the whole thing.

But Dan beat him to the first word. "It was her, wasn't it?"

Brandon merely nodded, still feeling like a fool and still hoping that no one noticed what he'd been doing.

"So, are you gonna go over there?"

"No." He shook his head, trying to take the moral high ground. As well as act toward his own self-preservation.

"What?"

His head snapped back a little at the vehemence in Dan's reaction.

His friend continued, steamrolling any thoughts Brandon might have on the issue. "You have to go over there and break them up. You have a chance to save one of your fellow men from the same thing you went through. You have to do it."

Brandon's brain ached. What had he suffered really? Two nights of achingly hot sex. Some excellent pastry. The loss of his memory and some uncertainty.

Dan leaned forward, his voice and expression melodramatic after several beers. He issued his call to arms. "You owe this to your brothers. And to yourself. You have to go over there."

CHAPTER 12

Delilah swished the straw in her mojito, watching the small green pieces of mint swirl in the glass. She wondered if any were stuck in her teeth. And if they had, would they repel the completely boring Jeff? Or could she maybe create a small vortex in the drink and work a little spell to make him more interesting?

Delilah doubted she had the power to actually make Jeff interesting. She might be able to work a little spell that would put him off her, but that was likely best accomplished without magick. Perhaps a discourse on the state of her tax filing system. Or maybe just a well-timed belch.

She stopped the straw, afraid that the motion, combined with the focus of her thoughts, would cast on him right there in Gin's. She really couldn't let that happen. It was horribly unwise and unsafe to cast if you weren't intending to. Besides, it wasn't her place to interfere.

It wasn't her place to interfere.

It wasn't her place to interfere.

She repeated it over and over in her head like a mantra. As

though, if she said it enough, she would abide by it. Hadn't she learned her lesson the last time?

Well, hadn't she?

She wasn't really certain that she had, because she was still so tempted to do it again. So here she was, in Gin's on a Thursday night with a man she didn't know and didn't want to know. She never should have agreed to this.

In an effort to appease her worried brother, she'd allowed Yasmin to set her up on this date. She always thought Yasmin had better intuitive skills than this. Maybe Tristan and Yasmin had both just gotten so excited that she'd agreed to their blind date that they lost their heads a little. Well, after this oh-so-rousing success, they weren't going to get another chance.

She looked up and smiled at Jeff as he droned on about his work with the Jet Propulsion Laboratories. Her bland expression matched the enthusiasm she felt for the formulas he was spouting. She almost laughed out loud. He really was a rocket scientist. And, Lord, listening to him, it sounded like the dullest job in the whole world.

He hadn't even asked yet what she did for a living. He'd only given her a look that bordered on appalled that she didn't want to share the Gin's Special Buffalo Wings with him.

Maybe she could cast a spell on herself to make herself more interested in what he was saying. But, gods forbid, if he actually thought she had a good time he might just ask her out again. And if she'd made herself like him she might just say 'yes.'

So she focused her thoughts on analyzing him rather than actually listening to him. He was too uptight, which made him seem older than he probably was. Way too buttoned-down to suit her. She needed someone without a perfect part in his hair or starch in his collar. Jeff's manners were impeccable. Too impeccable, she sighed in frustration, they were in a bar! He was eating Buffalo wings with a knife and fork.

He leaned forward, clearly expecting some response from

her. Desperately she searched her brain for what he'd been talking about and couldn't come up with anything. So she just gave a small "hmmmm" while she nodded.

Unfortunately, that had him off and running at the mouth again.

She resigned herself to being stuck for a while longer, upset that she hadn't thought ahead and didn't have a friend lined up for a mercy call. Yasmin would have done it, but this had been her set-up. It would have been wrong to ask her to provide a way out.

Jeff droned. Delilah discretely checked her watch, wondering how long she needed to stay in order to politely tap out and call it a night. At least another half hour. No, make that twenty minutes. She wouldn't survive another half hour.

She was so focused on appearing focused on Jeff, that she felt the harsh shove at her hip before she saw anything.

Jostled to the side, she looked up, startled, already having figured out that someone had slid into the booth next to her, mercilessly bumping her out of the way.

She could not have been more surprised to see Brandon or the sweet smile that spread across his face at the sight of her.

Blinking a few times, she rapidly took in the scene, once again regretting that she hadn't finished that second forget spell on him. She also saw that Jeff was just mortified by the intrusion. At least it shut him up for a moment.

Before she could think of anything to say, Brandon gave her a sad pitying look and odd words started tumbling from his lips. "Lilah, baby, come home."

"Huh?" What the hell was he talking about?

Jeff's spine got straighter, if that was possible. He huffed and crossed his arms.

Brandon gazed deeply into her eyes and kept talking. "We miss you."

We?

"Delilah," Jeff's tone demanded attention and both she and Brandon turned to face the other man. "Do you know this . . . gentleman?"

Clearly 'gentleman' was not what he thought Brandon was. Delilah thought maybe 'insane asylum inmate' was a better option. What did Brandon mean, 'we'?

She took a sip of her drink to cover for her confusion.

Brandon put his right hand out across the table as though to introduce himself, his left arm snaked possessively around Delilah's shoulders, but she was too confused to react. "I'm Brandon Stewart. Delilah's husband."

Immediately she choked. *Husband*?

Her wide eyes swung to his face, only to find that he looked perfectly serious. He gave her a sad smile as Jeff voiced her concerns. "Husband?"

Brandon didn't take his eyes off hers. Even as she sat there choking on her drink. Not that he volunteered to hit her on the back or ask if she was going to survive. He just looked sad. "Baby, have you been dating again? You know the doctors think that's a bad idea." Then, he turned his sympathetic face to Jeff, "She isn't well."

That was it! Her anger poured out in her voice, which she barely managed to keep from screeching above the noise level and broadcasting to the entire bar. "Brandon!"

Jeff looked taken aback. "You *know* him? Are you *married?*"

"No!" She shook her head violently. What was Brandon doing?

He made his next play before she could form words.

"She's not only married, we have a family."

He shifted his weight, pressing intimately along her from shoulder to thigh, as he fished in his pants pocket for his wallet. He drew out the leaning and fishing a little longer than necessary. Especially considering she was boiling mad. She was *married?* To *him?*

He deftly plucked a studio portrait of two small children, clearly his own. Delilah had to hand it to him, the little blonde-haired, blue-eyed cuties could easily have been hers. One boy and one girl smiled at the camera, sweet and perfect for all the world, heads pressed together.

Brandon made sure she saw the photo before he handed it over to Jeff. "That's our Tiger and Muffin there. Well," He smiled like he was all chagrined, "Tyler and Madison."

Then he turned to her, still sweet and sad. "You can't do this again, baby. Come home."

She simmered, but didn't speak.

Jeff's expression changed from confused to mad to upset as he looked from one of them to the other. When he appeared to have made up his mind, he tossed down his napkin and rose. "Well." It was all he got out. Delilah got her only satisfaction from the fact that the goon was in a booth, and he didn't make it all the way to standing before he hit his thighs against the table and had to scoot out, ungracefully, to the side. "Goodnight."

He raised his weak chin high and stamped out of the bar like a child.

Delilah let loose in a low growl, and it cost her every effort to keep her response to mere words. If she'd had her way, her focus was strong enough to create a small wind around her and make her eyes burn red. But her witchcraft had cost her enough already where Brandon was concerned. Even though she was mad enough to burn all bridges and say to hell with it, she kept it in check. "What are you doing?"

He laughed. "What, you don't remember Tiger and Muffin?"

She drew a deep breath and held her emotions on tight rein.

The waitress chose that moment to saunter her bare belly up to their booth and ask if they wanted anything else. Delilah merely ground out the word 'no.'

The waitress didn't seem to notice, simply smiled and said

'thank you,' instantaneously producing a check and sliding it to the middle of the table, before she sauntered away.

Great, Delilah thought, the obnoxious Jeff had downed five very over-priced snobby beers and she was stuck with the bill. She didn't think this could get any worse.

But Brandon had her pinned into the booth, the fake sad look gone from his face. The humor now missing as well. Which was just fine, since she didn't have any of her own.

She asked him again. "What are you doing here in my booth?"

"Running your date off. Sparing him memory loss and who knows what." He reached out and snaked her mojito away, before taking a healthy gulp.

"That's mine!"

His smile resembled a shark's. "After everything else we've done, sharing a glass isn't going to kill you." He took another drink, draining half of what remained and a lot of her sanity. "I had to save the dweeb from you."

"He didn't need saving." She tried again to push past him, but he didn't budge.

"So you weren't going to take him home and screw his brains out and make him forget everything?"

She was so shocked by his blunt but accurate assessment of their first night together that she didn't think, just blurted out, "No!"

That startled Brandon, and he asked, "why not?" out of genuine curiosity, before she could regroup.

"I didn't like him." *Crap,* that was a whole other can of worms. She sat back, at last resigned to this going from bad to worse.

It was Brandon's turn to be startled. "Then why were you trying to pick him up?"

She started with a sigh. It seemed only appropriate. "I wasn't picking him up. I was trying to figure out how long I had to sit and listen to him before I could beg off. I miscalculated, not having figured in the 'pissed-Brandon' factor. Contrary to popular belief, men do not need to be saved from me. But now, if you'll excuse me, I have to pay for Jeff's drinks."

Before she could pluck the cash register tape off the table, it was in Brandon's hand. "I've got it."

Delilah tried to reach for it. "No, I do. You shouldn't have to pay for Mr. Boring-rocket-scientist's overpriced beer."

He didn't let go. "Was he really a rocket scientist?"

"Yes."

"Sorry."

That startled her. "About what?"

He shook his head. "I didn't mean to run off such a good catch."

Did he mean as in 'husband material' or 'money'? She couldn't tell.

He didn't explain. He did sit there for a moment, looking pensive as he counted out bills and laid them on the table along with the check. "Why me?"

Oh God, what a question. And there were a million ways to answer. She tried to find one that didn't involve filleting her soul and serving it up on a platter. The best she could come up with was, "I liked you."

He nodded. "Okay, here's how it's going to go . . ."

She did not like the sound of that.

Brandon didn't seem to notice. "You and me, we've got two nights behind us, but no dates. We're going to start making up for that tomorrow night."

"I have to work tomorrow." It bothered her how quickly and easily the lie tumbled from her mouth.

"No, you don't." He didn't even act upset that she had lied to him, and he sure didn't believe her. Was he out for some kind of revenge? His words got even stranger. "Tomorrow, we are going to start dating. We are going to be exclusive. I figure after everything else between us, we owe each other that much. And maybe you'll explain the whole thing to me one of these days. We'll see where this goes."

His eyes caught and held hers and she had to wonder if he was as crazy as he'd told Jeff she was. He wanted to date her? No way.

But he smiled and it seemed genuine. Then he backed carefully out of the booth, deftly avoiding a waitress coming behind him with a loaded tray. His hand locked onto hers and he pulled her smoothly out after him. "Come on."

She wanted to say no. Wanted to tell him good-bye. Her instincts were screaming, but not a one of them was about harm. She felt completely safe with Brandon. Even if she didn't know why. As a double-check her hand shot out and jostled what was left of the mojito.

The leaves went clockwise. It was all right.

Whatever 'all right' meant.

CHAPTER 13

"You do it."

Delilah's head turned at the sound of the voice. She knew that voice. Her heart knew that voice. It belonged in a time when things had been okay. That's how she knew she was dreaming.

Her own mouth opened to respond, her brain knew the words before they were spoken, but she said them anyway. "You do it. You're better at it."

Still the small hand had held out the cluster of long grasses, plucked from the field behind their house. They lived at the edge of town, both literally and figuratively. A Wiccan family on the fringe of society, trying to keep the balance between civilization and nature.

Even back then, when they had been young, Juliet had been the littlest and the best at magick. As though their parents had gotten better and better at focusing their talents into their children each time they brought a new one into the world. It had been Juliet who encouraged Delilah to get better, stronger. So she held out the grasses for practice.

They had stood there for an eternity. At least it had seemed that way to Delilah. Juliet's small fist around the grasses, held out directly between them while Delilah concentrated.

She'd been nine. Juliet seven. Tristan twelve, but less involved in the effort to master the grasses.

Delilah had caved long before her sister. "Jules, I can't do it. Not like that."

"Sure you can. You just have to want it." Where Juliet had come up with that bit of sage advice Delilah would never know.

But it didn't matter. Delilah had wanted it. There was nothing wrong with her desire. Merely with her methods. She wanted herbs, flame, small hand motions. Things Juliet never needed nor used. But she couldn't fail in front of her baby sister, her cheerleader. She tried again.

Eons later, the plain grasses bloomed into bright, peach colored flowers that smelled of the apple pie she planned to help her mother bake that evening.

Tristan had worked on his own skills. With a sprinkle of water, he made pebbles levitate and spin. He could whip his pencil through the air and leave tracers of blue light. He could make tiny alterations to wind, the kind that would conveniently pull a few papers out of a girl's grasp as she passed by in the hallway at school. Papers that he could pick up for her. If only he could keep his own awkward body under his control. But that wouldn't happen, because junior high was junior high, and there were certain inescapable truths. She and Juliet found those things out for themselves in later years.

But that afternoon, the afternoon she had first made the grasses bloom with only her thoughts, she'd gathered them from Juliet's outstretched hand and run into the house. Her mother then pulled down her best vase and arranged them in the center of the table and lovingly poured water on them, even though she stopped doing this for Juliet's creations long ago. They stayed on the table for a month before they finally withered and dried as the grass stalks they had originally been, as they had been meant to be.

In the dream, small Delilah knew this all this, knew how long her precious flowers would last. And she knew that she should still take this moment to admire them.

Her smile must have burned a thousand watts, for her whole family had smiled with her. Even Tristan, and back then he seemed determined not to smile about anything, at least not until junior high was finished.

Small arms went around her. For some reason, Juliet looked up to her. Aside from magicks, Delilah was clearly the older, more experienced sister. When she looked at Juliet though, something was wrong.

The voice that came from Juliet's mouth was not her own. Well, it was, but it was a voice Jules would not obtain until adulthood. "I knew you'd be okay."

Delilah jerked back, her nine-year-old body reacting with her adult knowledge. *I'm not okay. I'll never be okay again.*

But her mouth didn't speak the words. Not that it mattered. She would never speak to the real Juliet again. So she stood there with Juliet's arms around her, her sister's small face gazing up at her.

Juliet smiled. Her eyes . . .

Delilah had to blink twice to figure it out.

The eyes were blue.

Not Juliet's eyes, but her own. Staring back at her from her sister's face.

Her lungs expanded on a strangled sound, sucking in air as though she'd been underwater. Even as she came awake and struggled to right herself, a great weight kept her pinned. She was bound and suffocating in the dark, haunted by images of her sister. Seeing Juliet as a reflection of herself and scared to think what it all might mean.

Delilah thrashed against her bindings, only to discover that she wasn't being held prisoner at all. She wasn't tied, but tangled in bed sheets. The weight she felt was a heavy arm across her waist.

Brandon's arm.

She must not have thrashed as hard as she thought, because he slept like nothing had happened. As though someone on the other side of his bed flailed themselves awake in the middle of every night. At last she lay still, unable to fight against Brandon, who won merely by being larger and heavier. And unable to fight against the memories of her dream, which were burned into her brain whether she understood their meaning or not.

She talked herself back into a state of half-sleep where she became unaware of the passage of time, as well as the unmoving man beside her. For a while she drifted through half dreams, before the contact with Brandon's skin showed her his dreamless sleep. Delilah latched on to that and tried to relax.

Later, his alarm went off, startling them both. Tired as she was, and not willing to deal with what she'd done and how she'd wound up in his bed, she rolled back over while he showered then dressed.

Utterly confused, she found herself alone in his apartment after he kissed her good-bye and left for work. Pretending to sleep through the whole 'leaving' part had been an attempt to avoid anything else between them. But he hadn't left it at that.

What he left was a lengthy note telling her all about the date they were going on that evening. He was planning to take her to Othello—where she worked—which just would not do.

She sat there in his bed, clutching the sheets to her chest, protecting herself from the lecherous gaze of . . . no one. So why did she feel so exposed? She debated with herself over what she should do. She could call him on his cell, as he'd left her all his numbers on the note. Or she could do what she'd planned all along: snitch a piece of hair, a well-worn garment, and his toothbrush cup.

Cautiously, she climbed out of his bed and back into her clothes. She pulled her fingers through her hair, and spelled it smooth and shiny. It was a little measure of control in a world that was suddenly spinning way too fast for her again. While she worked on her hair, she told herself that she wasn't going to do anything wrong. She was just going to look around.

His living room was sparsely furnished and managed to feel empty even when Brandon was in the house, but her spell to search for personal items turned up the remote control. He would have had a lot of contact with it if he was anything like David and her brother. But if she took it, he'd definitely notice it was missing.

If she cast on him again it would have to be subtle. If he realized she'd spelled him then he'd just shake it. Some people seemed to have that ability naturally. She herself apparently was not one of them. Brandon, however, had already proved himself capable of doing just that.

So the remote was out of the question, but the toothbrush cup still seemed like a good idea. A lot of contact, but it was nothing special, just another plastic cup from his cupboard. She could take the one he'd been using, slip in a replacement, and he'd never realize it.

Only her fingers suddenly wouldn't work when she tried to pick up the cup. She'd gone completely klutzo. First it had slipped into the sink. When she grabbed it again, it rolled under the toilet around back. It's third attempt at escape had landed it square *in* the toilet. That rendered it unusable on all fronts.

She'd pinched the rim and lifted it gingerly from the bowl—thank god the man had good cleaning habits or a good maid service. She rinsed it in the sink, then delivered it to the kitchen where she set it into the dishwasher with its dirty dish friends and pulled a replacement that she put back, upside down, on the rim of the bathroom sink.

All of this, of course, was carried off without a single bobble or foible. And left her with no cup.

She sat down and closed her eyes and focused. Quickly she cast a small spell to see if anything had been cast on her. What a great irony it would be if Brandon were Wiccan, too. Or even a pure magician without the religion to follow. He could be having great fun countering her spells.

But when she looked, she found nothing. Not a single spell cast on her.

Her fingers simply weren't working. She managed to break every hair she tried to extract from the brush. To top off her frustration, every piece of his clothing was freshly laundered. The hamper was completely empty.

She could not get what she needed.

If she couldn't cast on him, she was stuck with him.

She'd almost sat down and cried. Right there on his living room floor. While he was off at work.

And what was he doing leaving her alone in his house? He didn't trust her.

Delilah amended that. Well, obviously, he did. But he shouldn't.

Maybe he had a camera on her. She'd looked around but couldn't find anything. He did know where she lived. So he could always come after her.

Eventually, she'd called it a loss and picked herself up off his pretty hardwood floor. Making sure she had everything that was hers, she turned the lock when she left. The man hadn't left her a key. Since he thought she drugged him and wondered why she didn't take his wallet, why was he leaving her here alone? For that matter, why had he asked out a woman he thought capable of the things he thought her capable of?

She found it hard to trust a man who trusted her. At least

given what Brandon knew of her, he *shouldn't* trust her. And why hadn't she made an effort—any effort—to defend her bizarre actions?

She'd started the walk home with her eyes straight ahead, watching the traffic around her and wondering how the world could go on so benignly, when so much was just beyond the edges of what you could see. But, within moments, her thoughts had turned back inward—to Brandon, to the dream—and her feet followed their own path home.

She was almost there when she was jolted from her blind state by the music from her cell phone. The faceplate showed that, not only was it Tristan calling, but he had called three times already this morning. Realizing that she had to do it sooner or later, she hit the *send* button and connected through to her brother.

"I see you have deigned to answer my call." Then he got right to the point—commenting on her date with Jeff. Which now felt like it had happened over a million years ago. Somehow he wound up with entirely the wrong idea.

"No, Tristan. It was a complete disaster." Delilah sighed into her cell phone as she rounded the last block to her apartment.

"Yeah, right." There was a smile in his voice that she couldn't understand. "I'm just glad that you had a good time with a date for once."

"But I didn't. Jeff was boring. And later, he was arrogant. Don't tell Yasmin, because I know he's her friend, but he was awful. What makes you so certain I liked him?"

Tristan's voice faltered through the line. "You didn't go home last night."

"How do you know that!?" Delilah spilled the words before she realized that they were as good as an admission that she hadn't spent the night in her own bed.

She really had to cast a spell on herself to be sure that she thought before she blurted. It was happening way too much lately, really since this whole thing with Brandon started. Which just went to show you that she really needed to ditch Brandon.

Something more than her words must have broadcast to Tristan, and she added 'keeping her thoughts closed' to the growing list of spells she clearly needed to work on herself. His voice couldn't mask the trepidation underneath, belying how concerned he was about the answer. "Was it the Rotisserie Guy?"

She could lie but, really, what good would that do?

It was likely that Tristan would just laugh at her for trying. Then, if it did work, she would carry around the guilt of lying to the one person in the whole world who truly loved her. So she bucked up and did what she could. "I plead the fifth."

That didn't work for Tristan. "Rotisserie Guy! No."

He said the 'no' the same way you would if you'd found out your perfect soufflé had fallen.

Delilah countered with a slight change of subject. "How did you know I didn't go home? You weren't scrying on me were you?"

A warped image formed in her head of Tristan and all his adoring clerks at the shop gathered around a crystal ball trying to watch her on her date. Luckily, or maybe just intelligently, she'd cast a protection against being viewed remotely a long time ago. If they had checked in on her, Tristan would never have made the mistake of assuming it was Jeff she'd been with. Still the whole idea gave her the willies. Thank god her brother had morals.

Indeed, he offered up a far more common method. "I called your house all night, you didn't answer."

"Maybe I was just sleeping heavy."

"You already admitted you were with the Rotisserie Guy."

Yeah, that blurting thing had been a mistake. She sighed again, finding herself at a distinct disadvantage against her brother's concern for her. "Can we stop calling him that?"

"So tell me his name, or better yet, bring him by to meet me. Since you're actually seeing him."

"Never mind. 'Rotisserie Guy' will be just fine." She didn't even address Tristan's idea that she was really 'seeing' Brandon. She so wished this conversation were over.

Tristan must have sensed that, because he claimed there was a commotion in the store and that he'd have to leave soon as it got busier with the Friday afternoon rush that would turn into the evening crush. They said their good-byes—even though Delilah knew the discussion of 'Rotisserie Guy' was far from finished—and he hung up to go train the new girl about the midnight closing before he left her in Yasmin's capable hands.

Delilah mentally amended that Yasmin was not a capable matchmaker, but she kept that to herself and just wished him well with his trainee.

She hit the *end* button on her phone as she looked up and down her own apartment hallway. She hadn't paid much attention to getting here. She'd walked the ten blocks from Brandon's house in a daze.

Turning the key in her own apartment door, Delilah stepped over the threshold into familiarity. With a deep breath, her whirl of thoughts and feelings at last came to a stop and settled.

Trying her best not to think at all, Delilah padded into the bathroom and turned the hot water to full blast. She stripped her clothes away and wished she could strip her memories just as easily. Not only Brandon, but all of them.

She stepped into the spray of the shower and simply enjoyed the heat for a few minutes. It wasn't long before her thoughts demanded attention. She tried, like she had so many times before, to figure out what had gone wrong in her life. But she couldn't find it. Couldn't pinpoint a moment of mistake, the obvious signs she had missed or ignored.

She and David had married in a whirlwind of romance, happy and in love. She'd had the white dress and the flowers in her hair. Her mother and father beamed, her brother and sister were in attendance, all of them smiling and happy for her.

They'd all loved David. David loved them. He'd known her family was Wiccan, and accepted her religion. He'd embraced her love of it, if not her faith as his own. He had no issues with what she or her family was.

Yet none of them had foreseen what was to come.

Delilah pushed the water off her face and thought back to her wedding day, to the days before and after it. David gave no warning that she could see. She'd gotten no cold feet, no inkling that something was wrong. Even in hindsight, she could see nothing.

Maybe nothing had been wrong.

Maybe it was her own fault as much as anything.

She squeezed her eyes tight to combat the twisting in her heart. That was enough for one day. Even if she could figure out what had gone so wrong with David, it wouldn't solve a thing about Brandon.

And the Brandon issue needed to be solved.

Apparently without witchcraft.

That meant that she had a date tonight.

She'd have to call him and tell him she couldn't go to Othello. But he would find somewhere else. He was persistent that way.

That meant she needed something to wear. Something suitable for a date. Something suitable for telling him she couldn't see him anymore. Something that said it was over.

She didn't think she owned any date clothes that said 'it's over.'

Damn.

CHAPTER 14

Brandon let out a relieved sigh. "Five thirty is excellent. Thank you."

He smiled as he parked the desk phone in its cradle and leaned back in his chair for a moment before he called Delilah to tell her. He was going to have to come in to the office this weekend to be ready for the round of investor presentations that started on Monday. They were too important to neglect. Still, he'd gotten virtually nothing done today.

Like usual, he'd come into work before Dan did, but this time he was whistling. Why, he wasn't quite sure. Delilah was a handful herself and she brought a handful of problems he didn't want to deal with. But his mouth kept saying things that kept her around.

Dan caught him grinning and joined in. After a few comments, it was clear that Dan was pleased that Brandon had given the girl the what-for. That took a bit of effort to untangle. The smile disappeared from Dan's face as Brandon explained that, no, he hadn't taken Delilah out of the bar and told her off or worked her over. He had, in fact, asked her out. Brandon didn't say he actually *told* her they were dating.

Dan was not impressed.

Then Delilah called, saying the reservations he'd wrangled at Othello wouldn't do—as she worked there. At least he now had a place to match to the kitchen in his memory. But there was the problem of getting other reservations for a Friday night in Hollywood.

He called every nice restaurant in town. And, no surprise, they were all booked. He was tempted to have Angela at the front desk call and make reservations for him under some famous B-list star's name.

Finally, he'd done the unthinkable and groveled to Dan.

Who'd yelled.

"Take her to *Pink's*, for God's sakes."

Brandon had felt his jaw clench. "She's a chef. I can't take her to a hotdog stand."

"Please, she screwed with your head." Then he conceded, Brandon could tell by the sigh. Dan tried one last time before he really gave up. "They really are the best hotdogs in town."

Brandon didn't speak.

Dan picked up the phone and called his cousin who worked in the kitchen at Spago.

She'd called Brandon back forty minutes later with the reservation.

Now he had to call Delilah and tell her dinner was going to be earlier. He wasn't going to get *anything* done today. Anything. Except seeing Delilah.

Grinning like the fool he knew he was, and wondering why the date pleased him so much, he dialed her cell number. "Hey, Lilah."

"Hi, Brandon."

That was it, no inflection, no nothing—good or bad. He'd never met a woman he could read less.

"I got us reservations at Spago. Is that all right?" Who could argue with Spago? Still, he crossed his fingers.

"That's fine—"

He cut her off before she could say anything else. "They're at five thirty. It's a Friday, everything else is booked."

"Five-thirty!"

No, he thought to himself, *do not back out on me now.* Taking a deep breath, he steeled himself. If the time didn't work for her, then she could eat steaks off the grill on his back patio. He'd have to buy a table and chairs, but it was still only noon. He could do it. He waited.

Finally, her voice came through. "All right. I'll see you there."

She sounded ready to hang up. "I'll be by to get you at four forty-five."

"Okay."

"See you then."

He hung up, wondering again what he was doing with a woman who was so much work. At least he didn't have to rush out and buy a patio set.

He scrounged through the office refrigerator for lunch, determined to stay in and do something—anything—work related. There was also the problem that Dan wanted to harass him over his choice in dates and Brandon didn't want to deal with it.

At three-thirty he called it a day and snuck out without telling Dan. Even as he did it, he wondered what his problem was. He and Dan always checked in with each other. It was the only way to keep things running. But he was gone before he could figure out why.

At his house, he wandered through the rooms, looking at it new, as though there would be some sign indicating that Delilah had been there. The woman sure had gotten under his skin. He just hadn't figured out yet what to do about it.

With fresh eyes, he saw where he lived. Of course, it was totally after the fact. He hadn't intended to run into her and wind up here. But it wasn't too bad. Right?

He cringed.

Right from the front door the place began screaming 'bachelor pad,' and it didn't quit screaming it. Ever.

The living room was a shrine to a TV so big it threatened to eat the viewer. Aimed at the TV were a sofa and mismatched chairs, slouchy for watching football on Sundays. The old non-descript coffee table seemed to serve as an altar to the widescreen, and bore circular testaments to all the beers of worship that had sat on it.

Out back, his tiny yard was enclosed with beautiful vines blooming as they climbed the wooden fencing, but he'd had nothing to do with that. The house came that way. The cement patio was home to two shiny silver testaments of manhood. There was a grill so souped up, it looked like it would take off into orbit at any moment. A matching outdoor bar with an inset fridge had a great liquor and beer collection. But there was nowhere to sit. He'd have to remedy that.

The bedroom had only one small nightstand and a California king sized bed, made neatly for the first time in . . . well, ever.

He stopped cold and stared.

She'd made his bed.

And that was why he had to keep seeing her.

Why the woman had drugged him then lied to him about it was beyond him. Especially when she was clearly such a poor liar. That the same woman would practically catch on fire for him after he'd almost badgered her into coming home with him, and then in the morning make his bed—that was too much of a mystery. That was something he'd have to figure out before he was through with Delilah Goodman.

He climbed into the shower and sudsed himself up. Then got out and toweled his hair dry, combing and watching it spring back into the large ringlets that more than one ex-girlfriend had been jealous of. He wasn't so fond of them himself, but there was something about having his hair past his collar that said he was no longer under his father's military roof.

After he got his hair where it could air-dry, he took a look at himself in the mirror, then promptly quit. There wasn't much he could do about the way he looked, and he wasn't about to get into it with himself. Delilah must have found him acceptable because she'd taken him home that first night. That was as much as he needed to know.

He pulled nice slacks and clean, shined shoes from the back of his closet. He chose a gray button down shirt, fresh from the cleaners, but only consented to wear it by sliding on one of his softest cotton tees underneath it. There would be no jacket. He only owned two, and didn't wear them unless someone died or got married. That was part of the benefit of working for yourself.

Four twenty.

Time to head over to get Delilah. He wanted to be a few minutes early. To see what she did before she went out. He figured those few unguarded moments would be worth gold.

But his car was a mess.

She'd been in it last night. The passenger seat was clear, but the back had fast food wrappers and receipts from oil changes and car washes. Last night, the darkness had obscured a multitude of sins. Luckily, Delilah hadn't paid any attention to the fact that it was no longer a clean car. Although to look at it now, you'd never know it had ever been detailed. There was not enough time to get it done and still be on time to pick her up. So Brandon opted to do what little he could.

She might forgive him his general male slovenliness, but he didn't know if she would be able to get past the fact that he ate fast food. Regularly.

While he cleaned the junk out of the car and into the waiting trash can, Brandon wondered if he could throw himself on her mercy and get her to make him breakfast tomorrow. His mouth watered just thinking about homemade breakfasts and what would have happened if he were still around in the morning to be cooked for. Then he stopped himself and wondered if she actually had any mercy to throw himself on.

He still managed to make it to her place a little early, but because of the building security he had to buzz up to her apartment. He found 'Goodman' on the list, just where it had been last time when he hadn't known her full name. He heard the change in static as she answered and her voice lilted over the crackling speaker, still giving nothing of herself except words. She said she'd be down in just a minute.

Brandon frowned. *No way.*

His sister swore that—contrary to popular belief—there were some women who were ready on time or even early. Brandon had never met one of them. After concluding that Delilah merely told him she was ready and was actually going to make him wait in front of the building, he began to pace. Right there on the sidewalk on Franklin Avenue for all the world to see. Of course that's what she'd done. It wasn't like she hadn't lied to him before. He figured some fellow male would come up and sympathize before Delilah showed up.

So he didn't even turn when the apartment door buzzer went off, signifying that someone had come out.

"Is something wrong?" Her voice sounded worried.

She worried. That was something to know. He'd begun to wonder.

She was in a soft, red, somewhat clingy dress that begged to be touched. "You're ready."

"And that's a problem?" She scrunched her eyebrows, looking at him like he was suggesting they try to shoot pigeons out of the trees and roast them for dinner.

"No." He stumbled through it. "It's not a problem." He opened his mouth again, then thought better of it.

Turning away, he opened the passenger door to his car for

her. But when he looked up, she was still standing in the same spot.

Her tone was almost demanding. “You were about to say something. You might as well spit it out.”

“I’ve just never met a woman who was ready on time. Early, in fact.” Great, this was already starting out so very badly. “I didn’t say it because I was afraid you might take it as an insult to your gender.”

Instead, she smiled. Then laughed. “No offense taken. My sister was that way.”

She swallowed the last word as her smile changed from natural to forced. Instantly, she started moving from her spot on the sidewalk, sliding past him and into the passenger seat. She didn’t look at him at all.

Well, he thought, things were definitely weird with Delilah around. But never boring.

Closing her into the car he went around to let himself in and started the journey to Spago.

Twelve blocks later she hadn’t said anything, only given him sideways looks that said she didn’t like something. At a loss to figure it out, he finally broke the silence. “What’s the matter? You hate Spago?”

“No, I love Spago.”

“I have spinach in my teeth?”

She shook her head.

“Good, because I didn’t even eat spinach today. So that would be very concerning.” He waited a beat while his attempt at humor fell flat around him. He tried again. “Really bad breath?”

“No.” For some reason she laughed at that, the sound washing relief through him.

“What then?”

“Honestly?” At least she unfolded her arms and turned to face him at that point.

All he could do was say, "Yes" and brace himself.

"I don't trust men in button down shirts."

He almost hit the brakes right there in heavy traffic on Sunset. "I was wearing a button down shirt the night we met."

"I didn't trust you." She shrugged.

"You took me home!"

"So?" She looked out the window. She altered the subject slightly, leading him away from the questions he was forming. "If you must know, my husband always wore button down shirts. He said they helped him present a better, smarter, more honest face to the world."

Brandon saw where this was going—ex-husband, button-down shirts . . . He was nodding by the time she said exactly what he expected.

"He turned out to be a liar and a cheat of the worst sort."

He was still nodding, trying to figure out if he should express sympathy or outrage. He decided to try her own tactics and went solely for facts. "So you're divorced."

"No."

That time he did step on the brakes.

Cars honked at him as Delilah scrambled to grab for the dash, a scared look racing across her features. Well, too bad, because that one was her own fault.

Angry at all she'd played him for, Brandon hit the gas, startling the other drivers and squealing the tires as he pulled off the road into the nearest parking spot he could find. Then he jammed his fingers into his hair.

For a moment he just looked at her, sitting there staring all wide eyed at him like he was the crazy one. Then he yelled at her. "You're *married?*"

"No." Her voice was calm and she finally quit looking at him like he was insane. "Widowed."

He blinked at her. He was so confused. That option simply hadn't occurred to him.

At least she didn't look so upset anymore. "I was in the process of divorcing him when he died."

His mouth said, "I'm sorry" even though he really wasn't. If the man really had cheated on his wife, then Brandon had little sympathy. He'd watched his own little sister go through half a dozen cheaters before she found her husband. So maybe Delilah's ex had gotten what he deserved.

That led to another train of thought. One he didn't like much and didn't want to believe. But, given his own history with her, he had to wonder—had Delilah been involved?

After a deep breath, he realized he wasn't in any danger of getting killed off tonight. He hadn't cheated on her. It was a silly thought anyway. So he got himself together and smiled at her. "I wore the shirt to impress you. To look nice at Spago."

She smiled at that. It was a brilliant smile that made him forgive her for sins real and imagined.

"So you don't mind if I take it off?"

Delilah went back to looking at him like he was crazy. She hadn't said a word. For once her expression told him everything.

"I have a nice, soft, expensive, grey t-shirt on underneath it." He already started unbuttoning the damn thing. "You don't mind if I go out to dinner in a t-shirt?"

Again she looked at him like he was crazy. She shrugged. "Spago is about the food."

He shucked the buttons on the cuffs and peeled down the sleeves, stripping right there in car on the side of the road. If he could look past the memory loss and the questionable ex-husband, he could imagine for a moment that he'd found his dream girl. She was ready on time. Preferred him in a t-shirt. And she could cook.

He tossed the shirt into the backseat and almost blurted out 'what do you think of this year's draft picks?' but knew he'd only be disappointed if she didn't know who they were. It would be too much to wish that she kept up with football, too.

He pushed his thoughts back on track. "You dressed up." *Was he trying to talk his way back into that shirt?*

She shrugged again. "It's cotton. Feel."

Delilah leaned closer to him, urging him to test the fabric. Even though there was nothing sexual in her manner, his mouth watered. She didn't need to know a damn thing about the draft.

He reached out and, though it was a little awkward there in the car, stroked his hand down the side of her waist. Her breath sucked in and the look on her face changed from proving a point to noticing his touch. For a moment he wanted to ask if they should just turn around and skip Spago all together.

But the whole point of this was that they should date. At his insistence. Sometimes he was really stupid. So, with great force of will, he pulled his hand away, "Yup. Soft."

Then he put the car in gear and pulled out into traffic.

CHAPTER 15

The blinds let in a soft glow. She liked that they allowed some sunlight in and yet still kept her private in the big city. God forbid someone might have looked in and seen her with Brandon last night. She needed her cocoon. Maybe more than most. She always figured the high fences were because there were so many people here that everyone had to lord over their own space. Even the balconies had high walls.

But Delilah was more aware than most that wood and metal wouldn't stop people from watching, not if they knew what they were doing. An altar, a white plate of water and a glass of red wine could see beyond a privacy fence any day. Still only the strongest would be powerful enough to scry through the spells she had cast on her apartment.

So Delilah felt much safer here in her own place.

Still off-kilter. But not as lost and exposed as in Brandon's bed.

When she'd slept last night, she'd slept well. Deeply. Contentedly.

Then she'd woken early, her conscious mind harping at her

about men. Asking her what the hell she'd gotten herself into. And what the hell she was going to do to get herself out of it.

She was supposed to break things off with him last night.

Brandon simply refused. He'd done it so successfully that not only had she *not* broken up with him, here he was, right beside her in her own bed.

She frowned. When had she become such a wimp? She couldn't even break up with a guy she was determined to break up with. She even told him that she'd gone out looking for a dress that said 'it's over.' He'd only laughed at her. She could still hear his words. *That dress says a lot of things. It says 'look at me,' it says 'touch me,' it says 'siren.' But it does not say 'no' to anything. Certainly not to me.*

He'd climbed into the round booth at Spago opposite her. But very shortly, the respectable distance between them disappeared completely. His hip pressed along hers, his thigh and shoulder rubbing against her bare skin every time he moved.

She'd tried to slide away, claiming it was awkward. But he tugged her back, pointing out that he was a lefty, so they just fit.

Unfortunately for her breaking-up scheme he was right.

Brandon fed her scallops off his fork and watched her, green eyes ablaze, as the food melted in her mouth.

Eventually she stopped waiting for just the right moment and blurted out, "Brandon we can't date anymore."

He didn't even react. "Yes, we can."

She'd tried again. "No. You can't call me, come pick me up. None of it."

"All right."

Her heart had lurched unexpectedly at that. She was kicking herself for already being so attached to him when he smiled.

"I'll just roll over and say 'good morning, Delilah.'" He then fed her a bite of risotto with sun-dried tomatoes before she could mount a protest.

All evening he merely told her 'no' every time she tried to end it.

When he brought her home, she tried again. She said 'thank you' and scrambled out of the car as soon as he parked it. But she was too slow and he got out behind her and walked her to the front door. She was useless when he took her keys, letting them both into the building and leading her up to her own apartment. She was mush by the time he closed and locked the door behind him and kissed her.

She was still mush now.

Mush was bad.

Mush made poor decisions. Delilah had too much history of acting on bad decisions and causing serious problems to be with a man who made her into mush.

Yet here she was, lying in her own bed, off to the side rather than taking up the whole thing like she was used to. Her head propped up on one hand as she watched him come awake.

Jade eyes blinked and focused. Brandon smiled. "Good morning, Delilah."

Her brain and her mouth fought. Her mouth won and she smiled.

"See, that wasn't so bad." He leaned up and kissed her lightly.

When the kiss started to change from greeting to passion, Delilah jerked back, pulling the sheet up tight against her. "You should leave."

He frowned. "I'm not really sure what's going on between us. But why are you so anxious to get rid of me? Why can't we just play it by ear and see how it goes?"

Her voice ratcheted up a notch, and she pulled a little further away. "I know how it goes! It goes badly!"

Brandon reached out and grabbed her hand, tightening his grip when she tugged. He slowly slid her back, closer to him, until she was plastered naked along his side, and trying so hard not to notice the feel of his skin on hers. He tucked her head against his shoulder and she gave up, ceasing her struggles. "I'm not one for making promises early in a relationship, but I can promise you this: I don't cheat."

She didn't say anything, so Brandon filled in the space. "My little sister is one of my favorite people in the whole world, so don't get me wrong. She has abysmally bad taste in men. I've been in a handful of near fistfights with guys who cheated on her. Truly, she shouldn't have picked them in the first place. I threatened the life of the man who is now her husband if he hurt her. I wouldn't consider myself much of a man if I went out and did the same thing."

He took a deep breath and again continued when she didn't add anything. "So I don't know what is going to happen, but I know what isn't. You won't find me in someone else's bed or arms, and you won't hear nasty little rumors, and you don't have to wonder."

Still, Delilah could find nothing to say. Did she feel better? Yes. Did she want to feel better? No.

After a moment, he kissed the top of her head. Before her insides could unclench, he asked, "Will you make me breakfast?"

Quickly he amended that. "I'll help any way I can. I can open cans, peel foil, and I'm a whiz with a microwave."

She fought the smile that kept threatening and she caved. Totally and completely. For now. "Fine. But you just do what I tell you."

"Yes ma'am." He rolled away, far more comfortable with his nudity than she was. But still she watched his bare ass as he strolled into her bathroom.

When he was out of sight, she crawled out from beneath the covers and got herself dressed in jeans and a t-shirt. Her frazzled brain had her double-checking herself in the mirror, then refused to change clothes. She stuck with her first choice out of sheer stubbornness. She was *not* trying to impress him.

She passed a still-naked Brandon in the hallway and slipped

into the bathroom, hoping that he didn't intend to come to breakfast that way. She'd burn the food. Or herself.

Brushing her teeth, Delilah worked hard to keep her thoughts on track. She slipped her hair up into its usual ponytail, and put on just a little makeup, stopping herself when she realized what she was doing.

She was looking through the fridge when she felt his fingers in her hair. Turning, she was glad and disappointed at the same time that he was in clothes. His fingers trailed down her spine and hooked into the waist of her jeans. Tugging on the denim, he brought her upright and backed her against the counter. He kissed her soundly, the pressure of his hips against hers hinting at something more.

Her heart was racing when he pulled back. His finger brushed a few stray curls away from her face and he scrutinized her. "Why can't I seem to get enough of you?"

Breath escaped her lungs and she panicked, wanting to flee the whole situation. "Really, I have no idea. Do you want pancakes, waffles, quiche, puff pastries with egg soufflé? I can make baklava."

She was rambling.

Sensing her need to extract herself from the situation, Brandon stepped back. Just a little. "Baklava?"

"Well, with sausage and egg. I'll put tomatoes on top. Maybe some spinach." She peered into the fridge again to be sure she had what she needed.

"Do you usually cook like this? I can eat cereal."

She turned to face him, hands on her hips. "I don't think I own any cereal. And, yes, I cook like this all the time. My brother comes over four, maybe five, times a week and I feed him."

Brother! Her ears and heart pricked up, checking for Tristan outside the door. *He wouldn't.*

Yes, he would.

She thought about calling him and warning him away. But knowing Tristan and his overprotective streak, that would likely just bring him running. She could not have Tristan here, not now. Delilah started to panic again. The only real solution she could come up with was telling Brandon she was sorry. Lie about a nail appointment she forgot or something equally lame. Then shove him out the door.

With a deep breath for fortitude, Delilah turned to do just that. But she couldn't do it.

He was wandering the edges of her living room, looking at the tiny pieces of her life. Really, everything but the bedroom was all one big space. A small breakfast bar jutted out of the wall, creating the illusion of a separate kitchen. But the other side bled into the dining area, thanks to a wheeled island chopping block and a baker's rack that she had stuffed to overflowing. A spare cabinet was situated at the end of the bar, creating a little extra serving space and more storage for bakeware and gizmos.

The flooring changed to carpet just beyond the small table and Brandon padded around barefoot, looking at her bookshelves and trying to glean information about her. She saw him head toward the one photo she had of her and Tristan and Juliet—taken long before. They had all been happy, and young. Arms slung around each other, grins on their faces. Delilah couldn't answer any questions about it. Not without creating a whole bunch of new ones. So she interrupted his thoughts before he could get a good look at it.

"Did you decide what you wanted?"

He turned and grinned. "You choose."

"Baklava." She purposefully picked the most involved dish. "Get your butt back over here and help. Is there anything you won't eat?"

He thought for a moment. "Tofu. Quail eggs. Caviar."

"You don't eat caviar!"

His head tilted to one side. "Does that ruin your breakfast plans?"

"No." She laughed. "But it's so good."

"It's fish eggs." He made a face and she decided to drop the topic.

"Can you brown sausage?"

"Isn't it already brown?" He frowned at her.

Dear lord. "All right. Lesson number one: sauté pan." She held it up, along with a few other pans explaining the basic differences, pleased that he was actually paying attention. "Sausage does not start off brown." She held up the package of meat. "It's really kind of pinkish. If you've only seen it brown then you've only seen it already cooked."

She went through a few more steps, getting him set up with the right size flame on the burner and handing him the correct utensil. "Now, let it sizzle and keep stirring. Get those brown crispies on it and scream if you see smoke."

He nodded at her like a soldier with a mission. Delilah began assembling everything else. She melted a pat of butter and whipped a cup of half-and-half then poured six eggs into it. She crushed garlic into the mix as well as a pinch of salt and some fresh ground pink pepper.

Turning on the oven, she checked on Brandon who was watching the sausage like a hawk. While she prepped the baking dish, she started talking. "So who cooked for you as a kid?"

"My Dad. Mostly he made stuff from mixes, and he didn't want us kids in the kitchen. After he got home in the evening he would supervise homework and boil water for whatever was for dinner. He microwaved a lot."

"Your mother didn't cook?"

"I have no idea. She gave birth to Bethy and disappeared from the hospital."

Delilah couldn't comprehend that. She could barely keep her jaw hinged. "She just left her newborn baby?"

Brandon shrugged. "Dad said she'd been getting restless for a while. I was too young to remember. Apparently Bethy was an accident. Mom signed the birth certificate and took off."

She stood there like an idiot for far too long.

"Hey, don't look at me that way." He went back to watching the sausage. "Everyone has a sad tale to tell. Your parents were around?"

"Both of them." She cut and layered strips of phyllo dough into the bottom of the pan. Trying to think what she could tell and what she shouldn't. "Too much of the time."

"But everyone's got a sad tale: your ex-husband ran off."

"With my sister."

She didn't know why she'd said it. It had just tumbled forth. She never talked about Jules and David. At first she had raved to Tristan who had listened and understood. Still, that hadn't been *talking,* mostly just anger and rants to expunge the pain. This was the first time she'd ever spoken of any of it in anything near a calm manner. Now she stood there, cold, wondering what she'd just handed Brandon.

She heard his spoon clatter to the counter. Felt the shock radiating off him. He didn't turn, but she could guess the look on his face from the tone in his voice. He was trying to be calm and cool about it as he picked the spoon back up, but there was a pinched quality to his words. "Your sister?"

She, too, tried for cool and easy. "I couldn't make this stuff up if I tried."

He stirred the sausage, the sizzle of the meat seemed way too loud and the kitchen suddenly seemed cramped rather than cozy. "Remember I said I wouldn't cheat on you? Well, I wouldn't. Certainly not with your sister."

Delilah snorted. "Of course not. She's dead."

Again, silence reigned supreme.

She stood still, waiting for his response. It seemed to take forever before she heard the spatula move along the bottom of the pan again. Her shoulders sagged. She hadn't cast the 'think before you blurt' spell on herself. Clearly, that had been a colossal oversight.

Then again, maybe it wasn't. Maybe now Brandon would realize that she was a walking heap of trouble where relationships were concerned. So she waited. Waited for him to put the pieces together and realize that it could never work. She saw him working up to something. She wondered how he'd bow out, what he'd say.

What he said was, "I think the sausage is done."

Yeah, well, I bet a lot of things are done. But she didn't say it.

Slowly, she turned around, for once fairly certain of what she'd find. But she didn't get what she expected. Instead he'd turned off the heat and was holding out the sauté pan for her inspection. He looked as immovable as he'd always been.

Her voice wavered. "Yeah, it's done."

His didn't. "So, now what?"

There were a thousand answers to that question. As usual, Delilah chose the easiest one. "Use the spoon to hold back the sausage. You're going to drain a little of it into the eggs while I whisk."

There in the middle of her kitchen, they worked in concert, neither of them really acknowledging the bomb she had just dropped. "That's enough."

"What do I do with the rest of it?"

"Here, pour the grease in this can. I give it to the little yorkie next door." Delilah gave him a real smile, although she wasn't sure why it came, or how it came so easily. "I'm the only one she doesn't bite."

That was because of a spell and not any sausage drippings, though. She didn't mention that to Brandon. He surely wouldn't be around long enough to find out what she was.

She pulled out fresh washed spinach leaves and rolled them before cutting them, making neat strips, then chopped mushrooms into paper thin slices. She had Brandon help her layer in the sausage and veggies. They added shredded cheese before pouring the egg mixture over it, then adding the next layer.

Brandon growled the whole time. "This smells so good."

"Wait 'til it bakes!" She carefully slid the dish into the waiting oven, then turned the timer for about half an hour.

"Thirty minutes?"

"About that."

"You didn't measure anything."

She shook her head. "I never do."

"So," he maneuvered closer to her, stalking her like prey, "what are we going to do for about thirty minutes?"

"Talk?" She deftly stepped away.

He crossed his arms and perched himself there at the counter. He managed to look like he wasn't disappointed that she wouldn't just climb right back into bed with him. "Do you have any kids?"

"No." Well, that single syllable answer wasn't helping the old 'talk' idea along very well. "But apparently *we* do."

He caught her reference to two nights before and laughed at her.

Her heart hammered like she cared when she asked him, "When do you get to see them? Clearly they don't live with you."

"Holidays." He fished the wallet out and held the picture up for her to see again. "Their names really are Tyler and Madison. And we really do call them Tiger and Muffin. I could never have come up with anything that good on the fly."

She interrupted, wanting the more pertinent information first. "Tell me about their mom."

Green eyes flashed sideways at her, as though he was holding something back. "She's sweet. And sometimes a little flighty. She was a pain in my ass most of my life, but I love her with all my heart."

Delilah's own heart hitched and she began to hate him for having that power over her. Maybe she should have just slept with him. Lord knows it would have been easier.

He leaned down to catch her eyes as he waved the picture in front of her face, maybe just to rub it in that he still loved his ex. She had decided she didn't care when his words came through. "And they don't live with me because they aren't mine."

She looked up.

"They're my sister's."

"That's why they look so much like you."

"And maybe why they look so much like you." He plucked out another picture, this one of the whole happy family at the same portrait studio.

Sure enough, while his sister didn't really look anything like she did—none of the features were even similar—both the mysterious Bethy and her husband had Delilah's same light blonde hair and blue eyes. She laughed. Maybe just as a relief.

He put the pictures back. "I have no exes. No one I married anyway. Just the one missing mother, a sister with bad taste in men, and a father who can't cook." He inhaled. "Although, I don't think anyone can cook like you do."

She followed suit and inhaled, too, enjoying the smells as the egg baklava baked. In her best southern belle voice she added, "It's a gift," and curtsied.

CHAPTER 16

Tristan eyed the baking dish that sat in the middle of the table.

Delilah eyed him eyeing it and wondered what he saw.

Grabbing a plate and fork, her brother made himself comfortable in a chair that had likely just cooled from where Brandon's hot little ass had warmed it only minutes before. Tristan, as usual, helped himself. "What is it?"

"Egg baklava."

He ate a bite and smiled, then looked at her. "What? No smart ass remark?"

"Sorry, I baked them all in with the eggs."

He took another bite and chewed, delaying his comment just long enough to make her start believing she was safe. "Or maybe you used them all up on Rotisserie Guy."

She moaned, then thought before she spoke. She tried really hard to sound like she had no idea what he was talking about. "Rotisserie Guy?"

"Yeah, when did he leave?"

Oooooh. She hated when he pushed. So she pushed back. "What do you mean?"

"Please." He gestured at the dish with his fork, hazel eyes flashing with humor. "You made this for yourself? Then ate all that? Without waiting for me? I'll bet you fifty bucks there are two plates in the sink." He smiled. "Or I can get a pendulum and start asking questions. Every answer on Rotisserie Guy is going to go clockwise."

Delilah groaned. She'd thought she was so lucky when Brandon had declared that he had to go into the office and removed himself from her apartment before Tristan showed up. Instead Tristan seemed to know everything, as usual. And he often figured it out without magick. She was so screwed.

"What do you want, Tristan?" She turned to face him, exasperated.

"I think the real question is: what do *you* want?"

"*I* want to be left alone."

As she had suspected, that didn't work. "I can't leave you alone, Delilah. You cry yourself to sleep at night and pick up strange men in bars when I do."

"So what?" She plopped her butt down in one of the chairs, recognizing this conversation as a long one, and one she'd need to conserve her strength for.

"So that's not safe. It's not good. And it scares me."

She'd managed to hold onto her anger until that last part. "It shouldn't scare you. I'm okay."

"I really have to disagree." He ate continuously through the conversation. "You've been upset and angry and who-knows-what ever since you came out of your little emotional coma after David and Juliet died."

"Emotional coma?"

"You shut down, Li. Completely." This time he set his fork flat on the table to talk straight to her. The fact that Tristan stopped eating was as bothersome as his words were.

"That's not true! I did not shut down. I *couldn't*! I did all kinds of things: buried my husband and my sister. I got a job and a new apartment. I cleaned out our house and sold it."

"Yeah, and you did it all—all crazy, exciting, scary, new stuff —on your own. And with the emotional range of a spoon." Frank eyes mirrored her own. "I was really afraid you were going to kill yourself."

He'd never mentioned any of that before. But her brain began to click to all the times he had just showed up, when she was at her lowest. He'd let himself in and found her asleep on her couch and carried her to her bed on more than one occasion. She didn't question why he came so often for food. Maybe he had needed the reassurance that she hadn't done anything crazy. And she had certainly needed to feel useful. "You were?" Her voice was small, her chest caving in as she absorbed what he said.

Tristan nodded. He picked up his fork and ate a few more bites to give her time to say something. Anything. But she didn't have anything to say.

"I'm surprised anybody hired you or let you into the building. You just seemed to me like you weren't even in there."

"Thanks." She studied the pattern on the floor, upset that he thought so little of her.

"Then you got angry. And you were angry at the whole world. You pretty much have been all this time."

She shrugged, not wanting to hear any of what he said. Mostly because she figured it was true.

Tristan didn't stop though. "Look, you had every right to be as mad as you were. No one deserves what David and Jules did to you."

Delilah felt even smaller, if that was possible. "They didn't deserve what I did to them either."

Tristan actually smirked. He still must not have figured out what she'd done. "That did get pretty ugly there for a while."

Not wanting to continue where this was leading, she altered

the subject just a little. "Why are you telling me this now?"

"Because you actually accomplished something crying your eyes out the other night. You're a little better each day. I think you're finally starting to come out of it. You actually gloated over that silly rotisserie chicken." His expression turned serious. "It was good to see you closer to happy again. Maybe you should spend all the money on infomercial crap."

She laughed.

Tristan joined her. "That's a good sound, Li."

"So, Big Brother, what do I do now?"

He sighed and got up to clean his plate, worrying her that his answer required contemplation. She would have thought he'd have that part all mapped out before he'd even started this conversation. Tristan was a planner, if nothing else.

When his plate was clean and he'd loaded it and the two he'd predicted he'd find in the sink into the dishwasher, he turned and faced her, arms folded across his chest. "You get rid of Rotisserie Guy."

Her breath came in sharply. Apparently that motion told Tristan everything he needed to know. But she didn't protest. Much. "I tried."

"You tried? What does that mean?"

"I tried several times."

Tristan had a *what-the-hell-are-you-talking-about?* look on his face. So she launched her best explanation.

"I cast a 'forget' on him. Then he broke it. So I told him to leave. Then he found me at the bar with Mr. Rocket Scientist—who was, by the way, the worst date ever—and he ran Jeff off. *Then,* I told him I was breaking up with him and he said 'no'!" She was practically wailing by the time she got to the end of it.

Tristan laughed. "He just said 'no'?"

"Yes. More than once." She watched her brother try to hide the humor he was finding. "What's so funny?"

"I'm just having a hard time imagining this guy who

counters your spells and tells you 'no.'" He laughed again, then sobered up. "You quit casting on him, right? You know it's unfair. You *know* it."

She nodded like the chastised child she was. Jules had cast 'forget's on her. She knew what it was to feel manipulated that way.

"It was only the one time." Delilah didn't add that she'd tried several other times and couldn't get the spell completed. Tristan didn't need to know that. She still deserved a few secrets.

"So you're keeping him?"

"More like he's determined to keep me. Although I can't for the life of me figure out why."

It was the standard 'big brother' grin he gave her. "Maybe he sees the Delilah you were before you got worked over. She's been starting to come back out lately."

"Or maybe he's just an arrogant ass. He believes his memory loss was because I drugged him to steal his wallet."

Tristan laughed again. "That's as good a guess as any if you don't know what really happened." Then he spoke straightforward again. "If he's really an arrogant ass, you should get rid of him."

She so desperately wanted to say 'yes'—that Brandon was just a jerk. But he didn't really seem that way. All she could do was shake her head 'no.'

Tristan tried another tack. "If you're keeping him, then I get to meet him."

Delilah groaned. It was like he'd taken over some of Mom and Dad's worst characteristics after they'd died. Like, now that there were no parents to insist on meeting and badgering the boyfriend, it was his duty. And, once he knew Brandon's full name, he'd spare nothing to check him out. Tristan would scry to see what Brandon did normally, cast on him to check all the angles. He'd likely even have the police run a criminal check and then do his own full Google search.

And he didn't pull his last punch either. "If you're keeping him, you have to come clean."

~

Delilah filled the dishwasher and hand washed everything that required it after Tristan finally left. The motions were rhythmic and she used the time to think.

Tristan talked of coming clean, but she wasn't planning on having Brandon around long enough to make it worthwhile. Although, she figured it would be a good way to run him off if all else failed.

As she dried the pans, she realized that she didn't want to be that crazy bitch he dated that thought she was a witch. She didn't want to have to prove anything. What was the point of telling him if he was just going to leave because of it anyway?

It would have been a real catch twenty-two had she wanted him to stay. She would have felt the need to be honest, and that in and of itself would have driven him away. Delilah reminded herself it was a good thing she didn't plan on keeping him around.

She stretched to hang the last pot on the rack mounted on the wall, realizing as she did it that her shoulders ached, and so did her legs. She'd been going for so long on such poor sleep that last night's deep slumber didn't seem to refresh her so much as it made her crave more.

With no pressing plans for the day, and knowing that if she stayed awake she would have to contemplate Tristan's idea of telling Brandon the truth, or at least consider introducing the two men, she figured sleep was the best option.

Her weariness pulled her into the bedroom and under the covers, but it seemed it was Juliet who pulled her under sleep. Her sister was waiting there in the shaft of sunlight through the window the moment she closed her eyes.

"Come'on Lilah. Let's go for a ride." Juliet tossed the keys and caught them again, the grin on her face and the light in her eyes infectious.

Somehow Delilah pulled herself up and followed. This was the Jules she had known for so long. The one who had never betrayed her. So for a little while Delilah was able to follow her younger sister without a trace of the bitterness that had settled in her heart.

They left the apartment—Juliet's old apartment—and made their way down to the garage. A sleek black coupe awaited them, and as usual Delilah asked to drive. Juliet shook her head and Delilah found a measure of comfort that some things were immutable.

Juliet had scrimped and saved for that car. It was far more than she could afford. She'd eaten nothing but Ramen noodles for months on end to save the down payment, then she continued to be frugal to make the remaining monthly payments.

As Juliet guided the car up into the Hollywood canyons Delilah stared out the open window admiring the glorious weather of the day. Red blooms lined the drive and houses crowded close to the street like they might climb into the car and come with you. They reached the crest of Mullholland and the Valley opened before them, squares of streets as far as she could see. The car made the sharp turn easily, and they followed the peaks of the hills, one of their favorite drives since they had been children.

Delilah ran her fingers along the leather door trim, admiring the workings of the coupe and thinking again that she'd like to drive it. As usual with these dreams, she seemed to know it wasn't real. She had an innate understanding of the future that would destroy them all. Still, in the dreams, she didn't yet bear the scars of that what she knew was coming.

So, after a moment's contemplation, Delilah asked what she

had never dared in life. "Jules, did you push the deal on this car?"

The corner of Juliet's mouth quirked up, but she didn't answer.

All three Goodman children had been schooled in the religion of the craft as well as the magicks. There had been no question about it. Her parents had withheld certain skills until they felt the kids were old enough to use them wisely. With Tristan and Delilah it meant they simply hadn't been taught the secrets until they were of age. For Juliet, with her peculiar brand of thought magick, it meant the Goodmans cast a series of binding spells on their youngest daughter.

They had lifted the last of them on Juliet's twentieth birthday. And Juliet had never fought them in that regard. She knew she wasn't to use the craft to harm another, to advance herself, or for material gain. But Delilah always had a nagging doubt about the car.

With their parents gone, Juliet had acted as though it was all okay. She cited the circle of life and that she would merely wait for the two to reincarnate when asked if she missed her parents. And she went on as if nothing had happened.

Delilah had never really wanted to know about the car. She didn't want to get upset about it. Later, when she might have thrown it in her sister's face, there were far bigger concerns than a mere car. But here, in the safety of her dream, where she was no longer so angry, and the answer wouldn't hurt, she tried again. "Juliet, did you give the car salesman a push to cut you a better deal on the car?"

Juliet still didn't speak. But this time she lifted her hand as she drove around the curve. Her thumb and forefinger were held just a smidge apart. Still Juliet had grinned, almost as though she were proud of herself.

Just a little bit.

CHAPTER 17

Brandon typed the message carefully.

"You said I can't call or come pick you up. So I am texting and you have to drive over." He thought for a moment and added, "Dinner. Steaks and corn—I can grill. Come at five. Bring a salad? and an overnight bag. See you."

He hit 'send' and slid the phone into his pocket, wondering if she'd come. The better part of him said that he'd get the steaks and get ready, and if she didn't show, it would be her loss. Another part of him fought the idea that it wouldn't just be her loss.

Still he couldn't figure out what it was about her that he simply had to have. He'd dated other women that he'd been very interested in. Yet he always managed to play the games, waiting before he called, keeping his distance and not being pushy. He'd been through women who did the hard-to-get thing and it always turned him off. Even when he admitted it was no worse than playing the forty-eight hour rule.

Maybe it was because Delilah didn't *play* hard-to-get. She *was* hard-to-get. He didn't expect a return call from Delilah. If he was lucky, she'd simply show up.

He pushed the thought to the back of his head and settled in to work. There wasn't a lot of time to get the presentations prepared. Not if he wanted to find a patio set and get the steaks and be ready to go by five.

Strange ideas came to him and plagued him during the day. He pushed them out of his brain, but they continued to nag at him.

Delilah's husband cheated on her and wound up dead.

Brandon could laugh away the coincidence. But she said the man cheated with her sister. And later said that the sister was dead, too.

He entertained thoughts that maybe the two had died together, and that was how Delilah found out. Except she said she'd been in the process of divorcing the husband when he died. So she'd known.

Divorces often got ugly . . .

He shook it off. His thoughts were what was ugly. He tried to convince himself that he knew her. But he really couldn't quite lie to himself that badly. In the end he knew *things* about her. And he wanted to say he knew *her*, but he couldn't. Then he fell back on the fact that his instincts about women were pretty sound.

Except for that one crazy stalker ex he spent six months trying to shake. And the one who tried to bang as many of his friends as possible and rub his face in the fact that he was losing out. Luckily, he hadn't really cared. So maybe he didn't really have such good instincts after all.

Finally, he decided that he was in it up to his neck and it was better to just deal with things and try to get some work done. Maybe tonight he'd ask her flat out if she'd killed her husband and her sister.

Four hours later he called it a day. He had everything as ready as possible for Monday morning, even though he would have to come in early. And he'd managed to keep only every *other* thought to Delilah and the evening ahead.

He locked the office behind him and hit the road. Three stores later he was standing in front of a table and chairs that he really liked but was uncertain about. It just didn't seem like solid furniture. And his imagination was fighting him, the image of Delilah in temporary furniture made it seem like that's what he intended. He knew that wasn't what he wanted, even if he wasn't certain about what he did want. Then again, maybe she was completely temporary. He wasn't even sure she'd show.

"It looks as though the fate of the world rests on that table and chairs."

The voice startled him, but he turned to see a man in a green vest who worked for the store. Brandon thought of Delilah resting on one of those chairs. "I think maybe the fate of *my* world rests on the table and chairs I choose."

He was about to admit that he'd gotten way too melodramatic for the moment, when the man nodded and stuck out his right hand. "I'm Mark, and I may have just what you need."

Following the clerk, Brandon made his way through the huge store. They ended up outside under the awning that housed the garden department, standing in front of a wrought iron set that was both beautiful and permanent. Mark pointed out pillows for the seats and Brandon stared at them before deciding that Delilah might like the blue and yellow floral print, but he had to survive his friends sitting on it, too. Red was definitely better. He thanked Mark and had the whole thing rung up.

When the big SUV was loaded with a heavy box containing the square, glass-top table and another with four matching chairs, he hauled it to the grocery store and had the butcher cut him two filets. He picked out fresh corn and refused to buy anything for a salad, telling himself Delilah would bring it.

Brandon repeated the thought like a chant a few times, upset that he was so uncertain whether or not she was coming.

Halfway home, he passed a liquor store and doubled back. He picked out a good beer, a red wine, and fixings for gin and tonics. Then grabbed a set of plastic outdoor beer pilsners at the checkout.

He groaned the entire way to the car.

Why?

Why was he so obsessed with a woman who only wanted him when he was right in front of her face? Even then, half the time she was determined to shove him away. Yet he kept coming back for more punishment. When had he become such a masochist?

Looking in the stuffed-full trunk of his car he thought he could pin-point the day. He'd started the night Delilah had taken him home.

Well, there was nothing he could do about it now. Except go home and assemble his new furniture.

He was covered in sweat and had pulled out every piece of his toolbox by the time he finished. The table base required a Phillips head screwdriver, the top a flathead. The chairs took a different size screw and then needed tightening with a hexbolt. And everything really needed two people to make the job go smoothly, but Brandon was determined that he was smarter and better than the furniture and he was going to win.

There was a certain satisfaction to be found in standing over the completed set. It looked good there in the middle of the patio. It invited you to sit. To stay a while. The bright red cushions shiny and new.

Brandon, on the other hand was anything but shiny and new. He needed another shower. He slowly gathered his tools and dragged himself inside. A little knot of worry grew in him as five o'clock approached.

Cleaned up, he kept himself busy preparing the steaks with a meat rub and a dash of pepper. He shucked the corn and wrapped it in tinfoil. He started the grill, closing the lid, letting it get rocket hot. He went back inside and ran a comb through his hair which was now almost completely dry.

When he was out of things to do, he checked his doorbell to be certain that it worked. Then he opened the patio doors wide so he'd be sure to hear her and sat down in one of the new chairs with a beer. Only then did he allow himself to look at his watch, telling himself it only *felt* later. Surely it wasn't yet five, he was just anxious.

It was five after five.

No big deal. Maybe his watch was a little fast.

Slowly he finished the beer.

Five twenty-five.

No Delilah. No word.

Son of a bitch.

He stood up and called himself any of a handful of names he knew.

Well, that was that. That was the end of Brandon and Delilah. That deserved another beer.

He thought about eating the steaks, but wasn't hungry. He tried to call her names, too, but he only had some for himself. She'd been honest. She flat out told him she didn't want to date him. He was the one who pushed. And he knew better.

Brandon tipped his head back and stared at the ceiling. It was that moment, when things were finished, and right then he realized just how deep he'd gotten by how much it hurt. How pissed he was. And how much it didn't surprise him.

He sipped the beer.

When the doorbell rang, he stood up wondering if the college student selling magazine subscriptions who was likely at his door would like a filet. He looked at the grill, disgusted with himself. He'd left it on, hoping he was wrong. With a flick of his wrist, he cut the gas as he walked by.

He was looking down when he opened the door, so what he saw first was a pretty little set of feet encased in red slip-on sneakers with ribbon bows. It bothered him that he wasn't sure if they were Delilah's feet or not.

"Am I still welcome?"

At the sound of her voice, his head snapped up to her pretty face, passing the huge bowl of salad she carried. Her face wore a weary look. "I'm sorry I'm late. I didn't mean to be."

She said the last part as though she knew he needed to hear that.

He was grateful, but for some reason his words didn't come out that way. "You could have called. I've been sitting here, waiting."

Brandon held his face steady, even though he hadn't intended to give that much away. He didn't want her to know how tight the strings that held him were.

She didn't seem to notice, instead she shook her head. "Traffic was piled up on the surface streets from some accident on the freeway and my cell phone died. Tristan called and wouldn't get off the line and my phone just gave out on him."

Relief shuddered through him. She'd been trying to get to him. Her phone had died.

Then he registered something else. "Tristan?"

"My brother. He wanted to meet you. But I guess not." She handed over the bowl. "Here's your salad. Enjoy your steak."

She turned to walk away.

Only then did Brandon see that he'd planted himself in the doorway, not allowing her in. His feet were spread apart and he could feel the scowl on his face. Instantly, he changed it. Tucking the salad into the arm that already held his beer, he reached out for her, managing to snag her arm. "I'm sorry. I'm being an ass. Please. Come in."

She looked at him with uncertain eyes. It seemed neither of them was ever certain at the same time. Slowly, her arm still loosely in his grip, she made the decision to change directions and walk through the door. She didn't smile, but lifted the salad bowl from his awkward grip as she passed.

Brandon used the opportunity to catch her, carefully tangling his fingers in her loose blonde hair and turning her for a kiss that weakened his knees. When he pulled back, he handed the information over freely. "I'm sorry. It's just that I was sitting here waiting for you. And I decided that you'd ditched me."

She shrugged, there wasn't much she could say. She'd already explained herself and Brandon accepted that. So he wasn't really prepared when she tucked the bulky salad bowl to one side and grabbed him. This time, for the first time since that first night, *she* kissed *him*.

Just as abruptly, she let him go and walked away, leaving him more than a little stunned. Still, he managed to find his feet and follow her into his own kitchen.

She found adequate counter space and opened her shoulder bag, producing salad forks and a bottle of what looked like homemade dressing. He turned the grill back on, happy as a little clam now that she was here. He put the corn on and carried plates and silverware out to the table. When she asked, Brandon happily fessed up that it was all new.

He slipped easily into the role of host, asking how she liked her steak done and demanding that she sit in one of the new chairs. "Can I get you a drink?"

"God, yes." Delilah shook her head, finally relaxing. The sight of the tension easing from her shoulders made some of his own tension ease up. "It's ten blocks you know. But it's the weekend, so I wasn't expecting bad traffic. It was a parking lot. I almost just ditched the car and walked. By the time I got serious about doing it, suddenly everything cleared up."

"Then you need a good drink."

Delilah took a gin and tonic, rambling sweetly about anything and everything while he tended to the grill. He'd stuck a tiny umbrella in her drink for fun, and occasionally she jostled it, making the paper garnish swirl in little circles. She frowned at it a few times, but kept talking.

When the steak was done, he poured them each a glass of red wine and sat down with her. She looked good on his patio, daintily eating steak and praising him for it. He plowed through salad filled with nuts and grapes and frilly little lettuces he couldn't identify. But it all worked together, even if he didn't know what it all was. Kind of like him and Delilah.

She told him again that he had to meet her brother. "My mom and dad both died and Tristan took over. He's worse than both of them."

Brandon laughed. It didn't matter. "I can handle your brother."

She looked skyward, like she was sure he didn't know what he was getting into. But he'd handled worse. Hell, he'd been worse. Delilah would make her own decisions anyway.

They were stuffed, sitting there talking, when the bugs started coming out. So together they cleaned up, hauling all the dishes into the sink in several trips before Delilah packed her bowl and salad forks back into her bag. Patiently, he waited until she finished, before turning her around and kissing her like he'd wanted to all evening.

She kissed him back, arms around his neck, and he'd never been more certain of anything.

Until she pulled away.

"I have to go."

"What?"

She seemed distracted, nervous. "I have to work tonight. I'm going to go home."

"You work at three a.m." The words tumbled over each other. He wondered how she was slipping away so fast.

Delilah opened her mouth to mount another argument, and he realized that he had to let her go. If he had any hope of holding onto her, he couldn't do it by badgering her or following her home anymore. "Okay."

"Thank you."

Brandon held himself in check. He didn't want to be the one to ask, but she was walking away and she wasn't saying anything. Deciding he'd be more upset about not having something on the table than about not holding onto his pride, he asked what he had to. "When can I see you again? Are you working all week?"

He hated that he sounded desperate. He hated that he *was* desperate.

"Monday, Tuesday and Wednesday. Then I'm off Thursday." She smiled. "So I can see you Wednesday night."

At least she didn't seem to be playing him. Brandon had to accept the fact that for whatever reason, he was far more invested than she was.

He kissed her one last time before watching her walk out his door.

CHAPTER 18

Delilah made cakes and pastries like the devil himself was at her heels. Flour made snowy white patches against the stainless steel countertops in the kitchens at Othello. Bowls of berries sat plump and at the ready. She popped one into her mouth each time she passed by. Her whisk was a rapid metallic scrape against the bottom of the copper bowl and the egg whites didn't stand a chance against her. She was driven to turn out as many desserts as she possibly could. Not that she could figure out why.

She expected Tristan to come by her apartment as he always did Sundays after dropping in at Blessed Be and checking the previous night's receipts. She wondered if there was ever a day he didn't start with a cup of coffee and a ledger. Since the store wasn't open on Sundays and he didn't hang around or spend time running the store, it usually didn't take long for him to arrive.

With her frantic drive, she'd worked a whole shift in six hours, then arrived home ready for a shower to see that someone sat on her couch watching TV. Brown hair fell in soft waves, the top of his head all that was visible on the man slouched there.

Her heart kicked up at the notion that it might be Brandon. But it wasn't. It couldn't be—she hadn't given him a key. Not unless Tristan had gotten here first and let him in. That thought alone was enough to give her the willies. If and when the two men met she needed to be right there in the middle, running interference.

She hadn't spilled all the beans the night before. She'd gotten as far as telling Brandon that her brother wanted to meet him and grill him like one of the steaks. That seemed like enough information for one evening. Then, feeling guilty about not telling him the whole truth, she'd completely chickened out of staying over, too.

She did have to get up and go to work, which she could have easily done from his place. But, since she hadn't yet confessed and been forgiven, she hadn't felt quite right about it. And he let her go. Delilah had no idea how much his easy acceptance of her not staying over would scare her until he said 'okay.' She'd expected the usual argument and instead it was as if she tugged and he suddenly let go. It left her stumbling.

So she was grateful now that it was Tristan on her couch and not Brandon. His voice carried up to her even though he didn't turn. "I figured you'd be early."

"Because?" She prodded.

"Don't know. Just figured."

"Somehow I worked really fast. Nothing on today's menu needed a long bake time." She walked by, slinging the white jacket into the hamper just inside her bedroom door. Delilah didn't say anything else as she made her way to the bathroom and slipped into a hot shower. Tristan hardly qualified as a proper guest. In fact, he'd already come in with his own key and made himself at home. She didn't worry about making him wait.

Refreshed and clean, she emerged twenty minutes later, ready to do what she'd been doing all morning: set up shop and start cooking.

It didn't matter that she'd been baking for hours. Besides, this was different. This was her own kitchen. This wasn't just food. This was a meal for her family and she would sit down and eat it with her brother.

Making him turn off the TV, Delilah demanded that he help. But that was normal, so Tristan didn't complain. Unlike Brandon, Tristan knew his way around a kitchen fairly well. He couldn't cook anything for himself, didn't know how to put it together, but he could identify all the utensils and chop and dice with the best of them.

They didn't speak when she popped the remaining egg baklava into the oven to reheat. She cleaned and seeded red bell peppers and made Tristan cut them and asparagus into skinny even strips. She mixed the veggies and sprayed them with olive oil before sautéing them in white wine. She turned the task over to Tristan and set about scooping perfect balls of melon from a honeydew and a cantaloupe.

They were quiet, working side by side with only Delilah's instructions and the occasional question from Tristan, until they sat down to eat. Then Tristan broke the silence before popping the first bite into his mouth. "So, did you tell him?"

Delilah sighed. In true big brother form, there was no getting away from him. She couldn't even pretend she didn't know what he was talking about. She savored the melon on her tongue, then responded. "I told him you wanted to meet him."

"And?"

"He said okay." It wasn't what Tristan had been after, but she hoped he'd take it.

Of course, he didn't. "So you didn't tell him about the forget spell?"

"No."

"So you didn't tell him that you're a witch." It wasn't a question this time.

"No, because then he would have figured out the forget spell." She put down her fork. He was ruining her meal, big time. "Lay off. I will tell him before you meet him. Because I know if I don't, you'll find a way to let the cat out of the bag."

Tristan had the nerve to look offended. Delilah leveled a look at him that told him what she thought of that. There was no way Tristan would meet Brandon, grill him about dating the little sister, and somehow *not* mention that they were witches. Not when he was convinced that Brandon needed to either be told everything or be sent packing. Tristan didn't have room for any middle ground in Delilah's life.

Once again, she wanted to be offended by his need to take things over for her. To dictate how she should be living her life. But the fact was, he'd taken care of her when no one else had been there. He was doing it because he cared. Then there was the issue that he was probably right.

Still he insisted on protesting his innocence. As though he would let Brandon go without telling him. "I would never—"

She cut him off. "Stuff it."

Thankfully he managed to bottle it for the rest of the meal, and they only spoke of the mundane things that kept them a family. Her job, his store, Yasmin and the 'beginners' class' that always went awry somehow and left Tristan constantly grumbling and wondering why on earth he let her have that class anyway.

They cleaned up side by side, working easily in concert from years of experience. The only adjustments they made had been taking the number of working pairs of hands from three to two. When they finished, he hugged her and left, knowing she'd been up for twelve hours, cooking the whole time, and running on very little sleep. Delilah closed the door behind him, sagging against it, before dragging her weary feet to her bedroom.

Stripping down to her underwear, she slid between the cool sheets, unhappy that they didn't smell like Brandon this time. Her mushy brain turned to thoughts of him and how she could get him back here. Then it turned cold.

He'd let her go very easily last night. Was he getting close to being done with her? He'd asked when he could see her again, but there was no phone call or text message this morning. He should have been awake for a while by now.

It would serve her right if he just let her go, and she knew it. To have pushed him away for so long, to have fought and bucked at the attraction she'd felt, only to have him give up on her when she was finally giving in.

Her brain worked with that thought for a few minutes. If she was giving in, then she wanted to be with Brandon. She had to admit that much. So she took a moment to savor the thought. But quickly her brain threw in another issue. If she wanted to stay with Brandon she could no longer delude herself that she could put off telling him. Couldn't tell herself it wasn't necessary because she might be getting rid of him anyway. And that brought up the very real possibility that he might be getting rid of her once she told him what she was and what she'd done.

She tossed and turned for hours, peeling her eyes open when her alarm went off at two a.m. Delilah figured she must have slept, because she'd woken up. She didn't remember sleeping, and worse, she did remember tossing and turning for hours.

Still, she had a job to get to. So she hauled herself awake, threw on her clothes and grabbed breakfast, still blinking her eyes to try to come around. She checked her phone for messages and tried not to be disappointed that there weren't any. She managed to get herself safely to work, then, like the night before, threw herself into it. She was greeted by a refrigerator full of raspberries and a question. *"Can you do anything with these?"*

Chuckling to herself, she imagined she was a contestant on the dessert version of some cooking contest. Only she got eight hours instead of one, and she didn't have to face a panel of Japanese judges who said all kinds of things about the food that always seemed to translate to "It is good. I liked it."

Still, tonight's work was time consuming, and she worked the full eight hours. Delilah was glad it took all her time. She desperately needed the distraction. Even so, things needed bake time, and things needed to be whisked and stood over and stirred, which meant her body had to be there, but not her brain.

Surprisingly it wasn't Brandon that occupied her thoughts, but Juliet.

The dream about them driving on Mullholland the other day stuck with her. It brought back with it a host of memories of the days before she found out about Juliet and David. That discovery tainted all her memories. It seemed that what Jules had done in the end colored over and gave a new darker cast to everything that went before.

But now Delilah wasn't so certain.

The two sisters had always been very close. Before.

Juliet had been her best friend. Or so she'd thought. Then again, in many ways she truly had been a good friend for a long time. They always enjoyed driving around the city on sunny days. Especially in the winter when the Santa Ana winds came and the days were warm. The smog was blown away and you could top a hill and see Pasadena in the distance without seeing the layer of grayish-yellow that lay across it, or even simply enjoy that it no longer looked like the world faded away just beyond the freeway.

Days like that, the sun would come out and it could even be ninety in January. The sisters would take Juliet's coupe out and put the windows down and drive and talk about anything and everything. They would stick their hands out the windows and feel the air change to ten degrees warmer as they crossed from Hollywood to the Valley. When drivers flicked spent cigarettes out their windows, Juliet and Delilah would try to outdo each other getting back at the littering smokers.

Juliet could pick the cigarette up off the road and send it swirling on a gust of air right through the driver's open window. That was fun to watch. Invariably the person had no clue why their trash had come back at them. Delilah didn't have that kind of skill, so she had smoked half a cigarette herself one day and collected the ashes for just such a purpose. She'd put them into Juliet's ashtray, waiting. For her turn she would put her fingers into the gray soot and rub them together. The driver up front would suddenly suffer from ashes raining down on his head. Inside the car. Usually there was arm waving and sometimes the sisters could hear cursing if the cars were going slow enough or were close enough together. Delilah always hoped that the people would quit flicking their cigarette butts into the streets, but it was good fun, too.

She smiled at the memory of laughing with Juliet the way they always did when they went driving.

They had grown up further away, north of LA, and out of the big city feel. They'd moved into town when Delilah started high school and Juliet was in junior high. Things had gone well for Delilah.

Delilah was pleased to find that for once, her memories of Juliet were pleasant. And clear. She stirred the berries and sugar as they reduced to a thick glaze and let her mind wander off again.

The high school in LA had been recently remodeled and nicer than what she'd been looking at locally, before they'd decided to move. There were magnet schools here that allowed her to study what she wanted, and find other students with similar interests. There were even other students who'd declared themselves Wiccan and gone goth in the process.

Delilah didn't put much faith in them. She didn't find anyone who'd been raised in the craft the way she and her siblings were, so she'd kept her mouth shut. Aside from working a few binding spells on students who were trying to do something stupid or dangerous with their tiny magicks, she stayed out of it. Even when they'd come back and said they'd bought their materials from her mom's new shop. Delilah always just shrugged it off.

High school had been her chance. She'd been ready to reinvent herself and she'd been able to do it. She was no longer the quiet little girl with the strange parents. In LA, her mom and dad were mysterious and therefore fairly cool. She'd gotten a new, better haircut, something other than her mother trimming the ends of her long heavy hair that just hung there. Her mother always left it that way, very hippy-ish and very untended. But Delilah found her own style then. She'd found friends, traded her button down shirts and long skirts like her mother's for jeans and sandals, cute t-shirts and flirting.

LA had been good for her. But not for Juliet. Juliet hadn't been ready to change, to break out of the comfortable mold their sixties-era mother had made for them. She'd been ridiculed. Junior High had been hell for her. When she had decided to put Delilah in charge of her image, it was already too late. She couldn't shake the labels she'd been tagged with. She was behind the crowd always playing catch-up, or trying to. And it wasn't what Juliet wanted, how she wanted to look, and Delilah didn't know enough not to try to clone herself in her younger sister, much as their mother had done to them.

Juliet had been uncomfortable in her own skin. Her anger and hurt at her fellow students' rejection had caused her parents to put a number of binding spells on their youngest. She'd even gone to Delilah for help. Delilah did what she could, cast a few things here or there to keep people off her little sister's case. But she didn't do much more despite Juliet's pleading. She was afraid of her sister winding up in some scenario that might have looked like it was straight out of Stephen King's *Carrie*, so she didn't cast anything resembling a revenge and kept most of her work on her sister's behalf to a minimum.

A sharp smell hit her senses pulling her back into the present, and Delilah looked down to see that the berries had turned into a thick bright magenta sludge. Exactly where she needed them. Running the goo through a fine mesh sieve took her mental as well as physical presence and she managed to keep her brain in the kitchen for the remainder of the night.

The only thoughts she had that weren't about food, were moments of satisfaction that those memories of Juliet had been seen through fresh eyes. Her thoughts stayed positive for the rest of the night, even including a few self-bolstering thoughts that she would tell Brandon what she'd done. And he would forgive her for it.

Later as she was just taking off her chef jacket in the office, Margaret, the executive chef/owner, came in.

"Lilah!" She offered a huge smile, just the kind Delilah needed to see right then.

"Hey, Mags!"

The two women hugged and stood against the wall, exchanging the usual pleasantries, until Maggie asked about the circles under Delilah's eyes.

Delilah could only snort in return. "Man troubles."

"Well, since this is the first I've heard of you having 'man troubles' you must dish!"

For some reason, maybe because she'd been holding back, Delilah spilled the whole thing to her boss. Starting with David and Juliet.

Maggie hired her knowing that something bad had happened. But she hadn't pressed and Delilah appreciated that considerably. The two had gone out for drinks several times, always clicking and always understanding each other. Still Maggie never asked about Delilah's past. Their job schedules being what they were prevented the two from spending more time together, something Delilah had always regretted. She'd always felt Maggie could be the only true friend she'd made since the explosion that had changed everything.

Maggie sat with her chin propped in her hand, eyes wide as she listened to the whole thing, with the witchcraft part edited out. But Delilah told everything, right up to Brandon and how she hadn't heard from him. How she was starting to get nervous that he wasn't going to call.

Delilah figured Maggie would give her the old *just wait him out* and *don't worry,* answers. But she didn't.

"Look, this world is full of couples playing games and waiting on each other and never finding out what's going on. Personally, I think it's better to know. So I think you should call him now and set up a date. If he wriggles out of it then you'll know. That's got to be better than sitting around for days just waiting."

It sounded so easy when Maggie put it that way, that suddenly she had the phone in her hand and was scrolling through her contact list with Maggie looking over her shoulder.

Just then, the phone rang. Delilah jerked, almost dropping it.

Maggie grinned. "Is it him?"

Nervous now, Delilah blurted, "I can't tell. I'm stuck in my contact list!"

So she took a breath and answered it. Tentatively. "Hello?"

"Lilah? Are you all right?"

She grinned, recognizing his voice easily. Taking a bit of Maggie's advice, she told him. "You just startled me. I had the phone in my hand and was pushing the button to call you to ask you out."

"Were you really?"

There was wonder in his voice, and Delilah realized she'd truly achieved the air of indifference she'd been going for. Brandon really had no idea how she felt about him. That was going to have to change. "Yes, I was."

"Excellent. Does that mean you're available for lunch?"

"Yes. I am."

CHAPTER 19

Brandon sent Delilah off to bed with a kiss. He needed to get back to work, but enjoyed her willingness to kiss him right there on the street. It was nothing but a small touching of their lips, even though he'd wanted it to be more. Still it sparked him more than such a simple touch should have.

He smiled, thinking of her, tucked into her bed, sleeping the afternoon away while he worked.

Later, when he and Dan finished their presentation a bit early, the investors immediately said they'd seen enough. Brandon read the same defeat in Dan's eyes that he felt in himself. Before they could thank the father and son team for coming out, the two merely said they had another appointment and pulled out pens, asking where they needed to sign.

For a moment, neither Dan nor Brandon were able speak. The two men had simply followed them around the office and sat through game demonstrations and development graphs with very few questions. Mostly they nodded their heads as though they understood but weren't very interested. That they were ready to sign—and wanted to hurry the process along—came as a shock. But he and Dan shook out of it quick enough and produced all the necessary paperwork.

Dan wanted to go out to celebrate. But Brandon couldn't quite commit to an evening out with beer. He wanted to call Delilah. That, in itself, was new to him. To want to share his work success with someone other than Dan. Then again, there was something magnetic about Delilah.

He settled back into his office chair thinking that it was nice to have someone to tell everything to. Then he stopped himself. He hadn't told her everything.

At lunch, he mentioned that he'd gone with his sister and her husband to the kids' school fair the night before. Both Taylor and Madison performed along with their entire second grade and kindergarten classes. Then the five of them wandered around the cheap, fund-raiser fairgrounds.

They'd stuffed their faces with popcorn, bratwurst, and kabobs. Gone fishing for candy. Bowled down plastic bunny pins for more cheap prizes. Brandon and Madison even managed to stay in the boogie-off until the semifinal round. All in all, it had been a great night and he kept wishing Delilah was with him.

Until he'd gone into the psychic booth. Bethy had shoved him in, wanting to get the scoop from the psychic since Brandon wasn't telling her. He was a bit surprised that they even had a psychic at a catholic school fair, but maybe it was okay because she was billed as a 'fortune teller.'

The whole family went into the purple tent and Brandon forked out all the money, glad that it was helping the art program. The psychic was sweet and cute to the kids, telling them that their lives were open and they could be whatever they wanted. By the time she got through stroking Bethy's palm, 'Madame Jennifer' had firmly established herself as a hack.

So he was surprised when she took his hand but looked straight at his face. "You have a new woman in your life."

He nodded. He figured he looked like a single guy, so that wasn't a big stretch.

"She is afraid."

"Okay?" He didn't know what to say to that. The woman was right, but again it was an easy guess.

"She doesn't want you to know." Madame Jennifer's eyes clouded, as though she were looking at some world other than this one. She blinked a few times before focusing again on this plane. Her gaze strayed to Bethy and her family standing behind him, anxiously awaiting his fortune. "You might not want the children to hear this."

That shocked him. Before he could say 'no, it's okay,' Bethy hustled them out of the tent, leaving him there alone.

The psychic leaned forward, her face a mask of concern for him. Brandon just figured she was putting on a good show. Her voice was her own though, not the over-inflected, slightly gravelly voice of Madame Jennifer. "She's hiding something from you."

Duh.

He'd pretty much already figured that out. He told the two-bit psychic exactly that.

But she shook her head vehemently. "No, not that."

Of course she said 'not that.' If it were about 'that,' then she would be wrong. "She's hiding something else. Something dark. Something you should look into before you go any further with this relationship."

At that point he'd had enough. Pulling his hand away, he said so.

She reached for him, clutching at his fingers. "Look, I do this for fun, but sometimes I really do see things. You should be careful."

Her eyes had been a little wild, a little soulful, as though she really did fear for his life. And he almost believed her—until she handed him her card and blew the whole thing. She was just drumming up business.

He shoved the card back at her, and the expression on his face must have said exactly what he thought, because she got angry. "You can ignore me if you want, and I'm sorry I don't have any more information for you, but whatever's in her past is dark. Blackmail, murder, that kind of dark."

"Okay." It was the only word to come out of his mouth, even though it wasn't okay. She'd ruined a perfectly good evening out with the kids. And managed to badmouth Delilah even though she didn't know a damn thing about the woman. Brandon held onto his righteous anger, even if Delilah still did have a few things to answer to.

He'd turned around and stalked halfway out the tent when she blurted out, "You told her about your mother leaving. About the fact that your Pop only made bad macaroni and cheese. And this woman, she can cook. It's like, it's like I'm in a bake shop—I can smell brownies and cakes and custards. And pumpkin cakes. There's something about pumpkin cakes."

He'd just kept going, walked away, freaked out by those last words tumbling out of her mouth.

When Bethy asked what the fortune-teller had said, he only replied, "Nothing."

But he was shaken. Madame Jennifer had ultimately been very convincing. Maybe too convincing.

He spent the rest of the evening ignoring the things she'd told him. It had all been so much mumbo jumbo until the part at the end. Then he shrugged it off. He told himself she guessed the pastry part because he smelled like cake, just a little. Delilah often did.

He ultimately decided the whole thing was silly. But if it was so silly, why hadn't he told Delilah about it at lunch? It would have been so easy: *this funny thing happened at the school fair last night*. But he hadn't said it. Why couldn't he forget about it?

Brandon knew it was just one of those psychic's tricks. Whatever they say that's closest to your truth gets a reaction from you, so they keep going with it. But she'd hit some of it dead on. It wasn't like he hadn't been having concerning thoughts about Delilah's ex and his mysterious death.

Brandon did what he'd done before and pushed the thoughts to the back of his head. Still, they waited there for him. When he finished whatever task he set for himself, they would burble up again until he managed to get into the next item on his list. But always they lingered.

Eventually he gave up trying to fight it, and he gave up trying to stay focused on work. He did an internet search, trying out the name David Goodman. He looked for obituaries and found three. One was for an infant and the other two were for men in their seventies. The timing wasn't right on any of them.

After a handful of searches that turned up hundreds of thousands of links, none of which were useful, he tried 'Delilah Goodman.' There were several old pieces about scholarships she had won. But nothing much helpful. At least he enjoyed reading the articles about her. He knew he'd have to confess later that he'd checked her out online. Quickly he made a mental note to check himself out too, just to see what might have turned up had she done the same.

First he finished the article. Her sister Juliet was mentioned in one of them. Delilah had been a previous winner and Juliet followed. There was something about the 'Goodman sisters' that grabbed him, until he realized that Goodman was *her* family name, not her husband's. She'd either not taken his name, or had reverted back when they divorced. Brandon had no idea what the mysterious philandering David's last name might be. That would make it harder to find him.

But, his brain crackled a moment, it would make it easier to find Juliet.

Sure enough, when he typed in 'Juliet Goodman' a series of

articles came up and a good handful were about the correct Juliet Goodman. Those generally had 'death' or 'car accident' in the title.

Mostly they were short and uninformative. Juliet and David had been 'running errands' according to one article. David Burnham. Now he had a name. All the information seemed to agree that the car had taken a curve too sharply and slid off the side of the road down into one of the many canyons in Malibu. Several mentioned that the two were survived by Delilah Goodman, his wife, her sister. None mentioned anything untoward going on between the two and there was nothing, no matter how hard he looked for it, about a divorce.

He wasn't sure how much later it was that Dan popped his head into the room asking if Brandon was finished for the day, and were they ready for tomorrow? Figuring he'd seen enough —Brandon sure didn't want to read all fifty-two thousand links the internet provided—he agreed and finally followed Dan out for a beer.

They hit Gin's again. As though if he kept coming back it would prove that he hadn't been here just to see Delilah. Of course, she was working and he knew he wouldn't see her. He managed to relax for a while and forget what the psychic had told him.

Surely if anything had been suspicious, truly suspicious, the police would have followed it up.

The two men drank themselves just silly enough to stay on their A-game. They had another presentation tomorrow.

Brandon held his glass up. "Here's to Richard. He was an ass, but look what he got us."

Dan clinked their pilsners together with a heartfelt "Amen to that!"

Just as he was shooting the last of his beer, Brandon realized that Richard had given him Delilah, too. If the other man hadn't been such a jerk to her, they never would have met. He raised another salute to Richard, but he didn't tell Dan what this one was for.

~

Delilah woke up long before her alarm that night. Rolling over, she opened one eye, staring at the red numbers on the face of the clock. 1:04.

She blinked. It was full dark outside, although the street light just outside her window gave some faint illumination through the glass. With a deep breath, she closed her eyes again, telling herself she could get another hour's worth of sleep.

By the time the clock read 1:14 she quit lying to herself. There was no way she was going to get back to sleep tonight. Throwing the covers back, she slid from the warm bed, waking up the last little bit as her feet hit the carpet.

Without thinking, she went into the bathroom to brush her teeth and wash her face. When she finished, she was left standing there in front of her mirror, thinking, *Now what do I do?*

It wasn't like she could just turn on the TV and watch for an hour. The only things on were infomercials. If she ordered any more *as seen on TV* products Tristan would have her head. She debated dressing for work, but there was really no point. She wasn't hungry enough to make it worthwhile to cook something.

She sat on the edge of her bed in her jammies and tried to think.

It only took a moment for the idea to come.

She owed herself a spell. Or ten.

Inspired, she began bustling about. She gathered her implements from the living room side cabinet where she kept them. Never ashamed of what she was or where she came from, Delilah nevertheless understood that flaunting her witchcraft was a bad idea. So her sea salts and incense coals and her herb bundles and sacred dishes all stayed behind the closed doors of the sideboard until she needed them.

The piece of beautiful handcrafted teak had been handed down from her grandmother. As the oldest female, she had been in line to inherit it, as had her own mother. Once, she believed her family should buck tradition and give the chest to Juliet, the more powerful of the Goodman daughters. But her grandmother insisted the chest was hers. The tradition was in place for a reason—it would always be the oldest daughter who had need of it—and Delilah wasn't to fight that. Later, she realized Juliet had no need of a place to store herbs and wands she didn't use. And, of course, eventually, there had been no one but herself to keep it.

One day she would pass it on to Tristan's oldest daughter. Not that he was headed that direction anytime soon. The colossal explosion between herself and Juliet had affected him, too. In ways that Delilah was still seeing. The hardest part had been David—they had all loved him. All believed him. And he'd managed to fool them all.

Delilah knew her family—with maybe the exception of Jules—would have protected her if they could. But David had gotten inside and taken advantage. And none of them saw it until it was too late.

Only as she set out the hand-crafted glass bowls, the wand worn smooth from years in her grandmother's hands, and the small orbs of crystal, did she think again that the cabinet just might be handed to her own daughter one of these days. She refused to think of a child with green eyes and chocolate brown curls.

In fact, that was the very reason she needed to cast this spell. It was horribly clear that her thinking was anything but clear where Brandon was concerned. Here she was daydreaming about children with a man who didn't even know her religion.

In moments, she was set up at her coffee table/altar. The magazines were set aside and the ceremonial knife removed from the wall. She stripped down to her all cotton white t-shirt and undies. Then she took a moment to center herself, to take a deep breath and let go of any of her stress—or at least as much as she could.

She began.

She walked to each of the candles she placed around the room. One at a time, she cupped her hand around the wick and blew the candle to life. She repeated the incantation for each of the four corners, then knelt before the implements on her altar.

Through a series of spells she asked for sight and clarity.

Once, she'd been much better at reading people as she touched them. But that had been because she regularly kept up with her spellwork. Constantly casting on herself to make her stronger had the desired effect. Delilah hoped to reclaim some of it tonight.

Eventually, she finished the work. Her head felt clearer already, her vision brighter as though she had put in contacts. From where she sat, she blew out all four candles with a single breath—just a little magick.

As she stood up, her legs stretched and she realized she'd been there a bit longer than she'd thought. A quick glance at the clock told her there was just enough time to get ready. Just.

She showered as fast as she could. Then blew her hair dry only enough to sling it up into a ponytail. This time she pulled the hair tie out of her jacket pocket and put the net in at home.

As her fingers worked the elastic band around her hair, a vision of herself came through. She was lying naked sprawled across her own bed, looking totally wanton and quite satisfied. She blinked.

Where had that come from?

The mirror gave nothing away, until she gave up and decided if she didn't get her hair up, she'd be late for work. As she rotated her head to see what she was doing, her gaze caught the blue fabric rose on her hair tie.

This was what had triggered the vision. Brandon touched this tie that first night they'd been together. That vision of her laid out across her own bed sheets must have been what he saw.

Lordy, that was hot.

She wondered what else she'd see the next time she touched him.

And she was beginning to wonder less and less whether she should keep him around or not.

CHAPTER 20

Brandon worked his butt off on the presentation the next day, but it wasn't as clean and easy as Monday's. The investors didn't whip out pens and ask where to sign. They said they had to think about it. Tell the other investors in their pool. Make a group decision.

They'd be in touch.

They asked so many questions. Some of them horribly underinformed. And they'd taken the entire day to come to their less-than-thrilling conclusion.

After the trio left, Dan stood in Brandon's office rubbing his head. "I hate this crap. I know it's wrong and premature to write them off and blame them for taking up our time. But it's just as bad to hold out hope that they'll come back tomorrow with fistfuls of money."

Brandon agreed. "Who knows? But today is a total loss." He was ready to rub his own head.

Dan looked like he'd put in a week of labor in the mines. "I'm ready to go-round again tomorrow. But right now, I'm going to go home and watch some football and see if I can't pass out on my couch."

Brandon agreed. After all, Delilah would be dead asleep right now. He wasn't thoughtless enough to wake her up before a shift like this. So he wound up leaving the office only about fifteen minutes after Dan did.

Exhausted from the trying day, Brandon paid little attention to his surroundings as he locked up the office behind himself and dragged his sorry butt down to his car. Eventually he took one good look around before he backed his SUV out of the parking lot. Immediately a man appeared behind the car and Brandon slammed on his brakes. His first thought was that the man was either a moron or was trying to kill himself under Brandon's tires. But he was too worn out to start up a good round of LA road rage. Besides, he wasn't even on the road yet. And the world was full of idiots waiting to happen. So he sat there with his foot solid on the brake and waited for the man to pass, but it didn't happen.

Because he was fairly short, the man's head was just at window height and it was wrapped in a huge white turban. On closer inspection all the man's clothes were white, edged with embroidery in fine threads. It was a nice enough outfit that Brandon had to wonder if the man was an actor escaped from some location shoot down the street. Or if there was a Hindi wedding missing their priest right about now.

So he was startled when the man rapped his fist against the glass, then motioned for Brandon to roll down the window. How had he gotten there so fast?

Brandon was just surprised enough to do it, not questioning the move until the window was already halfway open. The voice was reedy and crackled with a thick Indian accent. Just the thing Brandon would have expected from a character like this. "You are very lucky, sir."

No, you're lucky that I didn't hit you, walking around a parking lot like that. But he didn't say it. Just smiled and nodded and started to roll up the window.

The man spoke again. "You have a long life with a true love ahead of you."

Oh god, not this again.

"For five dollars, I will tell you all that I see."

"Ohhhhh." This time he actually groaned out loud. Then he got himself together and smiled again at the man. A nice placating smile as he resumed putting the window up. "No, thank you."

"Wait!" The man's bony hands wrapped around the top of the glass, forcing Brandon to reverse the window direction or break the man's fingers.

Even though he wasn't heartless enough to just put the window up and damn the man's fingers, he was still done with this crap. So he put on his best don't-mess-with-me face. "What?"

"I do not charge for this. You need to know."

Truly impatient now, at the end of a long day, there was nothing Brandon wanted to do less than listen to this man. But he couldn't quite bring himself to be rude enough to drive away, although he desperately wanted to. "What?"

"There are strong magicks around you. On you. There are spells cast on you. Hexes."

"Okay. Thank you for that bit of enlightenment. I'm putting the window up now."

At that, the old man let go and took a step back, his brow wrinkling. Brandon put the car in gear and pulled forward to turn out of the parking lot. In the rearview he could see the Indian man shaking his head and frowning.

Well, he was probably disappointed he'd lost the sale.

Brandon drove away wondering if people really paid him five dollars. Maybe just to make him go away. And what kind of living did he make at that? Brandon read once that some panhandlers in Vegas made enough to put their kids through college. Still, the Indian man looked upset.

And what was that crap about spells and hexes on him?

Brandon got mad. That crap was doing exactly what it was supposed to do: make him uptight and make him want to go back and pay the five dollars to find out what the old man meant.

He shook his head most of the short drive home. But he believed he'd cleared most of the infection of ideas by the time he pulled into his own driveway and closed the gate behind him. He wound up sitting on the couch, watching football just as Dan had suggested. He microwaved a frozen dinner and missed Delilah's cooking, but ate it anyway all the while telling himself that it wasn't so bad.

But it was that bad. After a long, drawn-out game that first looked promising, his team lost. His microwave dinner had been one that he'd enjoyed in the past, just not now. Brandon wanted to tell himself the company had changed something. The formula for the sauce was different or it had been frozen too long, but he couldn't quite brush it off that easily.

He knew the truth. The truth was that re-heated food no longer qualified. The other truth was that re-heated relationships no longer qualified. He'd been having the same stale go-rounds for years now. Meet girl. Like girl. Sleep with girl. Wait for something to come up that keeps it from going any further. Find next girl.

It wasn't a very flattering look at either himself or the women he'd been dating. The fact was, he didn't even remember half their names, they'd been so interchangeable. While he didn't know if what was going on with Delilah was right or if it was going to completely blow up in his face, at least it was different.

Every time he saw her, he became more attached to her. More convinced that whatever was going on with him not remembering their first night wasn't her fault. He needed, more than ever, to know if she felt any of the same feelings for him.

Still, there was no way he was going to solve any of those problems while the football commentators re-hashed a game that had been thrown away at the end of the second quarter.

Eventually he hauled himself into his bedroom and rolled into bed.

But all night, thoughts bounced through his head about hexes and spells.

~

Something was different about Brandon. Delilah just couldn't quite put her finger on it.

Wednesday, she'd slept all day. Her shift had gone by pretty quickly, and by eight a.m. she was home and putting away the groceries she'd stopped for on the way back. Then she'd fallen, face first, onto the fluffy comforter and tried to force her body back onto Brandon's schedule. Though even he told her he hadn't known what that would be, given that he and Dan were presenting to investors again all day.

Still, she shook herself awake and out of bed by four o'clock and was clean out of the shower by four-thirty. She took the time to blow dry her hair and put on make-up. By five, she was sitting on her couch with a glass of wine in hand while she waited.

Delilah figured she'd be there for a while. One, because she deserved it after making him wait last week. And two, because she hoped that meant things were going well with the investors and they had a lot of questions or were busy with paperwork. So she sipped her wine and leaned her head back against the couch cushions.

He called not ten minutes later to say he was on the way.

Delilah had hopped up and gotten down to work. She was quite proud that the oven was heating and the rice was already boiling in the steamer when he came in through the front door she'd left unlocked. She decided right then she would just give him a key. She had a few spares in the pen drawer, but he was so hyped up about something that she only got to *hello* before he was talking a mile a minute.

"Wait. I'm sorry."

Delilah wasn't sure what he was sorry for, but she didn't have to wait more than a fraction of a second. Brandon hugged her close, lifting her to the tips of her toes, where he looked right into her eyes. "Hello."

Then he kissed her thoroughly before sitting on her couch, which was a good thing because her knees were about to give out. Luckily, she'd already had a beer in hand for him and she held it up. As he accepted it, he started talking again.

Not all of it made sense to her. In a moment she found her feet and made her way back into the kitchen, still listening. Sipping at her wine, she got to work on the remainder of dinner while she listened to him ramble.

"These guys are very interested. It seems their problem is they want to put in more money than they have. But they wound up not signing anything today. Which is frustrating."

"What exactly do they invest in?" She rubbed a thin layer of oil on the slabs of salmon in her hands.

"Well, we have a concept for a game. They put in the money, we hire the code writers and design people, and do a lot of it ourselves. Then we sell it to a big company and the profit goes out according to shares."

While she sprinkled herbs and chopped broccoli, he watched her with an intensity that threatened to unnerve her. It was like he was looking for a drug deal to go down or trying to catch a card dealer doing sleight of hand.

But he kept talking, explaining the finer points of their system. How video games were developed in other ways. Their track record and the idea they had right now that people would want to put their money into. He told her about games they developed and sold in the past and what kind of money and splash they'd been able to make.

She shook her head each time. Each time disappointing him that she hadn't heard of one of his babies. Eventually she begged him to stop his questions. She pointed out her TV, and how it lacked *any* kind of gaming system.

Brandon walked over to the set, looking at it as though it were an alien being of some kind. Which was funny, because hers was so much more basic than his, lacking all the wires and game controllers. Also hers was a *lot* smaller. He popped it on and—as Tristan had predicted a week ago—it was on one of the cooking channels. He sounded almost bewildered. "This is what you watch?"

She nodded as she pulled the fish from the oven, turning it and admiring the perfect tinge to the pink meat. She looked up at him long enough to catch the frown that marred his features.

"Why do you watch this? You're a trained chef. You can't possibly learn anything from your TV. Can you?"

"I get ideas. I don't know that I would have thought up baking raspberries and pears together. One of the shows made a pie with it, like, a month ago. But two nights ago I had a batch of raspberries and I made raspberry pear cream tarts. So it's worth watching." She set the timer and joined him on the couch for a few minutes, curling in beside him as he watched a round woman showing off a level measure of yeast for a bread recipe.

He frowned again and flipped channels, surfing like every man she knew. Only after the first ten channels went by, he cringed and apologized. "I'm sorry. It's just been a long day and my mind is off. Does it bother you if I channel surf a little?"

"Not at all."

But while he ran through the programs, watching each one for all of fifteen seconds, it seemed he continued to keep an eye on her.

When she got up to pull the fish from the oven,

When she removed the top on the steamer and forked out bright green broccoli onto two plates.

When she pulled a lemon sauce from the fridge and whisked it for a moment.

She wanted to believe that he was just so in love with her that he couldn't look away. But it seemed more like he was watching for poison. More like he was waiting to catch her at something than like he was making puppy love eyes.

He turned off the TV and came to the table. He ate everything she set before him, including the leftover fruit tart she cut into wedges for dessert, as though it were his last meal. He praised her for each thing until she thought he'd gone a little overboard.

"You act like you've never eaten good food before."

He practically shoveled another bite of his rapidly disappearing dessert into his mouth. "I swear I had a microwave dinner last night."

Delilah made a face and shivered through a round of the willies while Brandon laughed.

She smiled at him. "You could eat here."

"Not all the time."

There it was: the perfect opening to say 'you can have a key, then you can come eat whatever you find in the fridge.'

There was a small pause as they waited, while Delilah couldn't quite get her mouth to form the words. Then it was Brandon who filled in the space. "Besides, if I ate here all the time I'd get fat."

"No, you wouldn't. The preservatives in those frozen dinners will make you fat long before anything I serve you will." There it was again. Another perfect opening to offer him a key. But still she couldn't seem to get the words out.

"It wasn't frozen," he insisted, "it was from a box. I added water."

"Eww. You should switch over to frozen. I don't even want to think about the chemicals in food you don't have to chill."

Brandon, still laughing at her—though Delilah was convinced it was no laughing matter—stood with his plate, insisting that he clean up since she made everything. He practically forced her to sit at the table while he loaded the dishwasher and hand-scrubbed a few of her precious pots even though she'd volunteered to do it. They talked about nothing and everything and still he watched her.

Finally, he hit the start button on the dishwasher, filling the room with the subtle swishing sounds. Turning, he braced his hands on her countertop behind him, his eyes painfully serious for the first time all evening. Something in his stance made her heart go *uh-oh*. She'd seen him building to this all evening.

"I don't know how to ask it, so I'm just going to say it flat out. Please don't be offended."

Here it comes. Although she had no idea what *it* was, she was nervous right down to her bones.

"Do I get to stay tonight?" Immediately he began backpedaling. "Look, that's not why I came. I wanted to see you. And if the answer is 'no' I still want to see you. I want to stay for a while at least."

She wanted to stop him in his frantic explanation. Then again, she wanted to hear it, too. Wanted to know if he had a solution or even just a reason for all this craziness.

"I thought we could settle in, watch TV, whatever." He took a deep breath. Just when she was ready to jump in and save him, he started prattling again. "It isn't just about the sex. It was. But it isn't anymore. I just . . ."

He ran out of words or steam or something. His eyes looked away then and his hands searched for something to do before grabbing a hand towel and wiping at his fingers. After a moment passed in almost complete silence, he looked back at her. "Say something. Anything."

Delilah was just ecstatic that he wanted to stay. She wondered for a while if maybe she'd placated him with food too much and now all he wanted from her was the occasional good meal. It also made her heart lift to finally find out what made him watch her so closely all evening.

When she opened her mouth to push the words out it felt like she stumbled over her own tongue. But she managed. "Yes. You should stay."

His head popped up, his green eyes bright. "I should?"

She nodded. "Please."

As charged as the moment was, they did what he'd suggested and sat down side by side on the couch. He automatically picked up the remote control and began looking for some kind of programming. What he was looking for, Delilah had no clue. Apparently, neither did he, because he changed the channel every few minutes. It wasn't quite fast enough to be called surfing, but he couldn't seem to settle on any one thing. Delilah couldn't bring herself to complain, though. She was exactly where she wanted to be, curled into his side, with his arm around her holding her against him. She couldn't have cared less what they were watching.

After half an hour, he turned to her.

"I know I said we should watch TV, but TV really isn't holding my interest with you all pressed up beside me."

Delilah smiled. "Me either."

His return grin was all but lost as his mouth found hers. Heat from him flooded into her as his lips moved across her mouth. His tongue tasted her and tested the borders until she opened for him.

Delilah's arms twined around his torso, using him as an anchor to tug herself up flush against him. Every breath, in her lungs and his, rocked them just a little closer together. His hands roamed over her, as though they were restless and didn't know where to settle. Eventually they wound their way into her hair, tugging at the elastic and tossing it aside. His fingers found the back of her head and turned her so he could kiss her more deeply.

It was her hands that started undressing them, working their way under the edge of his shirt. Smooth skin and crisp hair passed under her touch as she slid the cotton higher. Brandon worked with her, pulling his arms out then finally giving her the shivers when he growled just a little because he had to break the kiss to get the shirt completely off.

He tossed it to the side, his hands and mouth already occupied with getting her out of her own shirt. Delilah felt her head fall back, as first his fingers, then his lips, made a path ever lower as he opened each button exposing just a little more skin. Somehow he managed to not touch her breasts, no matter how much she wanted him to, until he had the top entirely off her and flung to the floor to join his. Only then did he look her in the eyes as she felt his hand climb higher against the bare skin of her ribcage, until his thumb brushed the underside of her breast through the thin layer of her bra and she was unable to breathe at all.

Slowly and in maddening degrees, he stripped her of every piece of clothing, leaving her as bare and vulnerable as she could be. His skin was feverish to the touch and driving her crazy. Crazy to the point that she didn't pay attention to the tiny flashes of pictures appearing in her head at random intervals.

He was thinking things before he did them—wanting and acting on it. When he first laced his fingers with hers, she was given the picture—the want—for her to touch him, to open the zipper on his jeans and ease the pressure he was feeling there. As he dragged her hand down, Delilah acted on his need. Pulling her mouth away from his, she kissed her way across his chest, using both her hands to set him free.

She reveled in the feel of him, unable to see beyond him or this exact moment.

Following the cues she was unaware she was even getting, Delilah pushed her fingers into his back pocket, finding the condom he'd been thinking about and pulling it out in her fist. Quickly she stripped him as bare as she was, all the while Brandon was lifting her, moving her, positioning her over the wide roll arm of the couch.

He watched as he draped her there before snagging the foil packet from her grip and rapidly sheathing himself. His voice came out on a breath, only her name, only part of it, and she heard the question there. "*Lilah?*"

She responded with her own desperate *please*, and was rewarded as he entered her.

They moved together, Delilah's world shrinking with every touch. She existed only where his skin contacted hers, only in the scent of him, the taste of him. His name fell from her lips repeatedly, and his eyes made contact with hers where she could see the need shining there that mirrored her own.

She was hot and oversensitized by the time she gave a last gasp and fell, headlong into the contractions that seized her. Even in the abyss where she was, she could feel him tensing against her, his own release only seconds behind hers.

It took forever for the world to stop spinning around them, for her breathing to even out or her brain to be able to grab a single thought and hang onto it for more than a passing second. Brandon was a heavy weight, sweetly pinning her to the couch. She could feel every deep breath in his chest pressed against hers. Her hands felt the slick skin on his back, traced his spine while they lay there and recouped.

Eons later, he lifted his head. A small, sated smile wound its way across his mouth. Still it took him a moment to find his voice. "You look satisfied."

Her own smile claimed her lips, and for a moment she

managed a small stretch, even pinned as she was underneath him. "I needed that."

Brandon's green eyes blinked, his expression becoming more serious, even though she couldn't say how it had changed. He closed his eyes, pressing his forehead to hers. "I needed you."

CHAPTER 21

Brandon heard the door click closed behind Dan hoping the lie didn't show on his face. After all he wasn't really *lying* about having more work to do, it was just different work. He was just hiding things.

Delilah wrung him out last night. Both physically and emotionally. They'd made love three times, as though to make up for the dry spell. He didn't know if it was Delilah who demanded so much from him, or if he simply couldn't help but give it. But each time they came together, he handed over another piece of himself.

In itself, that wouldn't be bad. He'd been dating all those interchangeable women thinking that one day one would come along and be unique. Be one he couldn't live without. But in his imagination, in the path he'd always been certain love would take, it had been both of them there—giving and learning together.

With Delilah, he was unsure.

Oh, she contributed, she was *there,* in a way his previous lovers hadn't been. But he wasn't sure she was handing her soul over, piece by piece, the way he seemed to be.

And only later, right after she'd fallen asleep, had his brain actually begun to work and a few things had clicked into place. There had been moments all evening, where he'd been ready to ask for something, say something, and she'd nodded or tilted her head and done it. Without him asking. He'd not gotten the words out. But she'd answered.

The second time, after he'd carried her into the bedroom, she'd peeled herself off the covers and wandered into the kitchen. She'd come in carrying two slices of watermelon that he'd seen in the fridge earlier, and a glass of ice water. And, though she shared the water with him, she'd said she wasn't hungry for the watermelon.

There had been no comment, like *I just thought you might be hungry* or *I saw these there and really wanted one*. She'd seemed quite solid in her knowledge that this was what he'd wanted.

At one point, she'd rolled over to set the alarm for him, exposing a luscious view of her backside. She couldn't have seen him, it couldn't have been the look on his face. But he'd touched her shoulder and she'd popped back up, her mouth open and a wide-eyed look on her face. She asked him, *really?* Did he really want to do that?

Again he'd been so caught up in the moment that he hadn't realized he hadn't voiced his thoughts. Now, he was feeling stupid. Like he hadn't seen it because he'd been naked, and there'd been a gorgeous naked female within his touch. He was beginning to have serious reservations that he was being led around by his dick. It bothered him that he was only capable of having these thoughts when he was nowhere near her.

He considered the possibility that she was psychic. But it didn't seem likely. The skill seemed to come and go. Not that he was any expert, but that seemed odd. Now there were two random strangers who told him to beware. That strange little Indian man said there were spells and hexes on him. And Brandon was unable to shake off the vague unease caused by the fact that he still didn't have any answers to the memory loss of the first night they'd shared.

Sure, he had most of it back now, but it had been completely gone for a while. He'd hoped she'd volunteer the information sooner or later. But it looked at this point like even 'later' wasn't going to happen.

Though it made him sick in his heart to do it, and he desperately hoped that he wouldn't find anything, he had to look.

As Dan's car pulled out of the parking lot, Brandon smiled and waved through the glass window as though not a thing in the world was wrong. Then he immediately turned back to his keyboard. He'd specifically waited until the office was empty before he did the search. He had no idea how long he'd be here or what he'd find, and he had no desire whatsoever to explain what he was looking up.

He pulled up a search engine and typed in 'spells candles.' In seconds, a slew of links appeared on his screen.

He sighed. Of course it wasn't going to be that easy.

Wading through the flotsam that a search like this always produced, he thought about what he'd seen at Lilah's the night before. Candles, everywhere. All women, or at least most that he knew, loved candles, but he'd never before seen a collection like Delilah owned. She had a set of tall thin ones in primary colors: blue, yellow, green and red. There was a tall fat white one. A tall fat black one.

The black candle seemed odd to him. It wasn't a homey, I-sure-love-the-light-of-a-flame kind of candle. And there were a handful of others. All in wooden candle holders, most of which looked like they'd been carved from knots of wood. They were pretty. But combined with the rest of it, they were suspicious, too.

There were little glass bowls, one had white stuff in it. Maybe sugar, he hadn't been able to get close enough to see.

There was a wall rack with ceremonial knives. He wondered why he hadn't noticed it before.

The thing was, before he'd been too caught up in looking at Delilah. And, truth be told, they looked like decoration. They were pretty and artfully arranged. Just the kind of thing Delilah would have a collection of. She sure didn't have teacups or those little crying figurines. But the knives were now suspect.

He'd been thumbing through the list. Pulling up a website and closing it down again when it didn't provide any help. Then a picture popped up on one of the links and grabbed his attention.

His heart stopped cold.

The photo was captioned "witch's altar." Witches had altars?

But it was the things in the photo that made him sit back, that slowed his breathing. There were two dishes. A sun and a moon carving. A wicked sharp ceremonial knife. A wine glass of blood. A big black candle.

Oh shit.

Knowing he wasn't going to like what he found, Brandon forced himself to read the accompanying article.

It explained something called casting a circle, which was generally done with a circle of salt and four candles . . . in red, yellow, and blue with the fourth being green or brown depending on the various branch of Wicca being practiced. The piece went on to describe the items in the photo and that the altar could be changed or rearranged depending on the witch or the spell. It said 'practitioners' often preferred to choose a sun god and moon goddess that represented themselves rather than the standard in the picture. The sugar in the bowl was actually salt. And, to his great relief, the blood was merely red wine.

While the information made him feel marginally better, the very fact that all the items for a witch's workshop were on Delilah's bookshelf or wall only made him feel worse.

For an hour, he ran other searches, looking up 'casting spells' and 'modern day witches.' He thumbed through one article after another, a lot of them having to do with ritual sacrifice, the need to kill with the athame—the ceremonial knife—as a way to empower it for magick. There was an entire section devoted to creating spell energy from living sources, either by bloodletting or killing. It said witches could spill their own blood for a spell, but in many cases the blood of another was required.

His stomach turned.

Eventually he learned far more than he needed.

The stupid school-fair psychic and the creepy man on the street had been right about one thing—he was in trouble. Big, big trouble.

He knew the greatest danger was—even seeing all this—he still wanted her. He didn't want to want her. But, God, he did.

Oh crap.

His head dropped into his hands. That first night. She'd burned something and tried to hand it to him.

With renewed energy and renewed dread, he typed in 'forgetting spells.' Again a whole list popped up, but he didn't even need to click through to any of the links. Just in the short bit of information that accompanied each title, he could glean 'lavender sticks' 'burning' and 'candle.' As he scrolled down one said 'works best if victim holds burning sprig.'

Rage swam through him.

She'd clearly cast one of these 'forgetting' spells on him. Maybe she hadn't actually lied when she said she hadn't drugged him. But she sure as hell hadn't told the truth either.

He still didn't have that whole night back. And he, who always had to get to the bottom of everything, somehow just let it slide. Who knew what she'd done to him in the time he'd forgotten?

Obviously, she'd cast some kind of spell on him to make him acquiescent. And a love spell, too. A love spell sure explained how he felt about her. That craving that he didn't know where it came from. The sex that was beyond excellent. The need to see her all the time. That she was constantly on his mind.

Again, knowing didn't change the fact that he still wanted her. Part of him wanted to find a way for everything to be okay. The other part of him was just insanely angry.

Quickly, he searched for love spells, almost blinking when the computer couldn't spit them out fast enough. Most looked like recipes—lists of herbs and items with an accompanying explanation of how to walk the right pattern or when in the spell to say or do what. A few contained warnings. Some had guarantees.

Furious now at how he'd been duped, Brandon closed all the windows and turned off the monitor so he didn't have to look at it anymore. In a rage, he stomped out of his office and locked it up behind him.

Climbing into his car, Brandon slung his bag in the back and cranked the engine. He desperately wanted to just march over there and wake her ass up. His fists gripped the wheel, taking tight turns while his foot stomped the gas and brake pedals like a case of road rage waiting to explode.

He was almost there when he turned the car around and headed back.

No matter how bad he hurt, how angry he was, he couldn't face her just yet. The wound was too fresh, too new. He wasn't ready to be logical in a fight. Not against a woman who was clearly not logical and who clearly held the upper hand. Who knew what would happen if he tried to fight her when he had no clue how to?

His place was the best option. He told himself his best bet was to head home. Cool off. Wait until he could see her without feeling that nearly suffocating desire. Because right now he was a swirl of anger. He'd been played, and it was all he could do to keep his lunch down.

He was almost home when his brain refused to go any

further. He might not be ready to confront her, but he also wasn't about to just go pop a beer and think it through. No, rationality was definitely beyond him. He turned the wheel again at the last moment, not yet ready to face the memories in his house.

She'd been in his home. He'd invited her in. With his new knowledge her presence felt like a violation. How many things had he done that weren't of his own design? Brandon really couldn't bear to try counting.

He found himself driving down Fairfax Avenue. His eyes saw the things he passed, the sunset he should have considered beautiful. The people walking by, bikers weaving in and out of the sluggish traffic he really should be watching out for. But his brain didn't register any of them. He couldn't process anything beyond his feelings.

He tried to simmer down.

When that didn't work, he turned the wheel again, and again. He found himself back in Hollywood, heading north. Which was a serious mistake. Now he was angry, betrayed, heartsick, and stuck in nearly standstill traffic.

He banged his fist on the steering wheel. His eyes hurt. He hurt.

It was more than just a little shock to find out not only was Delilah herself a lie, but his own feelings for her were, too.

He inched along, bumper to bumper with the other cars, until finally he'd had enough.

As a truck vacated one of the precious metered parking spaces at the side of the road, Brandon slammed the car in gear and squealed into the open slot. Taking two deep breaths wasn't enough.

He got out of the car, and angrily fed enough quarters into the meter to last until nine at night when it was no longer monitored. His feet carried him north on the sidewalk, and it was disturbing to realize he was moving faster than traffic. He tried to keep his head up, look around and pay attention so he didn't get mugged on top of everything else.

That's why he saw it.

Across the street. It looked like it had been there forever, and he'd driven up this street tons of times before, but he'd never noticed it.

Blessed Be—for the witch and the hobbyist.

Brandon crossed against the light, but the cars weren't moving anyway. His eyes were wide as he entered, taking in the smells and the feeling that he was suddenly pumped. He knew what to do now. And he was so focused on it that he didn't see the pretty brunette right beside him until she spoke.

"Are you here for the beginners' class?"

This was even better than he'd thought.

"Yes, I am."

CHAPTER 22

Delilah saw Brandon in the distance through the fog.

She had to squint to make out his features, but she knew instinctively and automatically that it was him. He was standing next to another person, icy fingers of white wrapping around the two of them, though they acted as if nothing were wrong. Delilah wondered why they didn't feel the cold when she certainly did.

It was a woman he was with. He seemed comfortable with her, but not overly familiar. He didn't have his arm around her or anything like that. But they spoke, a light-hearted conversation that didn't include her. They seemed to be finding a lot to agree on.

Delilah frowned and walked closer.

She wanted to talk to Brandon. She wanted to know who he was with. There was so much of his life she didn't know about.

She knew what he did for a living. Knew that he had a business partner, Dan. While she'd seen Dan at Gin's a few times, she wasn't sure she could pick the man out of a crowd. That didn't sit well—that something that was such a big part of Brandon's life could go right by her.

She knew he had a sister, complete with husband and kids. She'd heard about his father and the story of his mother. But she'd never actually met any of these people. Aside from the picture of his niece and nephew he pulled out the night he'd run Mr. Rocket Scientist off, she had absolutely no confirmation that any of these people even existed.

She walked a good bit of the distance between them. Or she thought she did. They weren't getting any closer. Still Delilah pushed through the cold. She wanted to get to Brandon. Needed to hear him say everything was all right.

She was curious about the blonde he was with. Was it his sister? For some reason Delilah didn't think that it was.

She was shivering now, the fog was licking at her, stealing little bits of heat as she pushed her way through. She got the distinct feeling that Brandon and whomever he was talking to didn't want to include her in their conversation. No matter how paranoid she told herself she was being, she couldn't shake the idea that they were talking about her.

For hours, she trudged through the cold. The wind picked up. She could see the blonde woman's hair whipping around, yet the woman didn't seem affected by it. She would just push the flyaway strands back behind her ear and continue talking. Delilah was frozen through.

Brandon either didn't notice or didn't care.

Still, she put her head down and fought through the wind.

At last, when she looked up, she caught the blonde's eye.

Delilah stumbled back in shock.

No longer interested in her conversation with Brandon, Juliet looked right at her.

Turning to Brandon for support, Delilah found none.

How could he? He knew how she felt about her sister. He knew what Juliet had done. But when he finally paid attention, it was clear he was angry with her.

Delilah was frowning, bewildered and confused.

But it was Juliet's voice that struck her to the bone.

Her sister didn't move her mouth, the words came into Delilah's head, in much the same way they had often communicated when Juliet had been alive. Although Brandon couldn't hear it, the accusation was plain as day.

You had everything.

When Delilah jerked herself from the last in a disturbing series of dreams, it was already two a.m. on Friday. Though she'd sunk deeper into things with him emotionally as they'd made love the other night, she still didn't tell him the truth. She meant to, but then he looked at her that way. Wanted her that way. There was always something more pressing than handing him the bomb that would blow everything up.

It had been a nice interlude to the week, but now her alarm was blaring in her ear, as usual, only she didn't feel well. Since she was never sick, she chewed a Tums and went off to work, figuring it would pass. It seemed that she was right, once she got busy, everything was fine. Until about seven that morning, when she started feeling nauseated again.

The pastries just didn't look right—not like anything she'd want to eat anyway. The smell seemed *off* to her. She had decided to throw the whole batch in the trash and go with her back-up recipe—chocolate mousse. But she couldn't—the idea of chocolate turned her stomach, too. Though her brain logically recognized that the pastries smelled the same way they always had, she realized she just suddenly didn't like the smell of cooked fruit.

That was a terrible dilemma. What was she going to do with her life if she didn't like the smell of cooked fruit?

So she didn't throw out the tarts. If she had, she'd just have to bake something else. And nothing—*nothing*—seemed appealing. She was feeling worse and worse as the morning wore on. Just barely, she managed to keep going, but before the night was half over she left Maggie a note that she wouldn't be in for her Saturday shift. There was no way this would simply pass. There was no way she'd be able to cook.

All through her shift Delilah fought her stomach. It wanted to turn over. To rebel. Suddenly, she hated all food. Particularly the smell. So she tried to limit herself to cooking things that weren't horribly fragrant, then bailed as soon as she could.

When she got into her car, her fingers scrambled for the Tums again and she popped two directly into her mouth. Though they tasted like mint flavored chalk, which did nothing to help, she forced herself to chew frantically until her stomach settled just a little. She managed to drive home, although twice she pulled to the side, thinking she would have to climb out and lose what little was in her fragile stomach. Somehow each time she waited it out and the feeling passed.

She was sweating by the time she arrived in her garage, praying for Tylenol and sleep. Of course, today the elevator had never been slower. The hallway was a long winding challenge before her and Delilah wanted to fall against her apartment door as soon as she got there. But even after she fumbled with the key and got the door closed tightly behind her, it wasn't the haven she had hoped for. She didn't feel better just for crossing the threshold.

Immediately, she stripped down and hopped into the shower, since she could still smell the food on her clothes and in her hair. With frantic strokes she scrubbed it all away hoping that had been the trigger and now that it was gone she would begin to feel better. Even as she washed, she wondered. She usually liked—*loved*—the smell of food, particularly dessert. Still, she stripped it away as best she could.

Normally, she ate as soon as she got home. But this morning

she skipped that step and practically flung herself at the bed, hugging her pillow tightly. And trying not to moan.

Delilah stayed there, just praying for the feeling to pass, until she heard the key in the lock. For the briefest of moments she hoped it was Brandon, come to take care of her. That was what you did when someone you cared about was sick. But then she remembered, she'd chickened out of giving him the key. And she hadn't even come close to confessing what she'd done and what she was.

No, the person coming through the door was Tristan.

Li?

Li?

She mentally thought in return, *I'm coming,* complete with sigh and attitude.

Delilah hauled herself out of bed, mostly for her own preservation. The last time she'd been sick, right after David and Juliet died, Tristan tried to cook for her. He'd only succeeded in making her worse. She wondered if Tristan's cooking had been a test. If she ever ate it again, he'd know she'd lost it entirely. But she'd have to be practically catatonic to eat anything Tristan made.

She ran into him in the hallway, where he was beginning his search for her. Which was silly. If she wasn't right there when he came in, he knew to help himself to the fridge. Then again the tone of his thoughts had been practically frantic.

Her arms came up to his, desperately trying to stop him from waving some paper around. Just watching the motion was making her feel worse. "What is it?"

"This!" He held up the small yellow sheet. It was a receipt from Blessed Be. There was no way it could be good. Not with that look on his face. He checked previous night's receipts every morning, but not once had he ever brought one to show her. His voice was as frantic as his thoughts had been. "It's

Cassandra, the new girl. She let this go out of the store last night."

Apparently, Tristan had absolutely no concern for her illness. For a few moments, neither did she. At least this was more interesting than lying around and feeling bad. Anything that took her mind off the nausea was welcome. So she didn't make any comments about how she felt or about how he failed to realize it.

He waved the yellow slip in her face as though she should be able to make out the tiny moving script. It was all Delilah could do to form a word. "What!"

Instead he read the list to her. "A Jasper ball. Tapers, two black, two green. Tansy. Salt. Athame. The Almanac of Spells."

He looked at her as she digested the information.

"Oh, no, Tristan. All for *one* person?" That was like handing a novice an instruction manual for how to light a thousand pounds of fertilizer. "I told you to stop selling that almanac. It's like *The Anarchists Cookbook,* it could be dangerous."

"We're very careful about who we sell it to." He paced back and forth in her hallway, blocking her in.

Not that he didn't already know it, but she said it anyway. "Clearly you aren't."

He just shook his head in frustration, at his wits end. "It's Cassandra, she didn't know."

Delilah caught his attention for a moment, her stomach finally taking a back seat to Tristan's trouble. "Why didn't Yasmin catch it?"

"She wasn't paying any attention. She was running that damned beginners class." As much as he hated that beginners class, his logical side acknowledged all the business it brought in to the store and wouldn't let him shut it down.

Delilah was about to pace, too. They had to find out who bought that list of ingredients, before somebody got the whammy. But her mouth didn't take the same direction. "Why was Cassandra running the checkout all by herself?"

He shook his head. "Because she's good. She learned everything really quickly, and she's actually quite intuitive. So I figured if anyone was up to no good, she'd sense it and alert one of us."

"So if you haven't already, *call her*." Delilah pushed past him, into the living room where she could finally pace a decent distance and think. "Ask her about the sales last night."

She waited, watching while he dialed the number from his cell list. "Hi, Cassandra? It's Tristan."

Delilah didn't need to hear it, and now that her focus was off Tristan, her stomach rolled again. Another Tums would only make things worse, so she scrambled through her kitchen for a peppermint. Finally finding one shoved in the pen drawer, she unwrapped it and gratefully popped it in her mouth. The mint was sinking into her tongue and starting to work just as Tristan was coming around the corner.

"She doesn't remember much. Just that she thinks she sold that stuff to a guy, and that she didn't get any bad vibes off him." He hung his head. "So that's no help, and now she feels guilty."

"She won't feel guilty for long, Tristan. You're good at putting people at ease. The fact that the buyer was male is helpful. There are a lot fewer male buyers at Blessed Be than female. We just have to figure out which guy he is." Delilah smiled.

Tristan didn't. "She said she'd never seen him before."

As though that ended the whole discussion. Were they witches or not?

His hands made wild flights, gesturing complete nonsense and he spoke. He started in again before she could speak. "You know how you can't buy certain cough medications without showing your ID, because you could use it to make crystal meth? Well, I just sold the equivalent of the parts for a pipe bomb. Only Cassandra didn't know enough to ID the guy and my only saving grace is that the government doesn't know enough to arrest me."

"Tristan, it's done. There's nothing else we can do about it right now. Maybe we can scry for the buyer later."

He turned to her, his face showing that her words made him suspicious. "Why can't we look now?"

"I just don't feel that well." And Tristan had never been any good at it. Juliet had been the best at finding things, she just had the gift—she wished something found or known and, within a few hours, the knowledge or the item would present itself. But, like every time she had that thought, Delilah pushed it back down. It didn't matter that Juliet had been the best, because she couldn't help them now.

Tristan gave up and gave in—she could read it in his shoulders. "All right, why don't we eat some breakfast then?"

Just the mention of food brought all her nausea back.

Delilah awoke at one a.m. on Saturday morning for no apparent reason. Two o'clock she would have understood. But one a.m. made no sense at all.

By one thirty she was wide awake and bored. So she noticed when her stomach started rolling again. Which made it impossible to use the time to cast spells again. She hugged her pillow against her stomach and thought that, the next chance she got, she needed to bulk up her immune spells. Then she tried to fall back to sleep.

By three o'clock she'd sat in front of her TV for an hour and had eaten two Tums and drunk a glass of water. In very small sips. By five she was exhausted, as well as the proud owner of a pressure cooker that cooked with water instead of oil and claimed to keep all food juicy and flavorful and would arrive on her doorstep sometime next week. Not that she would be eating that food. For some reason, food next week sounded like a good idea. Good enough to spend her money on it.

She'd bought that from her savings, too, and began wondering if maybe Tristan wasn't right. If maybe she ought to blow the whole wad on infomercial products. But there was no way her kitchen would hold all the crap she could buy with David's life insurance policy and the half of Juliet's that had come to her.

Delilah rubbed her hands over her face. Thinking about this wasn't making her feel any better. But she'd spent over a year avoiding thinking about it, and look where it had gotten her: nowhere. Top that off with the fact that she had a great guy that she was almost completely incapable of dealing with, and it started to seem like a better idea to dust off the old memories and dive in.

Tristan had no issues spending his half of Juliet's policy. But then again, Tristan had no blood on his hands.

Delilah's money simply sat in the bank all this time, collecting a pitiable interest for no apparent reason. Until the rotisserie. Which even Tristan was keen enough to realize was Brandon's fault.

Her stomach rolled again.

She fought her nausea by ordering a set of marvelous kitchen shears off another infomercial. They promised to cut whole chickens and tin cans with equal ease. Besides, she'd grown tired of tightening the screw on her current pair.

By seven, she called Tristan.

At eight, he showed up with her requests. She wasn't sure if she was happier to see him or the plastic grocery store bag as he let himself in through her front door.

Delilah dove for the striped round peppermints, practically ripping the bag to shreds then fighting to free one of the little suckers. She sighed in relief when the first one hit her tongue.

Tristan watched with great amusement before he started talking.

Delilah knew the price for sending Tristan on an errand was suffering the third degree. So she readily agreed to it, even if she knew it wouldn't be pleasant. For the peppermints, saltines and sprite it was worth it.

When he started in, she answered to the best of her ability. No, she hadn't eaten anything since the day before. Yes, she *should* be hungry. That didn't mean that she actually *was* hungry. At last he gave up and sent her back to bed, where finally she slept.

She woke up at two in the afternoon, and checked her phone. She was totally bummed there were no messages from Brandon. But she was happy her stomach ailment seemed to have passed.

Now, she *was* hungry. It had been almost two days since she'd really eaten. In her desire for food, and soon, she sliced a hunk from a small loaf of bread then slit it sideways. She stacked it with roast beef, provolone cheese, thin sliced roma tomatoes, and green peppers. Usually she added sliced mushrooms but today she wanted extra oil and vinegar. Besides, the mushrooms looked like they were on the verge of going bad although she couldn't say why.

Maybe it was some sixth sense about food.

Then again, who cared? She turned her head sideways and bit into the fragrant sandwich shark-style. *Oh, that was good.* Delilah stood there, over her kitchen counter, and savored each bite. She didn't think about the mushrooms again until she was almost at the end of the sandwich. Maybe they really had gone bad.

Or, she realized, becoming absolutely still as she polished off the very last bite of the sandwich, maybe it was for another reason entirely.

Brandon hadn't called.

She hadn't confessed.

He hadn't forgiven her. Because he didn't know he should. And that only made the whole thing worse.

Because it was plain as day as soon as the thought entered her head.

Oh, crap.

She was pregnant.

CHAPTER 23

Brandon sat on his beautiful hard wood floor in his circle of salt, right in the middle of his living room, coddling the big glass of the last of the wine, and thought for a moment.

Tomorrow he would need to hit Target and buy a really good vacuum broom. He'd been thinking about getting one for a while and the thick line of white grains around him clinched it. There was no way he'd be able to adequately sweep that up. And there'd be no way to explain it to Dan or his sister either.

Four candles flickered around him. They were as closely aligned to the four compass points as he could get them. He wondered if the people at Target would figure out what he was up to, what with the weird list of things he'd bought: wooden table top, wooden candle holders, tchotchkes and matches.

He now owned a small wooden table, hastily made with four by fours cut down for legs and held together with peg construction. The internet said the spell altar could contain no metal. That meant a trip to Home Depot and an hour in his garage. It looked like crap, and wobbled just a little, but fit the bill.

He'd gone to the liquor store and bought a huge party wine

glass and two glass dishes. And a really expensive bottle of vintage merlot. He figured if it really was all going to hell in a hand basket then revenge ought to be served with a fine red wine. Delilah would appreciate the gesture.

Brandon decided to forgo the sun and moon representations on his altar. Yasmin, the friendly instructor at Blessed Be, led a discussion how some people just did the spells, were merely magicians, but that there was a whole religion associated with it. Half the class consisted of useless chat about worshiping the rivers and the air and the souls of everything around them.

At one point, Brandon asked about the need to sacrifice small animals. Yasmin at first looked shocked—as though she would never stand such an occurrence—then patiently explained that his was a common misconception. She went on to say what he'd read online was actually a subset of Voodoo or maybe Santeria, an entirely different religion that the uneducated often called witchcraft. He hadn't thought it would go over well if he raised his hand and asked if they could just get to the part about causing pain. Yasmin would have frowned on his revenge.

Well, Yasmin The Good Witch could just stuff it.

Still, it was noon on the second day.

Thursday night he'd cast his first stupid spell, feeling like a moron the whole time. He'd stopped twice to be sure the curtains and blinds were all tightly drawn, afraid his neighbors would see him and string him up for being a witch. Which, of course, would be the ultimate irony. He also didn't want anyone to see him being such a fool.

He'd carried everything he needed to his little unsteady altar, lit his candles, repeated the rhymes, and poured the circle of salt right from the bag, keeping himself inside.

The book and Yasmin both stressed the need for pure emotion. There was also the theory that strong emotion worked better. Well, he had that in spades. Even if he looked like an absolute idiot in his white cotton t-shirt and a pair of plain white drawstring pants he'd bought for the occasion.

Thursday night he'd packed it in early, needing to show up at work and put on a good front. He hoped to hear from Delilah. Something to let him know it had worked.

But she hadn't called.

All day Thursday he'd been pleased with himself. He'd cast a love spell on her. That would be the best revenge: he could leave her begging at his door while he shut her out. The taste-of-her-own-medicine seemed perfect.

But she hadn't called.

She must not feel it bad enough.

He wanted her begging. On her knees. Crying when he slammed the door on her.

Mad didn't begin to cover it.

He steadied himself with deep breaths. Begged off work early. Ate a microwaved dinner and told himself that, while he couldn't pronounce half of what was in there, at least 'deceit' wasn't on the list of ingredients. He napped.

Midnight was the right time. He'd listened to Yasmin at the beginner class. He hadn't liked all she'd had to say, but he'd paid attention.

Again he cast his circle, this time with the added anger that it hadn't worked the night before. He burned more tansy, drank more wine, threw down more salt. And he hoped.

Until the sun came up and here he was, still sitting in his salt ring. He was glad he'd brought the entire magnum of wine inside the circle with him. Blessed Be at least sold quality candles. The black and green tapers were burned only halfway, even though they'd stayed lit all night. Then again, he'd been lit all night too. But he was burned to the nub.

The wine was gone. The whole thing. And he hadn't had that much the first night he'd tried to cast. Now all he could do was sit right here on the hard wood and think. Or else he'd have to break his circle and that would end the energy of the spell. If he'd done it right, it would work for a while, maybe a week, before it wore off.

He sighed. He hadn't figured on getting himself drunk while he did it. So he hadn't brought any Tylenol into the circle. With a smirk, he realized next time he should—there wasn't any metal on a Tylenol bottle. It wouldn't harm the spell.

Not that he knew what in God's name metal had to do with anything. Or if it made any difference if he sat here being angry for a while longer.

But he *was* angry. So he might as well sit here. The pounding in his brain was almost a comfort.

There was water, and he contemplated drinking it right out of the dish, until he remembered that he had thrown a generous amount of salt into it several times as he said the stupid little rhymes.

As the room brightened with the new day, he looked at the altar. It was as crude as it could possibly be. The store offered some beautiful handcrafted pieces, but he'd only needed to get the job done.

It turned out Witchcraft was expensive. Whole, well-preserved herbs didn't come cheap. That was, unless you wanted to grow your own and bundle them and dry them, for which he did *not* have the time. Or, he could scour the countryside and pick them fresh. Although, given his level of education on the subject he'd likely either get arrested for picking something protected by national law or kill himself with something that looked exactly like a kitchen herb but was deadly poisonous to the touch. Wouldn't Delilah just love that? If her little plaything killed himself trying to work a counter spell? Of course, Delilah had a kitchen full of all the herbs she needed. Then again, Delilah had been at it a while.

The athame he'd bought—which he'd been assured was *essential* to spell work—was twenty dollars. It was the cheapest, simplest one they had. It looked it, too. Beautiful ones, like what Delilah owned, ran upwards of two hundred dollars—each. Yasmin assured him you couldn't buy spell quality with a better knife. The only way to get a knife that worked better from the get-go was to inherit it from a powerful witch. So he gladly handed over his twenty dollars for this cheap, tacky, little silver blade.

His ass hurt from sitting on the hard floor for too long. His chin prickled with beard growth. His head pounded every time he moved or thought anything. But his heart beat a steady rhythm that was its own for the first time in days. And that made him smile.

There was also a great irony to the whole thing.

He'd been raised catholic. In a move he never figured out, his father had walked his two kids down the street to the catholic church at the end of the block every Sunday morning. They didn't do the Wednesday night dinners, and he and his sister only went to Sunday school when it didn't require they show up early or stay late. His father wasn't Catholic, he'd only partially completed his conversion by the time Bethy was born and their mother had run off. Still, the two kids were baptized in the church and had done the whole first communion thing.

The three of them stopped going when Bethy hit eighth grade. It just faded out of their lives. But Bethy had gone back during college, married a catholic man, and even sent her kids to catholic school. And she believed. All of it.

She would have the mother of all hissy fits if she knew her brother was sitting in a salt circle casting spells. Dating a witch. So far, she'd had nothing but good things to say about Delilah. Unfortunately, all Bethy had to go on was the *idea* of Delilah. The reality was turning out far different.

Brandon laughed.

He was a catholic, by blessing if not in his heart, and they were one of the few remaining religions that still believed in that *thou shalt not suffer a witch to live* stuff. He wondered if he should tie Delilah to a dunking stick and hold her underwater until she confessed. No one still had a dunking stick, did they? Were they maybe on sale at Blessed Be? Unlikely.

He shook his head. Then regretted it, as the pounding swirled through his brain from the simple motion.

His thoughts were running away from him and he didn't like it. As much as he hated what Delilah had done to him, he wasn't a violent person. He'd always broken off relationships with a good attitude. Revenge hadn't been in him since he was fifteen and he toilet papered his archrival's house for trying to frame him for cheating to get him kicked off the basketball team. But that had merely been a petty act of treason against him, and he'd retaliated with a petty act of retribution. It had been fair, in a stupid, high school kind of way. Regardless, it was a lifetime ago. And he thought he had gotten far beyond the boy he'd been.

Now he wondered if the hate was some kind of residue of the spells she'd put on him.

Screw it. He couldn't wonder anymore. It wasn't getting him anywhere. And besides, his head hurt, his butt hurt, and he was out of Tansy.

He was going to have to go sleep off his drunk.

Brandon stood, stopping for a moment to steady himself on the arm of the couch as the room swayed dizzily around him. Then he shuffled his way out of the salt circle, destroying the neat line and supposedly the energy along with it.

As he turned to look back at it, he saw it was a mess. The empty wine bottle was on its side with the cork propped in the corner across the room. The big wine glass had a smear of red in the bottom--all that was left of his vintage merlot. He'd spilled more salt than he'd thought, leaving white crystals trailed across the wood in various places. But the hammering in his brain offered an easy explanation for those misses as well as the misperception that they hadn't existed.

Even so, he saw remnants of his feelings for Delilah scattered there among the refuse. The first feelings. The fake ones. They still clung to him, were still trying to worm their way inside. He was desperate to excise them. He just didn't seem to be able to.

A very strong part of him still wanted to see her and hold her. Sensed that she needed him. Reminding himself it was all false, he shuffled his way into the bedroom and threw himself at his bed. He moaned at the tidal wave that one action set off in his brain, and he waited it out while the room stopped its violent rocking. As soon as the sloshing quieted to a gentle sway, he closed his eyes and passed out.

CHAPTER 24

Delilah sat on the edge of her bed, repeating in her head every swear word she knew. And ignoring the fact that the repetition was likely creating powerful magick. She didn't care if she created a storm around her, when there was already one raging inside her.

Tristan would say it was her own fault. That fate had a way of getting back at you when you hadn't done what you were supposed to. Fate probably thought it was hysterically funny that she'd been agonizing over telling Brandon what she'd done and what she was. So when she hadn't done it in time to satisfy, she got this thrown at her.

Tristan would tell her she'd brought it on herself.

Tristan would be right.

Still, she felt terrible. Her stomach rolled.

Her brain rolled, too. And she searched for every reason she could cling to that she just couldn't be pregnant.

She was irregular. She'd thought she was pregnant a few times before. But it was just her weird cycle.

Delilah smiled until her stomach turned over on her again. Of course there had been that one time when she actually had been pregnant. And it felt just like this.

That made her stomach turn over again. Even more violently than before. Leaping from the bed, she ran to get a mint from the bag Tristan had brought. Even as the taste permeated her mouth and sinuses, bringing sweet relief, her hopes sank. In the name of honesty, she had to admit that only the actual pregnancy had brought on this kind of nausea. Only the actual pregnancy left her downing bags of red and white swirled peppermints as though they were an oxygen source.

Her mind searched for anything else that might mean it was all okay.

This stomach thing came on pretty quick. With pregnancy it ought to sneak up on you, right? She read all about it last time. Morning sickness—which was horribly misnamed because it struck at any time—was a result of baby hormones, which grew as the baby grew. So a sudden attack didn't make any sense. But she couldn't remember how it all started the last time. Of course, she'd known she was pregnant first that time. Rather than figuring it all out like this.

Delilah crawled back under the covers and huddled there with her pillow and her unhappy thoughts while her stomach staged its coup. She tried to imagine all the ways she might tell Brandon what she'd been up to.

She could see him in her mind's eye, all happy and thrilled. She'd say, *I'm having a baby* and he'd respond, *Just what I wanted, a baby!* She'd tell him *I'm a witch* and he'd just smile. *That's okay.* No, better yet he'd say, *I figured all that out a while ago.* Delilah didn't have the imaginary chops to create an image of him saying that he was a witch, too. That was why the initial forget spell had been so hard to enforce.

In fact, the whole thing was pretty ludicrous. There was no way this was going to go over well. At least now he wouldn't kill her because she was carrying his child. Right?

Delilah shook her head to herself. He would likely either be angry she'd cast a spell on him or just laugh at her and think she was crazy. People tended to think what they themselves didn't understand or couldn't do just wasn't possible. Delilah could fix that really fast. Blowing a candle to life was remarkably easy, but nice and showy. The problem was that it was too easy. It made people afraid of what else you could do. Afraid you might try to control them.

Even lying there in her bed by herself, Delilah had to wince. Because that was exactly what she'd tried to do to Brandon. Would he think it was okay because it hadn't worked? No, likely he'd be just as angry as he had every right to be.

The whole thing was so tangled she couldn't even find a spot of happiness in herself that she was pregnant. She sure hadn't been trying to get herself knocked up, but she'd always wanted children of her own. She'd just become convinced it wasn't going to happen after David and Juliet died. She'd become certain she wasn't fit to be a mother. But there was a certain inevitability to this she couldn't argue with.

Delilah hugged her pillow a little tighter and tried to blank her mind. She hoped she might find some rest if she could stop the hurricane of thoughts crashing through her brain.

Finally, she was able to get herself to eat again. Only the saltines and soda, but she sat on the sofa and slowly munched while watching really bad television, keeping the food constantly moving to her mouth. Just having something in her did make her stomach feel better. A decent serving of crackers convinced her mind it was just a stomach bug. Right? If she were pregnant, she would still feel the nausea certainly. Delilah consoled herself with the thought.

She didn't even notice when she dropped off to sleep. But slowly she was climbing stairs to a small apartment in Santa Monica. An apartment she had known before. She'd cleaned this apartment out just over a year ago. But everything was here now. For some reason that didn't seem strange.

Her brain associated the door with all things Jules. The memories came in a flood too fast and furious to be stopped. Consoling her sister's tears over the boyfriend who had dumped her after she'd gone to the tremendous trouble of really cooking for him. Saturday afternoons, tired feet, dropping her sister off and sorting through shopping bags before she headed home to David. Jules always helped her shove the shoe boxes down inside the other bags so David wouldn't ask about *another* pair of shoes. Delilah had other memories of dim red lights and pulsing music, wall to wall people, as she and David made their way into the cramped apartment, made more so by all the bodies. They always came to Jules' parties.

Her brain wondered now if anything had gone on between her husband and Jules at these parties. If the boyfriends and the tears were merely clever covers for infidelities. But, no, they assured her it had been a one time thing. Although something at the back of Delilah's brain nagged her that it hadn't been just the once. Still, in the end, it was Juliet's infidelity that hurt the worst. So it was her younger sister Delilah wanted to hurt the worst in return.

She knocked on the heavy tan-colored door, noticing the sound was hollow in her brain.

The way Jules pulled the door open showed that she knew it was Delilah waiting on the other side. The siblings always sensed each other, and Juliet had always been the best. Delilah could have cast on herself, made it so Jules wouldn't recognize the feeling from just beyond the door. Jules would throw it open and get the nasty surprise of her betrayed sister waiting for her. But Delilah didn't do that. She wouldn't cast against her sister. She knew how it felt and got her only satisfaction out of this whole mess from taking the moral high ground.

And, besides, she didn't have to spell Jules. She had enough ammunition, enough righteous anger, that she didn't feel the need to resort to parlor tricks. Delilah pushed her way into the apartment, wondering briefly if she'd find David moved in here. He hadn't been home—not that she'd seen anyway—in a week. He said he wasn't staying with her sister. Then again, he said he wasn't seeing anyone else either. He said he'd never cheat, and that he'd love her forever. Delilah shut those memories down before they could go any further. That kind of thinking could tear her up inside even worse than she already was.

But it didn't seem David was there. Which would hopefully make this easier.

Juliet quietly closed the door behind herself. She was four inches taller than Delilah, thicker, more athletic, and right now, even though her voice was soft, she stood her ground. "What do you want, Li?"

Delilah didn't really think she could provide a real answer to that. She was so conflicted, even if she knew what she needed to do here. And she didn't feel like giving the short version either. Didn't think it wise to tell her sister what it was she wanted—or more accurately, *needed*—to hand her more ammunition when apparently Jules had little compunction about using it against her. So she asked her own question. "Are you still seeing him, Juliet?"

Jules flinched.

At first Delilah figured she'd scored a blow just by using Juliet's formal name. The sisters had always called each other 'Jules' and 'Li.' The formal name had been intended as an insult.

But apparently Delilah had been wrong. Juliet flinched because of her answer. "Yes, I'm still seeing him."

Delilah's voice and emotions came flooding out in a screeching voice she didn't recognize. "Well, you have to stop. How am I supposed to save my marriage if you keep seeing him?" Delilah didn't leave room for an answer. "No more, Juliet!"

While she'd yelled, Jules had stood up straighter, gotten angry, and her words came out on the grate of steel. Somehow

Juliet managed to look wounded and offended and *dignified* as she responded to the fact that she'd not only cheated with her sister's husband, but she was continuing to do so. "I love him! He loves me! I'm just supposed to hand him to you?"

"No Juliet, you weren't supposed to take him in the first place."

That at least made her sister a bit contrite again. Where did she get off thinking it was okay to steal someone else's husband? Her sister's husband at that? What had she ever done to Juliet to deserve this? The answer, of course, was *nothing*.

And nothing could have prepared her for the next low blow Juliet delivered. "I didn't steal him. He came to me."

Delilah found some of her own dignity. Tried like hell to push down the hurt, to believe it maybe wasn't true, and to simply file it all away for later when she might be able to deal with it. If she couldn't deal with it, at least she'd be alone. "Oh, *he* came to *you*? So that makes it okay? Then there's more than one of your cheap-ass boyfriends I should have fucked along the way."

Juliet seemed to tower over her. Looking sad and sorry and a little bit regal. "I'm sorry you got hurt, but you have to face that it's over, Li."

Delilah didn't balk. "I'm pregnant."

She expected the shocked look on her sister's face. She expected Jules to stop and place her hand flat against her chest and need a moment to think. She didn't expect the whispered words she heard back.

"I'm pregnant, too." Juliet lifted the hem on her shirt revealing a maternity panel on the front of her jeans.

Delilah stumbled back. Juliet had gotten that shirt a month ago. She'd worn it to the house one night and Delilah complimented her sister on her top and asked if it was new. Her little sister had happily replied 'yes.'

She could see the shirt now for what it was. There were

gathers and pleats to expand with a growing belly. It looked cute. But Juliet had been wearing it since a *month* ago.

Delilah wasn't even in maternity clothes yet. She looked her 'little' sister up and down: Juliet was tall. She was hardly showing, but she had to be about four months along—or *more*—in order to need maternity clothes.

Standing there, bewildered and frowning, Delilah tried to sort through it all. The math didn't add up. Jules was too far along—her affair with David only started a month ago, a fling that continued, if at all, because Delilah had thrown him out of the house.

Her lungs let go as it all fell neatly into place and finally she breathed. "What are you going to do?"

Juliet didn't blink. "David's going to marry me."

What? "He's still married to me."

"You're divorcing him." As though that made everything okay. Delilah didn't recognize this person she was talking to. This person that she thought she knew better than anyone else in the whole world. She'd been wrong on so many fronts.

Delilah shook her head, trying to stick to the conversation in front of her, because the rest of it was just too overwhelming. "I don't think I am divorcing him now. We're having a baby, apparently. So we're going to have to act like adults and straighten this out. You'll just have to stay out of it, Jules."

Juliet shook her head, too. "This is David's baby, Li."

"But— . . . It was only— . . . you said it was just the once . . ."

Delilah fled.

She stumbled down the hallway. Flew down the stairs.

They'd lied to her.

Of course they'd lied to her. They were in bed together, and they had both scrambled around, throwing on clothes and lies as though they might fix what they'd done. Like everything was all right if they said it was a one time thing and they were sorry.

The hallway seemed interminable and her brain clicked over

the facts as she ran. Juliet was in maternity clothes—a month ago—at her house. Long before Delilah knew what a cheap excuse for a man she'd married and what a back-stabbing sister she had. Then Juliet had known she was pregnant, by David, before Delilah caught them.

And if her sister was sleeping with him and showed up in her maternity clothes, then David had to have known, too.

They'd lied. They'd flat-out, bald-faced lied straight to her.

Delilah climbed into her car and squealed out of the spot. Juliet was racing down the stairs and out the building, barefoot, calling after her. "Li! Li!"

Barefoot and pregnant. Delilah laughed, the sound sick even to her own ears. Then the urge slammed into her like a baseball bat. She'd felt it in her gut and her chest. It invaded her brain: the overwhelming need to turn around, to go back and forgive her sister.

Delilah looked in the rearview mirror and saw Juliet standing there, bare feet just apart, hands clasped in front of her heart. It was a stance in which Juliet found great power. It looked almost like she was praying. Indeed, it had a lot in common with prayer—except what Juliet was doing had no divine origins.

Delilah could feel her sister calling her back. Instilling her with forgiveness she didn't want to give. The feelings flooded through her as she turned the car around and circled the block. She loved her sister, the little sister she'd once played with. There was nothing she wouldn't do for Juliet. They had to work this out.

When she pulled up, she rolled down the passenger window so Juliet could lean over, the picture of contrition.

"Li," It was a sigh of sorrow and need.

Delilah looked in her sister's eyes. She'd been there for her sister, every time she'd been needed. All through the boyfriends that didn't work out. The lost games. High school. College.

She'd forged the path, in a way her mother had never been able to, a fully modern day witch in a world that still didn't understand. And she'd given it all freely to her sister. Who now stood at the passenger window, very pregnant with Delilah's husband's baby.

Juliet had cast on her own sister.

David probably had gone to her. Juliet had probably cast on him, too.

Delilah looked into those blue eyes so like her own. "Juliet . . . . Fuck . . . Off."

She'd flipped a bird and stomped on the gas, practically ripping off her sister's fingers where they clung to the windshield. She could feel all the things Juliet wanted her to feel. But mostly she felt tainted. Used and lied to.

For a moment, she wished she weren't pregnant. The baby was a surprise, but one she and David had been considering for a while. Of course, now she realized that all the while they'd been talking about a baby, he'd known he was already having one. With Juliet.

If either of them weren't pregnant it would all be so much easier. If she weren't pregnant, she would hand David over to Jules and tell them they deserved each other.

With her first clear thought in a while, Delilah realized that was exactly what she needed to do. Baby or not. She could even threaten David if he tried to get custody. He had his own child—Juliet's child—to be a father to. Delilah would find something better for hers. And if he tried anything . . . well, she could start a turf war with her sister the likes of which LA had never seen. David wouldn't risk that. As she felt Juliet's spell wearing off, she sighed, and took a moment to be glad her parents weren't alive to see this.

Racing home, she ignored all the speed limits and every vestige of sanity she possessed. It was a wonder she made it.

Judging by what came later, Delilah had always figured letting her survive that drive had been a bad decision on Fate's part.

In the remembered dream, her thinking brain took over—correcting for life's mistakes. As had happened so many times in her dreams that first year, her car raced off the side of the Pacific Coast Highway. The tumble down the long cliffside ended when she plunged into the water, jolting as the car slammed her around from the impact.

She sat straight up, breathing heavily and drenched in sweat.

Delilah hadn't had that dream in a long time.

Even though she'd suffered through it so many times before, she still required a moment to reorient herself. She was on her couch, game shows were on her TV, sunlight filtered in through the window.

It was long over. Just a bad dream constructed and reworked from a far too real memory.

She stood and stretched. She called Maggie and left a voice mail saying she wouldn't be in the next night either, she was suffering from a bad stomach bug that she didn't want to spread around.

Well, it was partly true.

She checked her messages—on the home phone and on her cell.

Nothing from Brandon.

She drank a coke to clear her head for a minute and ate more crackers while she thought. She could go out and get a pregnancy test. But she thought the best thing to do was sleep. She'd like to tell Brandon before she took the test.

She absolutely must come clean to him now.

Still, her eyes were pulling closed. She needed real restful sleep. For her and the coming baby.

CHAPTER 25

Brandon was pissed.

Somehow he'd screwed it all up and Delilah hadn't called. She should be in the throes of a good, deep seated need for him right about now.

If he'd done it correctly—which was a big *'if.'*

Yasmin the Good Witch told them that first time spells were often duds. It seemed Brandon was going to prove to be no exception. She'd also told the class to start with inconsequential spells, things in which it wouldn't matter if they went awry or not. But Brandon didn't really see the point in that. If he was going to do something inconsequential it would involve several rounds of beer and a willing babe he'd pick up at Gin's for the night.

Yasmin had thrown in other good advice, as well. Like they should practice a handful of different spells so they could try things out and see what worked best for each of them. Brandon was soundly ignoring that advice, too.

He needed more Tansy.

Monday afternoon at work he called it quits early. They'd heard from the trio they presented to on Tuesday the week before. While the men hadn't come up with the money for as many shares of the game rights as they ultimately claimed they wanted, they still signed for more than what he and Dan had originally thought might be possible.

Dan wanted to celebrate.

Brandon wanted to want to celebrate. Instead he was too wrapped up in his now very warped love life.

He drove straight to Blessed Be.

He played parking shark until a spot opened up on the neighboring block. At which point he beat out a little old lady in a big oldsmobile for the rights. Too bad. He wasn't usually such an ass, so he figured karma would let him get away with a little bit.

He locked the car down behind him and considered trying one of the instant protection spells they learned the first night. But with the way his spells were going he figured he was far more likely to tag the car with a neon *steal me* sign and find nothing but a bumper when he returned. So he merely hit the button on the key and waited for the usual double beep that signaled Acura was taking care of his car even if he couldn't.

He enjoyed the walk over to the store. Traffic was heavy, but moving and he was forced to wait for the light. He was certain he was breathing in the fumes of years of overpopulation, but he couldn't summon the will to care.

As he pushed it open, the door knocked a bell that let out a small tinkle to signal someone was entering the store. The bell system seemed kind of primitive to him. Weren't these people supposed to be psychic? Shouldn't they just *know* who was in the store or not?

He found himself wandering around, appreciative that the dim lighting and the seeming pulse the store exhibited hadn't been effects of the odd evening when he'd first come. They existed now in the broad daylight of middle afternoon, too.

He was standing, gazing at the racks of dried herbs and

wondering what the hell they were all supposed to mean and do, when he felt the woman next to him staring.

Brandon looked up.

She smiled.

He smiled back. She was pretty, with large gray eyes and a nice figure. She was dressed to be attractive, but her outfit didn't scream it the way so many LA women seemed to think was necessary. Her understatement didn't hide that she was actually quite beautiful, in fact. But it was something he noticed with his brain. It didn't grab him in the gut and wrap itself around his heart, not the way Delilah's looks did. He felt no pull whatsoever.

Then he reminded himself there was a very good possibility all those emotions, and even now the lack thereof, were likely due to Delilah.

Still, he couldn't make himself feel any real attraction for the woman. He grabbed the tansy, noting that it all said 'boleen cut/hand cut'—another important tip from Yasmin. Machine cut herbs were definitely inferior. Although he couldn't say he was seeing the benefit of these expensive witch-cut herbs either.

He picked up a small felt cutout and nearly laughed out loud. They had all looked so horrified and *offended* when he asked about sacrifice. And Yasmin herself had gotten that *how dare you* look on her face when she firmly explained that he was confusing witchcraft with voodoo. But here he was, ready to make a likeness of Delilah, for spell work—and all this at Yasmin's instruction. It seemed *they* were the ones who confused voodoo with witchcraft.

Still, the cutout was supposed to represent a person. It looked more like a fuzzy gingerbread man to him, but supposedly it would get the job done. They came in several shades—Brandon chose a pale piece to go with Delilah's milky skin, surely kept flawless with some kind of spell. He grabbed a round of white cotton, handwoven ribbon and a fat, pink candle.

He was glad Yasmin wasn't here. She'd tell him he wasn't ready yet. Not for 'poppet work.' But he was more than ready.

The question was, was Delilah?

He hadn't grabbed a shopping basket, and now he was forced to juggle the items in his hands. Poorly. He should cast a spell on himself to keep from dropping things, but he was saving his energy for Delilah.

"Here, let me help." It was the same woman who had been looking at him, was still looking at him in that odd way. Maybe he had something in his teeth. Or on his face. She graciously took some of the items he was grasping and held them for him.

He was about to ask what she wanted, when she spoke. "Do you know you've had spells cast on you?"

He fought down the urge to laugh hysterically and never stop. Only in this store would that be an appropriate pick-up line. "Do you want five dollars so you can tell me which spells?"

"Five dollars?" Realization dawned on her face and with it came a look telling Brandon he'd seriously offended her.

"I don't need your money." Huffy now, she began stuffing his items haphazardly back into his hands before she turned away with a sniff. "I was just trying to be helpful."

"I'm sorry." He couldn't follow her; he'd drop his stuff. He called out instead, for some reason trying to mend fences. He felt bad, and he'd been an ass all day. It was time to quit. "How can you tell?"

She came back around the corner, frowning. "I don't know. I can just feel it. I'm really sorry I bothered you."

She started to walk away again and Brandon fought for a semblance of normalcy in a life that was spinning way out of his control and definitely out of his realm. "You didn't bother me. I just had two other people this week tell me the same thing, and they both wanted money in exchange for my fortune."

She shook her head. "I don't want money. And I'm Becky, by the way."

He smiled. "Brandon."

They didn't even try to shake hands, his were stuffed full.

For a moment, awkward silence ruled what should have been an easy conversation for him. He never had a problem talking to women before. But now he didn't seem to have anything worthwhile to say. And the one thing he did want to talk about—revenge against an evil witch—didn't seem like a good opening gambit with someone he'd just met.

It was Becky who broke the stalemate. "Here, put your things down." She pointed to an empty bin belonging to a sold out item.

While he carefully piled the things, she carefully selected a stick from one of the bundles along the wall. He didn't see what it was, so he asked.

"Black birch bark. The smoke reveals things."

Brandon almost made a face revealing what he really thought of all this voodoo. Then again, he'd gotten candles and cotton ribbon and would pay three dollars for a felt cut out for his own voodoo.

He stood very still as Becky fumbled in her purse for a lighter, then put flame to the bark. She then held the burning stick near him, reaching up to accommodate his height. It smoked like a bad grill, making his eyes water. His body fought for the right to cough, but he didn't dare.

He watched as the smoke climbed in swirls around him. Becky must have seen something he didn't, because she frowned and nodded. "A binding spell. Several actually."

Well, he already knew that. Still he tried to be polite, and he wanted to learn anything he could about what had been done to him. "How do you read the smoke?"

Of course what he really wanted to ask was if it was just a trick. Obviously the smoke swirled like that. It was smoke.

"See the swirls? The way they cling to you? Black birch does that in the presence of spells." Becky waved it at him, shaking more of the acrid gray clouds where they would cling to him. How in hell would he ever explain any of this to Dan? He was just grateful he didn't have to.

Still he felt the need to be honest. "I don't see it."

Becky didn't seem offended by that, just smiled and took charge. "Hold on." She hollered over her shoulder. "Tristan?"

The voice came from the back of the shop. "What?"

"You cleaned this place out yesterday, right?"

"Yup. Always."

Becky smiled at him. "Look at—"

Brandon interrupted her. "You work here?"

"No," She shook her head like he was being silly. "I'm just in here all the time. I know the owner. Now, see over here?"

She waved the still smoking stick around the aisle. The smoke dispersed immediately. Then she waved it back at him. It clung. "See? Spell." She waved it along the aisle again. "No spell."

Brandon nodded, finally understanding what she was looking at. That was creepy.

Then, to make an additional point, she waved the bark at herself. It cleared almost faster than it rolled off the end of the stick. "No spells."

Becky took a deep breath. "I have to say, the way it's clinging," She pointed with her finger to the haze gathered around him, "Someone has really built it up, or else it's older but was done by a very powerful witch."

"How can you tell the difference?"

"Spells by strong, practiced witches make smooth smoke." As though that just explained everything. Becky went on to say the easiest thing to do was burn black birch bark in conjunction with sage in the presence of the person Brandon thought was responsible. He'd see the connection in the smoke, if he had the right person. The strength of the connection would tell if it was recent or not.

Tristan, the owner, came around the corner just then, and Brandon got a glimpse of his hazel eyes and brown hair. He exhibited that held-back aura that some men just seemed to have, like he was reserving judgment about . . . everything. But Brandon was already gathering his things, so all he did was smile and nod. His brain was elsewhere—there was no way in hell he'd be able to burn that stuff around Delilah without her knowing exactly what he was doing it for. Besides, he already knew who was responsible.

He thanked Becky and grabbed about five of the sticks before leaving her and the mysterious Tristan standing there in the aisle caught up in their impromptu discussion of the merits of various herbs.

After paying for his purchases, Brandon left Blessed Be with his brown paper bag tucked up under his arm so the logo didn't show. It wasn't like he usually ran into people he knew just walking down the street, but it would figure it would happen today. And if anyone—like say Dan, or god forbid an investor—caught him like this . . . Well, it would be easier to explain walking down Sunset Boulevard in women's underwear and heels.

So he kept a keen eye out as he made his way back to his car. And he made plans. His house was going to stink to high hell tonight. But at least he'd be able to see what Delilah had been up to.

CHAPTER 26

The car raced along the Pacific Coast Highway, just as it always did in her dreams. Only this time Delilah wasn't in it.

She stood at the edge of a bluff, able to see for miles, it seemed. She easily recognized the view. It was the edge of the property, back when she and David first bought it, before the house was built, before the neighbors came.

There had been more than one day when she stood here just like this. At the edge of the land, overlooking the hills and though she couldn't hear it, she was high enough to see the ocean licking at the shore in the distance. Square and modern, luxury homes cut the horizon into created and organic shapes while sailboats peppered the far background. At that distance they appeared only a shade darker than the surrounding water and sky, their curved triangles reaching up and out as they passed in the distance.

She felt all powerful here, and so she'd come. When she needed to get away, when she was sad, when she needed to think. Delilah would drive up to the property they were waiting to develop and enjoy the fact that they didn't live here yet. That there still existed a spot in the Los Angeles area that wasn't yet built to the heavens and crumbling down.

In the dream, she stood at the edge of a sheer cliff that was never this steep in life. Like most of Malibu, it was bedrock, shifted high into the air. Barring an earthquake that hit nine or higher on the Richter scale, it wasn't going anywhere. But now, in the back of her mind the land crumbled under her feet, inch by inch giving away, the soil she once believed so stable. The cliff side offered a drop into a deep ravine unlike any that existed in reality. And Delilah stood there at the very edge, not only unafraid, but certain of her invincibility.

Clouds scudded across the sky, darkening the day and interfering with her view. Delilah disliked them. They weren't what she wanted to see today. So she grasped a fistful of the reeds growing wild at her feet and yanked. With closed eyes, she opened her hand and blew them away. As fast as the deed was finished, the winds came, kicking up the clouds and taking them to somewhere else.

Delilah smiled.

The car kept coming up the turns, racing around corners, skidding on two wheels when it should have slowed down. But Juliet wouldn't slow down. Delilah knew this. She also knew that it would take her sister forever to get here, no matter how fast she drove.

Delilah altered the landscape while she waited. Using her finger in the loamy soil that formed the top layers of the ground, she cut a winding path at her feet. Then smiled when a tiny stream burbled up at the other side of the property and ran clear and pristine through the center.

Rubbing her hands increased the temperature, until she could lean back and open herself to the sun, enjoying the heat and the breeze that cut it.

David came walking up over the ridge, his suit and tie impeccable. Every hair in place. But he was unable to maintain his footing as she worked on the land. "What are you doing, Delilah?"

He looked truly puzzled, but she could clear it all up.

"I'm making it perfect." She continued her spells. The car raced up the hill in the background, and David stood in front of her looking as perfect as ever.

She didn't need to work on him. He merely was, but he was beautiful and he was always . . . perfect. He wore the right things, knew the right people, said the right things, and constantly told her she was beautiful.

Delilah smiled at him, and David smiled back. Only . . .

He was becoming a little see-through. Although the image didn't waver, she could distinguish the trees that were directly behind him. David was wearing thin.

But Delilah could fix that. With the wave of her wrist, she made him solid again. Exactly the way she liked, then she could go back to concentrating on the things around her. On making it perfect again.

Juliet was getting close. The car was rounding the last turn, and Delilah could see her sister's bulging belly nearly brushing against the steering wheel. Turning to her husband, she asked, "David, why is Juliet pregnant?"

"Because we're having a baby." His was fading out of solid again. He was starting to wink in and out of existence. But even his lack of presence wasn't enough for Delilah.

"We can't have that." She held her hands palm out toward him. Though she never made contact, the push sent him stumbling backwards. When he held out, clinging to his footing, Delilah gouged the earth beneath her with her heel, happily watching the land give way beneath him. He tumbled over the edge into the precipice, screaming the whole time.

She forgot him before the sound even ended. Then, she turned back to the problem of her sister.

A smooth round pebble appeared at her feet. Delilah tossed

it in the direction of the car. It didn't get anywhere near squealing tires. But that was okay. A large boulder had loosened at the side of the earth and tumbled down toward the car.

There was no need to watch, it would make contact.

Delilah turned back to the sun while tires screeched and metal screamed below her. In a moment, the noise ended and the breeze picked up again, whipping her hair and her clothes around her, the day once again perfect.

Only she looked down at herself and saw that the clothing she wore was in tatters. Her hair was a tangled mess. Her feet were dirty. How had she not noticed?

Moaning, she tossed her head from side to side, fighting her way out of the dream. When she came fully awake, she was in her own room and all was dark. Her chest heaved several times in relief as she blinked and became fully aware.

In the dream she killed David and Juliet with a simple wish. But there was nothing mysterious about that, it was beyond obvious where those thoughts came from.

But the tattered clothes were new.

And true.

David had been so perfect she never looked past the surface of him. She'd believed herself in love with him, and him with her, but she hadn't really known it. And she'd been so busy making sure that she had the perfect life, that she'd never examined herself.

Her parents died, one right after the other, and she had given the perfunctory, required grief its due, but then went back to making her world perfect—never once looking at herself. Never once seeing that everything around her appeared perfect, but she had been in tatters.

She was afraid she still was.

Now there was another baby on the way. There was Brandon, who was already here. And she could no longer afford to turn a blind eye.

~

Brandon was frustrated. He'd burned the black birch bark all through his house, and all he learned was that burning birch bark set off his smoke detectors. Luckily he didn't pay for an alarm system and didn't have to explain this to any kindly operator calling to check in on him.

The smoke did tell him that there were no spells in or around his house, except the ones on him. He'd have thought the bark didn't work, that it was all a trick worked on him in the store, but the smoke clung to him so badly it trailed him around the house. It was creepy and he wanted it to stop, but in the end his *'yeah, yeah, I get it'* hadn't made the gray fog quit its clinging and he'd had to shower to get the smell off.

After he was clean and dressed in fresh clothes, he went back to burning the tansy, thinking he had a better shot of actually accomplishing something that way. Three more times he'd walked his circle, poured and cleaned up his salt, and generally felt like an idiot as he cast his stupid little spells. Still Delilah hadn't called.

She was no more in love with him than she had been a week ago.

He was ready to call it all crap and just be done with it. But if he admitted that there was nothing to this witchcraft thing, then he was back to wondering what the hell she'd done or thinking that she'd drugged him. Oh, and now he'd wasted a huge wad of money on those stupid herbs and felt cut-outs. Not to mention the time he'd spent in that damn class.

There were logical problems, too, with simply scrapping his new beliefs. Although Brandon would have been the first to admit that it seemed like an oxy moron to have logic issues with *giving up* a belief in witchcraft, that was the heart of it.

Delilah drugging him just didn't make any sense. There was

no pimp breathing down her neck. She'd never taken his money or his internal organs or even his silverware.

It made sense that Delilah was a witch.

He'd also had spells cast on him. Too many different people told him this. Perhaps he was on a new and very elaborate prank TV show that featured random people no one would care about. Since that clearly wasn't the case, the spells couldn't be anything other than true. It was scary that the simplest explanation was the one where his girlfriend was a real witch.

That, unfortunately, all added up.

So if spells really worked—and he was now a believer—why weren't his working? His almanac said that anyone could become a witch. It was just a matter of practicing the religion. Anyone could harness the 'energy of the universe.' All that was required was a way to tap into it. Spells were one way.

So why didn't his work?

Yasmin's spells worked. She said the shop clerks were all experienced in the craft and could help. Delilah's spell obviously put the whammy on him.

If the 'energy of the universe' flowed in and around him, as Yasmin swore that it did, then why wasn't Delilah on the phone in tears begging for him?

The *Beginning Witchcraft* book from class recommended a senior witch or magician as a teacher. But what was he going to do? It was clear that Yasmin the Good Witch was in no way going to help with his revenge. He could ask Delilah. *Oh, by the way, I figured out about you casting spells on me. I was trying to get this love spell to work. Maybe you could tell me what I'm doing wrong?*

Yeah, she might be a bitch, mis-using him and not caring what he felt, but she wasn't stupid. She'd realize that he was casting on her. Not only would she not help him, she'd likely retaliate. And, as he was learning, he wasn't a very good witch. There was no way he'd be able to stand up to her.

There was also now the huge problem that he couldn't go back to Blessed Be.

When he was last in, Becky called the owner over, and she'd called him 'Tristan.' As Brandon walked out that night with his purchases, his brain put the pieces together and he jolted to awareness. Delilah's brother was named Tristan. And, though he'd seen the photos in her house, he hadn't studied them. Each time he looked, something came up. It was as though she didn't want him to get too good a look at her family. So he didn't think he'd recognize the brother from the photo. But now that he thought about it, something about the shape of their faces seemed the same.

Brandon was grateful that he hadn't recognized the name while he was standing in the store. It might have been the tip-off for the other guy to recognize him. As it was, he'd made it out without incidence.

Of course, there was every possibility that while he knew about Tristan, her brother knew nothing about him. Perhaps Delilah hadn't told her brother about her new plaything. Or maybe she just hadn't mentioned his name. There was also the possibility that she marked him. That her brother would recognize Delilah on him.

Which left Brandon feeling a lot like the tree that got pissed on so every passing dog would know who it belonged to. He lit another sprig of Tansy and ran the chant through again. Angrier now that he was starting to catalog the ways his life had gone to hell.

Still he couldn't go back to Blessed Be until he knew that wasn't her brother running the store.

His mind could argue the points for days. On the upside, it was LA, and there were likely a lot of Tristans. Just the name sounded very *Hollywood*. So this one didn't have any great likelihood of being her brother.

Except that on the downside, Delilah was a witch and this

Tristan was running a shop for witches. The almanac said that witchcraft often ran strongest in families, handed down through the women. But this Tristan was obviously neck deep in it, regardless of his gender.

Then again, her brother—if he was such a great witch that he ran a shop for it—should have recognized his sister's handiwork all over Brandon. Right? But the Tristan in the store had seen the smoke, had seen the way it clung to Brandon and followed him around, and at no point had he said, *You know, that looks like one of my sister's spells.*

Plus, even though they might have some similarities, his coloring was nothing like Delilah's.

Still, Brandon had to figure it out before he could go back. He reasoned that even if he did find someone to help him, he was still in deep dog shit. Brandon sighed, he didn't like these analogies. If Tristan was the brother, and there were too many clues to just discount that, then the second he figured out Brandon was casting against his sister, he would let fly.

Brandon had already been on the receiving end of one witch. Once was enough, thank you. Two would tear him into pieces. His family wouldn't have anything left to bury. And, being Catholic, they'd never buy the witchcraft angle. Bethy would have decided he was doing drugs, his family would bury him in shame and his sister would fear his soul was going to hell. Which, if he faced it, it seemed to be doing at a rapid pace these days.

A sharp pain pierced his thoughts and he looked down at his hand to see the sprig he'd been waving around had burned to a nub while he hadn't been paying attention. His fingers flew apart and the small piece of fuming stick dropped to the floor.

Angry at his own clumsiness, he stomped on it to put out the last of the red glow, then used a paper towel to pop the whole mess into the trash.

All out of tansy—again—Brandon decided to try another tack.

He got out the wide pink candle and the poppet. The book suggested that he color the poppet in like Delilah's face to help the spell stay directed at her. But, seeing as his art skills were so poor, Brandon was afraid he'd cast a plague or a pox on some poor deformed woman who had nothing to do with any of this.

Instead, he stayed simple, putting blonde hair on it, blue dots for eyes, and pink lips. Even if it did look like a host of other women in LA, he hoped it was enough to give the impression of Delilah, without it running amok. For a moment he feared it looked too much like his sister, whose coloring, if not her looks, were remarkably similar to Delilah's. Needing a way to distinguish the poppet as hers and only hers, Brandon hunted for something that didn't require any artistic skill.

Eventually he settled on the addition of the Wiccan symbol of the three interlaced circles. Using a bottle cap that he traced, he made a pretty good version right it the middle of the poppet. Now there was no way any energy in the universe could believe that the likeness was of Bethy. Satisfied, he turned back to the spell.

Above the flame, he wound the white ribbon around the poppet. Over and over until he ran out of ribbon. All the while he spoke the words binding Delilah to the feelings he wanted her to have for him. When he was done, he blew out the candle and went in search of a hiding place for his poppet.

This spell was supposed to be stronger than the burnt tansy. There was a tangible piece keeping the spell alive—the mummified felt cutout. The binding was supposed to last until he unwound the ribbon or destroyed the poppet in some way. The book recommended burning it.

Brandon shuddered at the burning idea. The almanac said it was a legitimate way to end spells. But, if anything happened to Delilah after he basically burned her in effigy, he wouldn't forgive himself. It was one thing to mess with her mind—which so far he hadn't really managed to do. It would be entirely another thing to cause her lasting damage. And, even as mad as he was, he was not capable of that. He wondered for a moment if Delilah was, then he cast the thought aside. His judgment may be screwy right now, but it wasn't that far off. He would never have been with her if he'd believed her capable of real harm.

The thought made him feel better about Delilah, but worse about what he was doing to her—or *trying* to do to her. He had to remind himself that she had cast on him first. No matter how much that sounded like playground logic to him, it wasn't quite enough to make him unwind that stupid little doll.

He needed to put it in a place where she would never find it, but he would either remember it or find it and thus unwind it later.

He wandered into the bedroom, the palm-sized Delilah in his fist. He wanted to put it under the pillow. If it were there, then he would see it every time he changed the sheets, and he could decide to put it back until the next sheet changing or untie her.

But if Delilah showed up—as she should *any minute now* considering the sheer number of spells he'd cast on her at this point—she might throw herself at him. What would happen when she found the poppet? Or if the two of them jostled it to the floor?

Surely Delilah would recognize what it was. Then he'd be right back at the retaliation problem—by a witch who was clearly much better at this than he was.

He sighed.

He looked around again, knowing he couldn't put the thing in the kitchen—a lovesick Delilah was likely to show up and cook for him at any moment. The living room simply didn't have enough stuff to offer any real hiding places. If he was going to put the poppet there, then he might as well just toss the thing into the corner like a dust bunny. At last he figured he could tuck the cutout under the edge of the mattress. He might forget about it for a while, but whatever. Too bad, so sad. Delilah deserved what was coming. It was her own fault if he didn't unwind it fast enough.

Just then his phone rang.

He lifted the mattress and shoved the felt and cotton under the corner before diving across for the phone.

Sure enough, the caller ID showed *Goodman, Delilah*.

Finally. He felt the tension drain from him as he hit the connect button. He smiled for the first time in several days.

"Hey, Lilah."

CHAPTER 27

Delilah tried not to burst into tears, tried not to be so upset, tried to tell herself it was just the hormones, because she was pregnant. Still, she sat there, holding the stick and re-reading the instructions. Not that there was much she could do about it. It was really hard to misuse or misinterpret a home pregnancy test these days.

She was pregnant.

The early predictor stick tested some revolutionary new hormone to be able to tell her days earlier than any other test.

Oh, yea, Delilah thought wryly as she tried again to hold back the threatening tears. She sat on the edge of the bed and sniffled. She felt sorry for herself even though she'd decided she should be happy about this baby. It still didn't make her happy about what she had to tell Brandon.

Her phone buzzed, startling her so she jumped about five miles high. That couldn't be good for the baby.

There was only one person she knew who'd be buzzing up right now. She'd called Brandon and asked him to come over, right before she did the test. She hoped that way she wouldn't give anything away on the phone—because she wouldn't know anything to give away. She hadn't even said a word about thinking she was pregnant. Nor that there was something she needed to tell him. A handful of somethings in fact. Just that she'd really needed to see him. Soon.

He said he'd be right over, although he must have rushed or hit the perfect opening in traffic to be here this fast. But, ready or not, she had to begin.

Nervous now, she picked up the receiver, "Hello?"

"Delilah! Let me up."

Brandon sounded so sure of himself. He didn't ask, didn't hesitate. So she merely said, 'okay,' and hit the *send* button on the phone to activate the buzzer.

No sooner than she'd set the phone back in the cradle, her brain crackled to life. She was in her bathrobe. She'd been crying. She looked like crap. Her hair was uncombed and her nose was likely red.

What on earth had she been thinking?

Oh yeah, she hadn't been thinking. All that her brain was able to register was that she had to take the test she'd bought last night, and if she didn't call him first, she'd likely never tell him. If it were negative she might have never said anything.

But that wasn't a concern—clearly.

She checked the bathroom mirror as she flew by. Yup, her face was definitely red.

Faster than she'd ever done before, and wondering just how quick Brandon might be today, she pulled out underwear and jeans and stepped into them so rapidly she almost tripped herself. Praying the elevator was as slow as it had been the other night, she yanked on a bra and whipped a red t-shirt over her head.

Running into the bathroom, she pulled a brush through her wet hair, the best she'd be able to do under the circumstances. At lightning speed, Delilah slicked on lipstick, rubbed in concealer and applied powder, hoping it covered the worst of the sins. She had time for only one more thing, if that. As a blonde, that had to be mascara. That would get her as close to presentable as she could be. She whisked the mascara brush at her face begging the gods to let her only get it on her eyelashes and not catch her hair or smudge it on her cheeks.

This time the gods took pity on her. They certainly hadn't before.

Heavy knocking came from her front door, but she wasn't ready yet. Delilah took a deep breath to steady herself and evaluated the face in the mirror. There was nothing about the woman who stared back at her that looked anything other than hastily-put-together. Nothing that said, *I'm pregnant with your baby. Love me, please. Keep me forever.*

Nope, everything about her screamed *unstable,* and *now what?*, and *oops.*

She walked as calmly as she could to her door and pulled it open.

Brandon sauntered right past her like he owned the place. "Delilah, baby, what's up?"

She frowned at him. Had he really just said that? Maybe he'd eaten a bad toadstool. Then again, maybe it was just her. There was certainly no way she could convince herself she was thinking straight right now.

She had to come clean. Had to. Just look what fate handed out for punishment if she didn't. Delilah was steeling herself with a deep breath, when he spoke again. "I thought we'd go out today. Do something. Or maybe just stay in."

Huh?

Then, at last, he looked at her. And he frowned. "Are you all right?"

Finally, he sounded like Brandon. That gave her the courage to speak. She opened her mouth, but once again Brandon beat her to it. She hadn't gotten a word out since he arrived.

"You look like you've been crying." He said it with the same inflection he would have used to ask what color her table linens were.

"I have."

"Why?" Still no real concern.

Now she was the one frowning and she reminded herself, *think before you blurt!* Then she realized if she took the time to think first, she'd never get it out. So she blurted, "I'm pregnant."

He stepped back like he'd been slapped, his mouth falling open. His eyes blinked rapidly as though the movement would help him process his thoughts faster. Then he looked at her, really at her, and she felt it like a sharp stab. Not the reaction she'd been hoping for. Well, it probably wasn't what he'd been hoping for either.

He leaned in, still scowling, his face just a few inches from hers. "Is it mine?"

"*What!*" She just exploded. "What? Are you serious?"

He stood stone still. "It's a legitimate question, Delilah."

Fury burned through her and she fought the urge to send the room into a maelstrom. As if that would teach him. He'd probably run screaming out the door and she'd never see him again. Although, after that last remark she was thinking she might not want to. Still, she had to get through this. Sanely.

Focusing her energy on a candle sitting silent on the bookshelf behind him, she held her tongue and her anger in check. The candle popped to life. The tiny flame dancing, once, twice. Then it winked out. It didn't satisfy her, but it helped.

She kept her voice controlled. "I'm tempted to tell you that it isn't yours. Just so you'll take your damned accusations and get the hell out!"

The stone façade that had been his expression broke and words gushed out of him, none of them making any real sense, "Really? How? I thought . . ."

Her anger broke, too, and she sighed, "Honestly, I have no idea. Because I thought we were careful, too."

She hung her head to cover the fact that she was fighting tears.

Quickly, Brandon was at her side, the Brandon she *knew*, his arm around her shoulder. He lowered her to the couch, tucking himself alongside her, whispering soothing words the whole way. "It'll be okay. We'll figure it out. Don't cry."

Then, as though he suddenly thought comforting her was a huge error, he abruptly pulled away. Putting space between them and a chill in his voice, he looked at her. "What are you going to do?"

She stared. Her mouth hung open as she gaped at him. How could he possibly think it was the wrong time to comfort her? She really did burst into tears then. But Brandon remained stoic.

Delilah sniffled. Well, this was how it would be then. "I don't really know what *I'm* going to do. I didn't even realize that I might be pregnant until yesterday. And I took the test all of ten minutes before you buzzed. So I apologize for not having it all figured out quite yet."

She stood and went to the fridge for a coke, only to realize when she opened the can that she shouldn't be drinking caffeine if she was pregnant. *Crap*. She poured the whole thing down the sink while she tried to keep herself together. Steeling herself for what was ahead, and making her first choice for her baby, she poured a glass of ice water instead, then turned to look at Brandon. "Do *you* have any ideas?"

He looked at her like she was an alien from another planet, not like she was the woman he'd helped create this baby with. "Are you going to keep it?"

She pushed her teeth together for a minute, trying to think of the right thing to say, whatever that was. When the right thing didn't come, she settled for not destroying the relationship she had with the father of her child. Delilah forcibly reminded herself that he usually wasn't such a dick. "I'm going to try."

He didn't say anything. Just looked like he'd been pushed too far into a corner and his fight-or-flight response was kicking in.

She did what she could. She cut the strings. "Look, if you want, you can walk out the door and forget about all of this. I don't need or want your money or your help."

So much for not alienating him. Her brain churned through a life without Brandon, a life as a single mother. She'd spend David's life insurance policy on this child. On the child she could have. Maybe to make up for the one she'd lost.

Brandon yelled, snapping her out of her thoughts. "Look, I just found out about this ten seconds ago. So I'll apologize for not having it all figured out quite yet." He threw her own words back at her and rubbed his hands over his face. He crossed his arms. He uncrossed them.

He stood.

He sat.

Delilah remained still, watching him. In her mind, she was making plans. She'd buy a house. Away from LA. If she moved, then she wouldn't have to see Brandon. She wouldn't see Tristan much either.

Scratch that.

She'd buy herself a condo nearby. But she wouldn't tell Brandon. If the price was right, she could have enough left over so she wouldn't have to work for a while after the baby was born. And if she could keep her commute short, she'd be able to continue working up until much closer to her delivery date.

If she made it that far. Contradictory thoughts tumbled one over the other. Maybe she shouldn't move until closer to her due date. Whatever that was. She knew she'd be heartbroken all over again if she lived in the new place she'd bought for the baby and then there was no baby. But if she waited too long, it might be too stressful to move.

Brandon paced.

Then turned back and faced her. "What do we do?"

"I need a doctor's appointment. To be sure that I really am pregnant." *At least before I go buying a condo,* she thought.

He came closer and grabbed the test stick from her hand. She'd picked it back up, clung to it, maybe as proof in case he doubted her. In case she herself thought she was crazy.

He looked at the blue lines in the little plastic windows. She watched as his eyes darted back and forth, comparing her lines to the ones printed right there on the stick. "This clearly says you're pregnant. Are they sometimes wrong?"

Delilah shook her head, and was getting ready to answer him when he asked, "Then why do you need to see a doctor to be sure?"

She stepped away, for the first time needing some space from Brandon. She took a deep breath to steel herself, finding the explanation to be harder than she expected. "I am pregnant. But sometimes the baby isn't growing, or the hormone levels aren't high enough. Things like that."

He frowned. "Like you might miscarry?"

She nodded, and turned away, tears forming in her eyes. She didn't want to miscarry this time. Sure she had a good excuse for the last one, but that didn't change the fact that there was no real way to rectify it.

Suddenly, she desperately wanted this baby. Involuntarily, her arms wrapped around her belly, as though she could protect the life growing there with her hands. There was no way Brandon would agree to get her pregnant again if this didn't take. This was her one shot. Delilah sniffled and again Brandon put his arms around her, crooning to her that they would figure it all out. Just as she gave in and leaned into him, he suddenly let go, backing away like she burned him. It left her stumbling, but he didn't seem to notice, or if he did, he didn't care.

He'd never done anything like that before. He was the one

who said they were going to go out. He was the one who decided they would be exclusive. He pushed for the relationship that created this baby. And now he started pulling away?

Her brain twisted around that fact. Tried to find a way for it to be okay that he didn't want to touch her.

Maybe he was overwhelmed. Maybe his brain was working too fast, trying to figure out how this happened, and how things were going to happen from here on out. He'd never pulled away from her before, but then again, she'd never told him she was pregnant before. Maybe no one ever had.

She tried desperately to give him the benefit of the doubt, even if the way he was looking at her cut like a knife, how he jerked away like she was the plague. "Brandon, maybe you should go. We both need some time to think about this, to figure out what we each want."

He opened his mouth, but she couldn't take any more of his pulling away, any more of his hurtful looks. So this time it was her turn, and she talked right over him. "It's okay if you don't want anything to do with this, with us. I'll understand. But I won't keep you away from your child either." She watched his face flinch at the words 'your child' and wondered what was going on in his head. Still she kept railroading him. "You call me when you're ready to talk about it."

He opened his mouth, once, twice, but no sound came.

Clearly, he needed time to digest. Her heart burned. His reaction was so strong. And she'd only gotten through a third of the things she needed to say. She was going to have to do this twice more. Even if Brandon could live with all of it, even if he could adjust to everything she was laying at his feet, she wouldn't ever know. Because he was going to just die from the shock of it all, if today was any indication.

With only a brief nod of his head, he turned and let himself out her door.

As soon as the door clicked into place, the dam holding back her tears burst. Her chest wracked with great sobs. Slowly, she slid to the kitchen floor, her hands covering her face. Her body and her mind let go of the tight hold she'd managed to maintain.

She was going to be a single parent.

Which was nothing she'd ever aimed for. Look at her past: she'd been willing to take a cheating David back when she found out she was pregnant. The irony here wasn't lost on her. Brandon was a good guy. He wouldn't cheat like David. Not even if Juliet came on to him. Somehow she knew that in her heart. But Brandon still wouldn't be here for her and her baby—simply because he didn't want to be.

She sniffed and managed to haul herself up far enough to reach the tissues on the counter. Then she sank back down to the floor, wiping her face even though she was nowhere near done crying.

Blinking a few times, she at least managed to get her pep talk started. If Brandon didn't want to be with her then she would deal with it. It was her fault, and she could own up to it. But if he didn't want to be with his child, then he wasn't the man she'd thought him to be. Even though she'd been so convinced he was. She started crying in earnest again. It wasn't supposed to be this way.

As she sat there huddled on her kitchen floor, Delilah entertained the very real possibility that she'd never hear from Brandon again.

CHAPTER 28

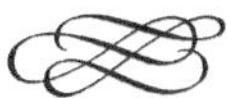

Brandon was still in a shocked daze when he pulled into his garage.

Delilah. Pregnant.

Well, he hadn't seen that coming in a million years.

He wasn't even sure how he got home. His brain was going a mile a minute, but none of his thoughts were about driving. He'd simply gone on autopilot.

For some reason, putting the key in his front door and unlocking both the deadbolts brought him out of it. With his brain working ahead of his feet, he didn't finish unlocking the door but turned around and went out into the front yard and looked up and down the street.

It was a good neighborhood. Right on the border of Hollywood and West Hollywood. West Hollywood was incredibly gay friendly, also there were a lot of Russian families that had been here since long before the tide had turned. People had their thoughts about the lifestyle in this section of town, but the fact was that it was open and friendly. Not as rich as Beverly Hills but not full of rundown apartment buildings like so many areas. It was as safe as you could get in LA. And he had great neighbors.

The yard wasn't big, but it would do. He'd want to put a fence around it. You couldn't have a small kid running out into the street, no matter how nice you thought your neighborhood was. There was a good green park at the end of the block, something he hadn't considered at all when he bought the place. Now he could envision a chubby blond toddler running in the grass there.

Just as quickly, he turned away from the scene playing out in his mind and finished unlocking the front door. He stepped over the threshold onto the hardwood floor and tried to think logically.

The fact was he was having a baby with a woman who had completely manipulated him. Who still was.

So many times Brandon found himself reaching out to her, putting his arms around her to console her, wanting nothing but to make everything okay. He'd thought about asking her to run off to Vegas, get married. Then she'd know how he felt, because he never really said it. Now, logically, he was glad he'd never said it.

Of course, there was every possibility he'd never really said it because he didn't really feel it. Well, he *did*. But since it was all conjured at Delilah's will, it wasn't real. Every time he remembered that, he stepped away from her and tried to put his hands back at his sides.

But that wasn't what he wanted to do. What he wanted was to tear his own hair out.

To top the whole thing off, this pregnancy came right when he was starting to fight back against everything she'd done to him. Poorly, mind you, but fight back nonetheless.

He looked around the house, taking stock. His bachelor pad days were over. It didn't matter if Delilah had offered him an easy way out, that he could just leave her be and never think about her or the child again, he wasn't that kind of man. His father hadn't been, and he hadn't been raised that way. He'd also been the child who had a parent just disappear. It didn't matter if it was your mother or your father, it wasn't easy. And he would not be the cause of that pain in some other child's life—*his* child.

Besides, he always figured he'd have his own kids someday. Brandon smiled wryly at the empty room, it had been like this forever it seemed. He never decorated or tried to make his space anything other than a place to sleep or to watch TV. Until he'd put a patio table and chairs out on the deck for Delilah that was. Still, it was time to make a clean sweep of all of it. *Welcome to 'someday.'*

It was his child. The heat settled somewhere deep inside him, warming him in a way he'd never felt before. At least he could be satisfied those feelings were his own.

Now about the mother of his child . . .

He needed to tell her what he knew. Had to convince her to lay off the spells. So maybe they stood a chance at forming something real. Or at least that he wouldn't feel—*be*—so manipulated.

He felt the need to give it a shot with her. Not to doom his child to a lifetime of getting shuttled back and forth between parents who really didn't speak. Who held radically different beliefs. From his own childhood, he remembered his own father's unflinching honesty. And how it had soothed him in what little way it could over the loss of his own mother. His father had made sure he knew it wasn't his or Bethy's fault. His father tried to keep the marriage together. Brandon knew the question would come up someday, *why aren't you and Mommy together?* and he didn't want to respond with, *I just didn't pursue it.* It didn't seem fair, because it wasn't. So, for his own conscience, he had to do his best to patch things up with

Delilah. So that, at the very worst he could say he'd failed, but he'd done his best.

First, though, he had to ditch his own witchcraft stuff. It wouldn't do to tell Delilah to lay off the spells when lately he'd been just as bad. He grabbed the burnt halves of the birch bark sticks, the candles and the dishes, and hastily threw them all into the trash. He dismantled the wooden altar and hauled the pieces out to the garage, putting them in separate places as though they might be tempted to reform when he wasn't watching. Grabbing the hefty Almanac, he figured he should throw it out, too, but hesitated as he held the large volume poised over the trash can. For some reason his fingers wouldn't seem to let go of it.

The thought passed through his head that he should keep it. It wasn't like the book would cast spells on its own. As long as he didn't do any work out of it, it should be fine. Besides, he was having a baby with a witch, and the book said that mothers passed the religion on to their kids.

He put it on the bottom shelf of his bedside table. He'd been skipping the chapters on the religion of Wicca, only wanting to get to the magick. Now, he committed to reading the whole thing front to back. He'd learn the daily ins and outs of the practitioners. He'd research online, too, and ask Yasmin what was right and what was mixed up from the uneducated. He wouldn't be one of them any longer. It was the only way he'd ever begin to be able to keep up with a blonde-haired, blue-eyed witch who likely didn't need spells to keep him enchanted.

With the house cleared of his forays into the craft, Brandon picked up the phone to call Delilah. She'd told him to call when he made up his mind. But he'd barely been home long enough to throw out his herbs and to renounce his revenge. She was likely still in shock herself.

Carefully setting the phone back in the cradle, he changed his mind. He wanted her here. Away from her apartment, away from her supplies. He wanted her with him. For a moment he was able to look around his place and see it populated with Delilah's furniture, see her pots and pans lining the walls of his kitchen. That was taking it a bit far. His brain knew that, but even the logical assessment did nothing to ease the comfort the vision brought him.

Brandon admitted what he was feeling must be generated by Lilah's spells. But that was too bad for her, she was just going to have to play out the cards she'd snuck him off the bottom of the deck. If she wanted to cheat, she'd have to live with the consequences.

He wanted her here. He wanted to influence her decisions about this baby. He didn't want her to be able to dump him and dash away as she had before. Besides, he reasoned, she wasn't likely in any shape to drive.

So he pulled out his keys and headed back the way he'd just come.

He used the same trick he had the first night he'd snuck into her building, randomly dialing numbers until someone buzzed him in. Only this time, as he climbed the stairs, he frowned, upset at just how easy it was to sneak his way into Delilah's building. He didn't want his kid growing up in a place that wasn't more secure. It was as good an excuse as any for the rest of what was rolling around inside his head.

For three flights, he harbored his small fantasies of Delilah living in his house, playing with their child in his yard. When the first child in his imagination was grown to several years older and there was a second blonde toddler in the imaginary yard, he shook his head, trying to clear it. It was like the spells got stronger and stronger the closer he got to her place. If only they wore off when he was at his house. But they didn't.

He stared at the door to her unit for a few seconds. He almost knocked, but he didn't know if she would answer. He'd stormed out in such a huff, with her words telling him in essence she would understand if she never heard from him again. There was every possibility she would check the peephole and never open the door. How long would he be able to camp outside her door and wait her out? Probably not as long as she could stay in there. So he reached out to first try the knob, just on the off chance . . . it opened.

Surprised, he pushed his way in to the apartment, only to find Delilah was more surprised by his move than he was. He was opening his mouth to chide her for leaving the door unlocked, when his brain put together the red eyes, disheveled hair and the fact that she was sitting on the floor of her kitchen. Her arms were wrapped around her knees. And though she was startled by his presence, she seemed too tangled, or maybe too shocked, to get herself up off the floor.

Brandon didn't know what to say, so he offered up, "Give me a minute."

Mutely, she nodded, biting on her lower lip and stopping her desperate attempt to get herself up and put together. Brandon walked off into her bedroom. He opened her closet to find that she had a horrible case of organization. He thought maybe she was just that anal retentive in the kitchen because she cooked. Now he wondered if she had her medicine cabinet alphabetized.

Still, that made it easy to find the duffle bag on the top shelf. He pulled a soft t-shirt off a hanger and a pair of jeans from one of the racks. He opened several drawers looking for underwear, stumbling across socks and bras first. Which was probably a good thing since he hadn't thought of either. He stuffed one of each thing into the duffle bag then tried not to get distracted by the drawer of frothy underwear. He decided to pull something out randomly, but came up with a red lace thong.

They needed to talk about her pregnancy, make decisions about their future. He didn't want to give her the wrong idea. Not that the red lace thong was a *bad* idea . . . He forced himself to put it back and try again. This time he came up with a sedate shade of purple, in cotton. Still a little skimpy on the cut, but he wasn't in a place to be choosy. He smiled a little, then headed into the bathroom, only to find it was just as organized as everything else. She could work wonders on his place.

He grabbed her toothbrush and toothpaste before scrounging around for her hairbrush and whatever else she might need. After a few moments he realized he was out of his league in here and gave up. Slinging the duffle over his shoulder, he headed back out into the main area where he found Delilah still curled in a tight ball on the kitchen floor.

Her voice was as wet as her face. "I thought you were going to call."

"You're in no shape to drive."

He didn't know why he'd said that. It didn't really answer her question. But he knelt down next to her, and he could tell he startled her when he scooped her up. Then again, what did she expect? She'd cast love spells on him. And probably—certainly—other spells, too. Something to placate him, so he wouldn't be angry when he found out. Like now. Again he went back to his mental argument about her needing to stay in the bed she'd made.

She protested, though only marginally, when he headed to the door with her in his arms. When he asked, she provided keys and he carefully locked the door behind them before heading down the hall to the elevator, Delilah's head resting against his shoulder. Maybe it meant she'd seen the inevitable and given in to him.

He could only hope.

CHAPTER 29

Delilah stared out the window on the short ride to Brandon's, but she refused when he offered to carry her inside. She needed to walk on her own.

That seemed to be what this was all about. All the things she'd neglected for the last year. Like taking a good hard look at herself. Like taking stock and being sure she was doing what she needed to do—not just putting up a good front and getting to work on time.

Since she was being honest with herself—finally—no matter how painful that was, she had to admit that she'd been neglecting a lot since long before David and Juliet had died. She'd been perfect on the outside. Had the perfect plot of land to build the perfect home on with the perfect man. But none of it had been perfect or even right. It just looked that way.

Maybe because she could manipulate things to suit herself so well, she'd been able to make things seem close enough, even when they weren't. The fact of the matter was she'd been able to achieve what she thought was perfection, but now she needed to admit she didn't even know what that was.

Still, she couldn't let Brandon carry her around and

completely take care of her. That would be like going back to David. David who earned all the money and didn't want his pretty wife to work. But he sure liked the fact that she threw the best parties. She'd taken good care of him. They'd had great vacations. It had been fun being David's wife. If not very fulfilling.

Delilah figured today on the floor of her kitchen was the first time she ever admitted to that.

She'd been crying when Brandon had showed up, just getting all of it out. Apparently there was a lot to get over when you killed your husband and mistakenly took your sister out with him. So while Brandon may be enjoying playing white knight and spiriting her away, she needed to get onto her own two feet, literally and figuratively.

She followed him into the house, only then realizing he had her duffle bag over his shoulder. He must have packed it himself, must have intended for her to stay the night. Taking a deep breath for fortification, Delilah prepared to walk home. Once she told him the truth, he wouldn't drive her. If he was very generous he'd call her a cab, and allow her to pay for it.

Still, she mutely followed him inside, vowing to herself to come completely clean. It was way past time. Still, it was much harder to do it than to think it. She found herself saying yes, she would like a Sprite if he had it, when he asked if he could get her a drink. Then Delilah was on his couch, glass in hand, before she could even think about saying some really illuminating words. Then she chickened out—again—thinking that she shouldn't tell everything with a drink in her hand while she sat on his couch. What if it spilled?

She managed to berate herself mentally, but not to say anything.

Delilah was grateful, if a little ashamed, that it was Brandon who managed to speak first. "You said I should call when I'd decided something, so I called."

"I meant the phone." She'd never expected him to show up or she would have stopped crying and washed her face. Even now, she had to wonder what she looked like.

"Well, I wanted to talk face to face, and I wanted to get you out of your place. So I showed up. You didn't specify which kind of 'call'."

He looked at her like he was waiting for her to crack a smile. She just couldn't, so she nodded and sipped at her drink.

"Okay, let's talk."

Here it was—he wanted to *talk*. There was going to be a big to-do about whose baby it was, and she just really didn't want to do this now.

Brandon apparently did. "Are you going to get an abortion?"

"No!" She pulled back like she'd been slapped, nearly spilling the drink. She didn't even need to confess to mess up his couch. She was about to get up and call the cab herself.

Screw him. She wanted to laugh. Somehow he managed to take the pressure off her to confess. There was no way she was telling this ass what she was. Then her feelings turned on a dime. Somehow that idea only made her feel worse.

"You won't change your mind?" He looked straight at her.

For a moment she didn't consider spilling the drink, she considered throwing it in his face. He didn't have to be involved. She'd made that abundantly clear, but the mere suggestion that he wanted her to—

His hand hooked her arm as she tried to stand and march out. His hold was soft, but she clearly wasn't going anywhere until he released her. "I take it that's another 'no'."

"Damn straight." Still he didn't let her up.

"Good." His breath came out of him like he'd been holding it.

Delilah blinked. She felt more confused than she was when she watched the lines appear on that pregnancy test. Come to think of it, she hadn't been anything but confused from the moment she met him. She looked back at Brandon and wondered how he had the power to scramble her so. His expression didn't change. Delilah still didn't understand. "I'm sorry?"

"I said, 'good.' I don't want you to have one, but it isn't my place to decide for you."

At last he let go of her arm and she managed to pull back. That was weird.

He asked another, point blank question. "Are you going to keep the baby?"

She answered him in the same dry tone he interrogated her with. "Yes."

He nodded, seeming relieved. He looked away as though he was getting his bearings. Then he looked back at her, right in the eyes, like he could see more than she intended him to. "If you decide not to keep the baby, then I want it. Boy or girl, healthy or not, I want it."

He still showed no expression, but the words got to her, chipping at walls that shielded her heart. As great a gesture as that was, it wasn't going to happen. She needed to be clear about that. "I'm not giving this baby away."

"Good, but count me in."

She nodded. She did admire his determination. Go figure, the man she picked up in a bar one night was better father material than the one she married and lived with for five years. There was no way Delilah could deny this man his child. Though it would cause uncountable complications, she was glad her child's father wanted to be a part of the baby's life. He wouldn't want to be part of hers after he found out about her, but at least her baby would know him. She sat back and waited for the next question.

It wasn't what she expected. Delilah began to wonder why she ever thought she could guess what Brandon would say at all. He was truly unpredictable.

"Tell me why you were still crying when I came in. Was it all just too much?"

He'd handed her an easy way out, but Delilah still wasn't ready to take it. She was starting to hate herself for being a chicken. "I was pregnant before."

He nodded again, that slow 'I'm thinking' motion that he did. "You said you were going to try to keep this one. Did you give the other baby away?"

"No, I miscarried. I was six weeks along when my husband and my sister died. Together. I watched them die."

She could see he was rolling that one around in his head for a minute. But he didn't judge—or at least if he did, he kept it to himself. "The stress was too much?"

"I won't ever know." She shrugged and pushed herself to tell him, to reveal the next piece of information. She could tell him these facts, it was just a piece of her life, not the whole thing—which she herself was only just now realizing. It didn't have to define her. Perhaps if she started telling him things—even the painful ones—maybe she would be able to just keep talking.

"We lived in Malibu, in this tiny house that we built on this property we found. It was up on a hill across the Pacific Coast Highway. It had a great view. I was up there, watching from the window when I saw his car coming up the canyon road to the house. I didn't know Juliet was with him. He was almost in the driveway and I was so mad about him and Jules. He didn't live there any more, he'd moved in with her or whatever—he wasn't with me. He just left me to handle all of it. He showed up at the divorce hearings and that was it. So I sold the house all by myself and I was really mad. I came out to yell at him, to tell him what I thought."

Standing now, she jumped to another part of the story, trying to explain how it all went down. Not that there was any way to make her part in it appear better. She had done it, she lived with it. She just wanted him to understand. "The roads are curvy, and someone came around the corner too fast. It was a sharp curve, blind, and the other driver was long gone before David and Jules went through the retainer wall—it was really short and the rocks were loose. They went right over the side. I went down after them. I just ran right down the side of the cliff."

Delilah took a deep breath and another sip of the drink. It didn't help. Brandon merely waited her out. "They went into the river and so did I. I tried to save her. But by the time the paramedics pulled me out of the water, I'd developed hypothermia and the baby died a little while later."

In a blink, he was up and his arms were around her. He pulled her close, a tight bear of a hug that didn't let go. One that said she meant the world to him. And she couldn't stand it, because he didn't know what she'd done. She couldn't accept his sympathy unless he gave it with all the facts in place.

Delilah pushed her hands against his chest and moved away.

Her voice broke. "I hated them both, but I tried to save her. She was my sister. Even though I'm confident she worked hard to take him away from me. I guess she succeeded. Somehow I hated him more than I hated her. Maybe just for being so weak."

"I'm so sorry, Lilah." He tried again to pull her close but this time Delilah managed to dodge him before she was tempted to sink into his embrace and just forget the rest of it.

"She was pregnant, too."

She stood up, watching as that fact jumped through the points in his brain connecting up all the things he'd learned.

"It was his?"

"Yes." She nodded as she walked a tight circle as though the action might keep Brandon away. Nothing she did ever kept him away. "The autopsy showed she was almost five months pregnant when she died."

"Oh, Lilah."

But Delilah turned her face to the wall, so she couldn't see his sympathy and so he couldn't see her. She'd hated both of them so much. But suddenly she didn't. She lost her niece or nephew that day, too and never before had she considered that as another blow to her heart. The baby had always just been a weapon Juliet wielded against her. Not a family member. Delilah never even found out if it was a boy or a girl.

He was standing, too, when he spoke next. "Did you hate her?"

How did he do that? How did he see what she was thinking? "Yes. More than anything. Except maybe him."

This time she didn't—couldn't—fight his arms around her.

His words were soothing, even though they should have made her angrier. He only justified all the mean things she'd felt. But the justification made it easier to start to let go. "Of course you hated her. She was your younger sister, right?"

Delilah nodded, her back pressed against his ribs. Her head fell against his shoulder, resting there and finally taking some of the strength he offered.

"She deliberately took your husband, then got pregnant with his child. I'm guessing it was just another blow that she was more pregnant than you."

Everything went out of her then. Like a balloon with a hole—in a second it was over. Somehow, Brandon made it okay that she hated Jules. He was the only one who ever realized Juliet had taken something else by being further along. She'd taken the first grandchild, and she'd made Delilah's early pregnancy trivial. She'd taken away Delilah's chance of salvaging her marriage.

How many times had David asked Delilah to try to forgive rather than carry it around with her? He'd tried to comfort, and he'd soothed a little. But he'd never made it okay to be angry. He'd been the source of so much of her anger, it wasn't possible.

Suddenly, in that moment with Brandon's arms around her, she wasn't so angry anymore.

Maybe because it wasn't a fault of her own so much that she harbored all this resentment still. Even against two people who paid the ultimate price for what they'd done. Maybe because someone finally understood, or simply let her be without trying to judge her or fix her. Or maybe it was because there was another baby on the way. Because her second chance had arrived.

She turned in Brandon's arms until she was facing him.

She was going to say 'thank you,' but his arms came tighter around her, telling her without words just how important she was to him. In that moment she couldn't destroy the little piece of serenity she'd found. She didn't tell him the rest, she didn't have the energy. She desperately needed just this one more chance to be held by him before he wouldn't ever offer again. So she allowed herself to sink against him and let him lead her to the bedroom.

Gently he pulled off her shoes and tucked her under the covers.

CHAPTER 30

Brandon was thoroughly dismayed with the time schedule the world had set for him.

He left Delilah in his bed the morning after their illuminating talk. She mumbled something sweet and rolled over. It was the second time he'd gotten up and gone to work, leaving her there alone at his place. Nothing special, just a normal day-to-day kind of thing, and he was surprised to find just how much he liked it. He liked the idea of Delilah waking in his room and making herself breakfast in his kitchen or watching her cooking channel on his TV. She could see pastry cream in larger-than-life high-definition at his house. It gave a little more credence to his visions of her moving in with him. Regardless of the fact that his desires were originally fabricated by her spells, they were certainly taking hold.

But apparently she hadn't stayed. She called him from her little apartment not three hours later to say that she managed to get an appointment with her doctor and would he like to come with her?

Brandon wholeheartedly agreed, mapping out the time in his calendar. The only real issue was trying to figure out how he was going to explain this to Dan who still didn't even realize how involved he was with Delilah. Then again, 'obstetrician, 1p.m. UCLA med plaza' pretty much said it all.

Brandon was caught in his musings, wondering why he hadn't told Dan what was happening. Was it because he knew the response he was going to get ahead of time and he just didn't want to deal with it? Was it because he didn't know how much to say? *Dan, Delilah's a witch and she . . .* Or was it because he was avoiding the legitimacy of everything he knew Dan was going to say? But Brandon didn't get the chance to follow that train of thought. He noticed the date on the appointment, "What? That's over a week away!"

He heard Delilah's resigned sigh across the phone line and he could tell she wasn't any happier with it than he was. "I know. It was the earliest they had available. And I'm not a high priority."

"How are you not a high priority?" That made no sense to him whatsoever. He was pretty certain the harsh pitch of his voice conveyed just that. He was sorry as soon as he'd practically yelled it.

But, thankfully, Delilah didn't seem to take offense. "I'm barely pregnant, so if something is wrong there's not much they can do. There's not much they can see or test at this point, and I'm not an in-vitro patient. The baby's just going to grow anyway."

Still, he was frustrated. "Don't they want to be sure that you're taking good care of yourself? Eating right?"

Oh, lord, as he said it, all these thoughts came into his head. Things he hadn't worried about before: Delilah's health, whether she was on medications, what she was eating and drinking on a regular basis. Could her witchcraft hurt the baby? There was often a lot of burning of various herbs. It probably wasn't as bad as cigarette smoking, but he really didn't know.

Her voice pulled him back to the present. "They handed me

off to a nurse who asked a bunch of questions, told me not to drink or take drugs—"

"Duh." He interrupted, then let her continue.

She laughed, "They're busy. I'm not a priority. I'm not in danger and there's nothing they can actually *do* for me now."

There was a shrug in her voice. He wanted to know *now*. "Is there another doctor you could see faster?"

"Probably, but there may be a reason if an OBGYN is available."

"Well, that's a catch twenty-two." It was probably a good thing she couldn't see his hands scrubbing through his hair. He already didn't like the doctor, just on the principle alone. Even though he knew he was being unreasonable.

"And this is *my* doctor. I know her and I like her."

Brandon resigned to waiting the week, totally bummed. He wanted an ultrasound now. He wanted to see his baby. *His baby*. The words tumbled around in his brain, finding a home, and putting a slight smile on his face. His baby.

He was getting loopy about it and almost missed Delilah's next words.

"They did recommend a book."

Brandon copied down the title and they talked for a few more minutes before hanging up. He was going to have to confront her about the witchcraft. He'd wanted to wait until she told him. He really needed it to come from her. But his baby needed that discussion to happen now. What if tansy smoke was toxic? Surely Delilah wouldn't keep drinking the wine so many spells seemed to require? Surely, he could initiate a tough conversation about his child with the woman who was going to be that child's mother. Well, the witch who was going to be that child's mother.

Telling himself she wasn't going to give the baby some rare herbal smoke cancer before he could talk to her, he took a deep breath and forced his brain back to work.

At lunchtime, Dan stuck his head in the door, and Brandon agreed to go along if they could stop at a bookstore. Dan caught on when Brandon perused the Pregnancy section comparing titles to the one he had jotted down.

"What? Who?" Then a layer of relief settled over Dan as though he figured it out. "You're just picking it up for your sister or something. It's a gift for someone!"

Apparently satisfied with his own answer, he stepped back, letting Brandon thumb through the books looking for the one he wanted.

But Brandon didn't leave it that way. Was it a bad sign that it was easier to start the conversation with Dan? "Nope, this is my copy. Delilah's pregnant."

The indignation switch flipped back on in Dan. "The same Delilah who drugged you? She got herself knocked up? That's what it was all about? Sperm thievery! She's one of those women who wants a baby but the sperm bank isn't good enough. Although this was really taking it to a new level."

Brandon laughed away his partner's zany explanation. "No. She's only a few weeks along."

Dan let out some air. "Then maybe it won't last. I'll pray for you, buddy."

An unexpected jolt of anger struck Brandon. "Don't." His voice was low and rough, in accordance with his surprise at the hurt he felt at the thought of losing the baby.

But Dan didn't see the pain in the response, his brain had already latched onto another tangent. This time he looked truly horrified. Not the expression Brandon wanted to see. "If she's only a few weeks along then you guys are still seeing each other. Really *seeing* each other."

Brandon just nodded and took the book up to the check-out line. Dan followed. "Was this planned?"

"No. Just happened." Brandon paid and got his receipt and wished the interaction with Dan was just as easy to terminate.

For once, Brandon wanted someone to tell him he was doing the right thing. But that wasn't to be and he knew it. Delilah was hiding things. Dan thought he'd gone off the deep end. And if he told his father there would be discussions of marriage that Brandon was not ready to deal with. If he told Bethy . . . well, his very catholic sister might just go get that dunking stick.

So he decided not to tell anyone who didn't already know. At least not for now. Still, Dan pestered him all the way back to the office and through most of the afternoon.

Brandon put up with the henpecking because Dan was his business partner and his best friend, and truly only had his best interests at heart. Even if he didn't see what Brandon really needed.

Delilah went home that night because she had to work the next morning, leaving Brandon with time to himself. Normally he would have found a game on TV, but instead he decided to read. Then he had to choose if he was going to read the pregnancy book or pick up the witchcraft guide. Both seemed truly important to his future with Delilah.

A future that he still wasn't sure existed. A future that still hung by a thread. He sat on his couch, staring at the ceiling for a while wondering if there was any way he could push this process along a little. At one point he seriously considered going down to the loading dock at Othello and just hashing it out. But then all those people wouldn't get their desserts. He had to afford her the same courtesy he'd want. He'd be pissed if she walked into his office one day and slapped all this at him.

So he resigned himself to waiting until there was a better time. It seemed he was doing that a lot lately. Making a decision, he picked the pregnancy book because it was on the couch still in the bag, rather than under his nightstand in the bedroom. Not the most astute method of choice, but he started reading.

Quickly he was pulled in by the information he was

absorbing like a sponge. There were drawings of what happened as a baby grew, recommendations for what the mother should and shouldn't eat. How much she should eat. How much weight she should gain. What she might feel. What she should record. What other women had experienced.

By the end of the first chapter he was overwhelmed. Delilah might be happy or irritable or sad and weepy—or any combination of those—for the next nine months. She might eat him out of house and home or not at all. She might run around like a chicken with its head cut off while she 'nested' or she might get put on bed rest.

The way Brandon figured it, the book should really just say 'We have no clue what is going to happen to you. Good luck.'

Even though he'd been up all night by that point he wasn't ready to stop. Wanting more information, and hoping that he could either support or refute what he'd just read, Brandon turned to the internet then, knowing full well he couldn't trust everything he read. If the bulk of the information agreed, then he'd go with it. He was really hoping he could get a little more definition to what was going to happen. Then he might be able to make a few plans. Or something. After an hour and a half, he had Delilah signed up for discounts at three different maternity stores and had a free package of very tiny diapers on the way.

He wanted to call Delilah and ask her exactly how far along she was, so he could put it into the due-date-counter and see when their baby would come. He would also be given a daily email with a new picture of the baby's development, but not until he produced that date.

Knowing he couldn't call her—he'd never interrupted her at work before—he tried to guess when it might have happened. For the life of him he couldn't figure it out. He needed Delilah to tell him what she knew. But she was at work until maybe as late as eleven and then she would head straight home and crawl into bed. She said she'd been so tired lately, with the pregnancy and all. And he didn't have the heart to wake her when he knew she hadn't slept well for the past few nights and hadn't eaten much at all in days.

Eventually, he gave up and went to bed.

CHAPTER 31

Delilah worked every night that week. Partly because she owed a few nights to the chef who took over for her the week before on such short notice. Also because there was a good likelihood she'd need a few more days here and there just to take care of herself. So she needed to rack up some extra hours just in case. It also didn't hurt to get in everyone's good graces early.

She ignored the fact that her work kept her away from Brandon—and the knowledge that she still hadn't told him anything. She saw him at lunch twice early in the week. Being out like they were, she couldn't really spill her whole story. *LeJune* was a great place for light lunch, not a good place to confess. Not in the middle of his workday.

It was just an excuse, but she clung to it like a lifeline. Logically, she knew that she had a better chance with him if she came clean sooner rather than later. But she would have had a much better chance if she'd done it before she realized she was pregnant. With a sense of fatalism about the whole thing, she ignored her obligation for a while, only talking to him on the phone. Using their opposing work schedule to keep it so they weren't ever truly alone.

If Brandon suspected anything, he didn't say it.

She'd dreamed every time she went to sleep. That hadn't happened to her in a long time. When it happened before, she'd tended to have the same dream over and over. First, right after David and Juliet had died, she relived watching the car go over the edge of the canyon every time she closed her eyes. That had been when she'd taken to the cooking sherry. She hadn't really drunk it, she'd just cooked with it and didn't cook off all the alcohol. It had been the only way to sleep without seeing it all again. The only way to rest.

Tristan gave her hell about it, and she gave up the cooking sherry. Delilah had been surprised to find that the dreams didn't return. She'd slept well for a while. Then her brain altered things. In the next round of dreams it was she who plunged into the water and died. Again and again. For a month she hadn't slept. But, finally, mysteriously, the dream disappeared as fast as it came. And the dreams hadn't come back.

Lately, however, she'd been dreaming all kinds of things. Maybe because she was pregnant. She'd read that in one of those books. But her dreams weren't repetitive. They kept morphing. Still, none of them were pleasant.

Twice this week she dreamed she managed to pull Juliet out of the river. Her sister gasped and coughed up water while David was washed further and further away. Delilah wondered what kind of sick construct her mind had made up. Over and over she watched the man she'd married drift away on a current she knew was going to kill him while she sat on the shore.

But in that dream, Juliet's baby lived. A sweet healthy baby boy that her sister named David. A baby that made Delilah's own arms ache when she held him because her own baby hadn't been strong enough to survive the dive into the water to save Juliet. In the dream, Juliet showed little compassion.

That one woke her up cold.

Delilah was running on little fuel and less sleep. A condition that only seemed to make itself worse as the days went on. She didn't toss her lunch like she had before, but maybe that was because she was eating so little. And the lack of sleep only made her more restless. The dreams didn't stop.

The worst had come the night before. It hadn't been as bad as the others. At least not on the surface. She hadn't woken up in a panic, in fear, or in tears. Instead, she felt so cold and so full of dread that she hadn't dared go back to sleep even though it was only eleven thirty when she woke up. She would just stay up until work rather than face that dream again.

It was too late to call Brandon, he'd probably already be in bed to get himself up and get to work at a decent hour the next morning. In fact, she'd been so exhausted that she'd been sleeping—or rather, *trying* to—pretty much most of the time she hadn't been at work. Which left her precious little time to talk to Brandon about all the things she needed to.

The dream re-played in her mind while she waited for the hours to pass. She'd watched *Oprah* in re-run and a few infomercials, but her brain couldn't shake the vision that kept creeping in.

She and David had been throwing a party at the house on the hill. There were numerous open white tents set up around the yard with streamers floating on a breeze she couldn't feel. A tiny blonde toddler ran past on the over-green grass. Dressed all in white, he dodged in and out of the manicured guests, all of whom commented on how precious he was. Delilah beamed.

Tons of people were at her party. She didn't know any of them, but she felt she ought to. David talked to all of them. They all stopped her to complement the champagne, the crustades, the canapés. It was truly the perfect party.

Then the whispering began. Hadn't the child been wearing white? There he was again, but dressed all in blue. Delilah blinked. She chased her son. He usually came when she called him, but this time he played coy and darted away. It was Juliet, wearing a bright and shiny smile, that scooped him up. He hugged her and called her 'mama.' Even though she called him 'David.' Just like Delilah's own little boy.

Delilah was angry, ready to point out that Juliet was not his 'mama' when the child in white appeared again. People were whispering about how much the two children looked alike. How much they both looked like Delilah's husband David, and that they were both named after him. Nearly identical, the two children cooed at each other, while Juliet pasted on a serene smile and explained to everyone that she had no idea who the father of her baby was.

David, her husband, stepped up at the time and embraced Juliet and her little boy, he was so glad they could come to the party. He kissed her 'hello.' With tongue.

Delilah smiled at them, glad that her family got along so well.

But the voice in the back of her brain was clamoring to wake her up. Screaming at her to not be so blind. Her eyes opened to the ceiling in her apartment and to pain. She stared at it for a while. The dream had been so clear, even though in the dream she had been a complete idiot, oblivious to what was going on right under her nose.

She'd stayed in bed for a while before she gave up and watched TV, but she hadn't been able to shake the disturbing, nagging feeling that she had been just as blind when David and Juliet had been alive. And, though she might have wished they'd lived, she had no idea how she would have lived with it.

She'd eventually turned off the TV and gotten dressed. Driving in to Othello and pushing herself through another early morning at work. Another day of eating very little and of still being haunted by her dreams when she was fully awake.

Not wanting to go back to sleep, Friday after work she stopped in Blessed Be to see Tristan. It was easier to confess to Tristan than to Brandon. So she used her key to let herself in the back just after nine thirty that morning. Tristan was exactly where she expected to find him—at his desk with a mug of coffee in his hands and his ledgers and receipts spread out across the desk in various piles.

He looked up as she came in and smiled before asking how she was doing, if she was still sick, and Delilah found she had a hard time getting her own information out there.

"Hey," Tristan looked at her sideways, "did you think that maybe you made yourself sick? By bottling it all up inside?"

"No, it isn't that." She sighed.

"How do you know?"

Delilah opened her mouth to tell him exactly how she knew, when Yasmin stuck her head in the office, her curls bouncing like her smile. "Morning, boss man."

Her deep brown eyes twinkled at Tristan but her stupid brother was oblivious. Yasmin had carried a torch for her brother as long as Delilah could remember. Only thing was she'd never put that torch to any herbs that would speed the process along. Delilah was so frustrated at both of them she was tempted to cast the spell herself. But then she repeated her little chant that she wasn't going to interfere, she wasn't going to interfere . . .

Having ignored Yasmin's pointed look and decided that he'd accurately diagnosed his sister, Tristan's head bowed back over his receipts. Delilah was getting ready to tell him what a jerk he was being when Yasmin's voice called out from the front of the store for him.

Knowing her chance to tell him about the baby was likely shot, Delilah followed him out behind the front desk just for the entertainment—as dull as that might be.

Tristan smiled at some girl on the other side of the counter, as he leaned over on his elbows. This time he made eye contact with the female. "Hi, Becky."

Delilah fought to not roll her eyes. Yasmin leaped into the conversation. "Becky said there's only one little birch bark shard in the basket. She wanted to know if we had any more sticks in the back. I didn't see any but thought you might know."

Tristan shook his head, still smiling at Becky. "We had a whole bundle come in last week." He paused, then thought. "There was that one order—. . . I saw a receipt for something like eight sticks—"

Still he muddled it. Then he shrugged. "That usually lasts us until the next order comes in. It should be here Tuesday, but there's nothing I can really do before then. Pan Pipes in Venice might have it."

Becky shook her head, and Delilah watched as Tristan noticed. Yasmin noticed him noticing, too. Delilah had to get out of here, she had enough trouble in her own love life without dealing with Tristan's mess. At least Tristan seemed gloriously oblivious to his troubles. It was a shame he was so hung up on hers. She wanted to lecture him on the evils of burying his head in the sand, but outing Yasmin at the front of the store—and in front of the oh-so-flirty Becky—was not a kind idea. She really should just take her thoughts and leave.

The problem was she was just too tired to move from where she'd perched her butt on the edge of the counter. Probably because she was pregnant. And it wouldn't help that she was crashing from a sugar high. She'd drunk three ginger ales during her shift and eaten a caramel cake, the only thing that looked appetizing in days.

Becky sighed. "It's probably my fault. I think I saw that guy grab a whole bundle of them last week. I should have said something, told him he only needed one. But I was busy talking to you."

Delilah saw the smile tighten on Yasmin's face. She had to tell Tristan about the mess he was in. So he knew even if he decided he didn't want to do anything about it. He just seemed so clueless.

Tristan leaned across the counter toward Becky, "Was he dangerous or just a beginner?"

"Beginners can be dangerous." Yasmin snorted and walked away, probably trying to get out of the charged air. Clearly, the woman was headed for a heartbreak. Delilah felt for her.

Tristan was too blind to feel, and he volleyed to her retreating back, "Glad to see you can acknowledge that."

Yasmin didn't turn. Her hands went into the air in a plea to the gods as she disappeared into the stockroom. But they all heard her, "That's why you *teach* them!"

Becky stifled a giggle at the obviously longstanding argument. "I don't think he was dangerous. Just . . . ignorant. And he did have some spells cast on him."

"Really?" Tristan leaned further forward and Delilah started to wonder if the two would wind up bumping mouths in a minute. If maybe she should leave them alone. Tristan's voice sounded very curious, as though beginners didn't come in here with spells basically spilled on themselves every day. "Just what was it that he did to himself?"

"That's just it."

Delilah hauled her tush off the counter edge. She'd seen enough. Time to go home.

Becky's voice followed her though. "Someone else did it. It seemed like he . . ."

The voices faded as Delilah grabbed her purse and headed out the back door. At the last moment she turned around, knowing she would have to get in her brother's face to tell him good-bye. Since she hadn't told him she was pregnant she needed to stay in his good graces, too.

All this niceness was starting to eat at her.

As she got near the front she cleared her throat just a little, so Tristan and Becky wouldn't think they were alone and lock lips or something right there over the counter. Also, Yasmin might not be so nice if she saw.

Tristan turned only partially. "Maybe he was one of Delilah's conquests."

Becky raised her eyebrows at that.

Delilah couldn't believe he'd said that, and to a virtual stranger. She jumped to defend herself before she could think better of it. "I haven't done that since—"

Tristan cut her off, but his attention was on Becky. "Delilah casts on guys in bars who . . . bother her."

Delilah let out a breath. At least that was only part of the truth. And not horribly embarrassing. She should have had more faith in her brother. She should have had more sleep.

Becky shook her head and spoke to Delilah. "I don't think this guy would have been a 'bother.' About this tall." Becky raised her hand over her own head indicating about six feet.

Delilah shook her head, she hadn't done anything like that since Brandon. Just look at all the trouble that one caused her. She was done. Finito. Quits.

But Becky kept talking. "Brown hair, a little bit of curl to it. Definitely sexy."

Delilah blinked.

Tristan finally paid attention, his focus sharpening on his sister as she focused on Becky.

Becky just kept talking. "Good looking. Straight nose. Green, *green* eyes."

Delilah's mouth fell open. The description fit. Perhaps a bit too well. Her brain was turning that over and coming up with 'no way,' when Tristan's voice broke into her thoughts.

He practically yelled. "Rotisserie Guy!? I met *Rotisserie Guy* and I didn't know it?"

Becky jumped back, obviously startled by Tristan's reaction and by the fact that she had been clearly cut from the conversation she started.

Delilah shrugged and tried to brush it off, even though it sounded incredibly like him. "Probably not."

She prayed that were true. How bad would her life get if Brandon and Tristan wound up in cahoots?

Tristan pestered Delilah to give a more thorough description of Brandon to Becky to see if she could make a positive ID. But Delilah had nothing more to give. What could she possibly say? His identifying marks are a mole on his left upper thigh and a bite mark on his right pectoral. If Becky had seen those, Delilah didn't want to know. And Becky sure didn't sound like she knew the guy.

Tristan pestered her for more information. "You have to figure it out. I want to know if that was Rotisserie Guy in case I see him again."

She was definitely in shock that Brandon might have been in here. And she wasn't thinking straight, because she tried to come up with something to add to Becky's description that would tell them if it was or wasn't Brandon they had seen. After a few moments Delilah was at her wits end, she couldn't come up with anything that worked, anything that really did him justice. Unfortunately, *he holds me like I matter* or *Did he seem really trustworthy?* wasn't going to cut it either.

"Come on Delilah. What's Rotisserie Guy's name?" Tristan nudged her.

She was angry by that point. She didn't want it to be him. "Brandon."

Becky blinked and perked right up. Which just made Delilah more upset. "This guy was named Brandon."

Tristan practically chortled. "It *was* Rotisserie Guy."

Delilah cracked. Her voice rose probably a whole octave, and she was too loud, though knowing that fact didn't seem to help her control it. "No, it wasn't *Rotisserie Guy*. What would my Brandon be doing in here? It's LA. There have to be a thousand brown-haired Brandons out on the street right now."

He gestured to Becky, but spoke to his sister. "Then give her something she can work with."

"Fine!" She turned to Becky, hoping the woman realized that Delilah wasn't mad at her. She was just put out. She hadn't eaten enough, hadn't slept enough, and apparently her brother believed she hadn't been pestered enough. "Did he look like he was the father of this baby?"

Delilah cocked her head to one side and gestured to her abdomen. And waited.

Becky looked shocked.

Tristan looked supremely irritated. "How the hell is she supposed to know th—"

Then he stopped, dead still.

So did Delilah. *Ooops*. She hadn't meant to spill it like that. Probably the pregnancy made her cranky. *Oh, crap.*

Tristan blinked once, twice, then he found his voice. "Li?"

All she could do was nod. If she opened her mouth, she'd crack and start crying.

Before she could finish, he took the step covering the ground that separated them, and engulfed her in a huge bear hug that didn't seem like it would ever end. Delilah hugged him back, already feeling better than she had just a few moments ago. She could hear and feel his smile for her.

This was why she let him pester her. Why she put up with him when he was a bear. Because he was instantly happy for her. She didn't have to explain. He knew. He understood.

Eventually when he stepped back, Becky was gone. Likely she'd excused herself from the suddenly personal scene.

Tristan held her at arm's length and looked her up and down, the smile still on his face. "Rotisserie Guy?"

She nodded. “Brandon.”

“Oh, Li, I’m so happy for you.”

She smiled, and felt like a ton of bricks had crashed on her. “Me, too. But I have to get home. Go to bed. I’m working again tonight, and I am so tired.”

As if to make her point, a yawn snuck up and overtook her.

CHAPTER 32

Tristan showed up for breakfast the next morning when she got off work. He called ahead and actually asked if he could come. He asked for a grocery list and made her clarify the whole thing to be sure he got everything right.

All in all, Delilah was entirely weirded out.

Tristan normally just appeared in her kitchen. He didn't knock, and lately he hadn't even *asked* her to feed him. He was like a baby bird—if he was there, then his mouth was open and he was hungry and it was just natural for her to supply the food.

None of that bothered her. But Tristan changing the game did.

He said it was because she was pregnant. Now he felt the need to take care of her. At least until he knew Rotisserie Guy had taken over the job.

But she sensed there was more to it than that.

Tristan suggested something with vegetables. Delilah complied, mostly out of curiosity. She wondered if Tristan figured out what she had—that Brandon already knew what she was.

She unlocked her own front door and let herself in, shedding the chef jacket as she walked toward the bathroom. She shoved it into the dry cleaning hamper and the checked pants into the regular wash, then stripped out of the tank, bra, undies and socks she was wearing.

She started the shower, and stepped back as she always did to give it a moment to heat up. Usually she stood there, breathing deeply, but this morning her reflection caught her attention and she searched herself for signs of change. For outward indications of the life growing within her. There was nothing she could put her finger on. No definitive signs of pregnancy. Her body looked the same as it always had.

Not that she would know what those changes would be. She hadn't been far enough along the last time she'd gotten pregnant to see any changes then either.

She wasn't sure if there was a glow or not. She didn't really think she had that. But at least she was getting caught up on her lost sleep. There was also a recommendation in the pregnancy book for what to eat to keep her stomach settled. Since she only cooked normal fancy foods most of the time, Delilah had little experience with special diets and it was all news to her. It was also working. Her stomach had settled dramatically and she was back to eating pretty much what she wanted as long as she had crackers and ginger ale the moment she woke up.

She was clean and dressed by the time Tristan arrived. Fruit was cubed and arranged in a big bowl in the center of the table. He set salmon down, and Delilah set to cooking it. Since the book ruled out raw or under-cooked meats, lox, a long-time family favorite, was out for the next year or so until she finished nursing. Delilah pushed that thought into a small compartment and ignored it. That was just too far away to deal with right now.

As usual, Tristan waited a while before he brought anything of importance into the conversation. He ate, he chatted about the store, he kept things mundane. Then he sat back. The look on his face indicated he was formulating words. Delilah knew what was coming.

"Does he know?"

She didn't bother asking about who 'he' was or what he might know. She nodded. "Yes."

Tristan didn't say anything. The raised eyebrows, the forward lean, the question in his eyes, all said *and?*

But where could she even begin? What should she tell him? It wasn't Tristan's baby after all, it was hers and Brandon's. Tristan was her brother, but Brandon had to have priority here. Delilah started simple. "He agrees about keeping the baby, and wants to be part of his child's life. We have an appointment in two days at the doctor's to get everything confirmed."

Then, at Tristan's frown and subsequent upset that she waited so long for an appointment, she wound up explaining exactly what she'd explained to Brandon just a few days before. She sighed. *Men.* But didn't voice the thought.

Luckily, Tristan didn't push further. She half expected him to pester her about Brandon's level of involvement and to press her for information regarding how and where they were going to raise this baby. None of which did she have an answer to yet.

She hadn't yet come up with a single reasonable method for sharing this baby. She and Brandon had not gotten that far into the discussion. They both wanted the child. For now at least, that was end of story.

At least she'd thought it was lucky that Tristan didn't push. Until he started his new line of thought.

"Li, if Brandon was in the store looking for spells on him, then you didn't tell him about you—about what you are—did you?"

This time she did sigh. He deserved it.

Tristan shook his head. "*And* he figured it out on his own."

Yeah, she'd come to that wonderful conclusion all by herself.

It had woken her out of a deep sleep the same afternoon she'd done the banner job of breaking the news to Tristan.

Brandon had shown up at Blessed Be, trying to see the spells that had been cast on him. Her spells. There was only one reason for him to do that: because he knew they existed.

"Li?" The single syllable held a world of concern.

But all she could do was shrug. "I won't see him until the appointment, our schedules completely conflict until then. But I *will* tell him then. We have to make a lot more plans after we figure out when the baby is due and everything. The appointment's in two days."

"But Li, what are you going to tell him? I mean, *how*, because apparently, he already knows."

"I'm just going to confess and hope for the best."

Though Tristan seemed willing to leave it at that, Delilah couldn't. Her brain scrambled round and round working itself into ridiculous knots. But she couldn't seem to stop herself.

Brandon knew about her.

Now she knew that Brandon knew.

But did he know that she knew? She shook her head at the stupidity. Then went back. If he didn't know that she knew, then he just might buy her confession. It might seem more spontaneous. That very idea produced waves of guilt that combined with hormones to threaten the food she'd just eaten.

It was dishonest to not disclose all that she knew. Even though she had been planning on telling him all along. Unfortunately, planning was all that she'd done. If she had bucked up and just told him when she first had the chance, she might have avoided this whole mess.

Then again, she might have had to go crawling to a man who hated her—rightly so—and explain that she was pregnant with his child. That would not have gone over well. Basically, the whole mess was her fault from start to finish, and there was no good way to detangle it now.

Not that any of it mattered now, because she couldn't go back and change it. If she could, she would never have cast that stupid 'forget' spell in the first place. Damn thing hadn't worked anyway. But if it had, she wouldn't have Brandon. And she wouldn't have this baby. This baby that in a few short days had become the very center of her universe. She was going to have to simply accept and deal with the consequences of her actions. And that sucked.

The appointment loomed ahead of her like the countdown on a time bomb.

CHAPTER 33

Brandon managed to talk Delilah into having lunch with him the day before the appointment. Her extra shifts at the restaurant allowed them no more time than that. Not unless she wanted to sleep at his place.

Even though he wanted that, he was still far too suspicious of his own feelings. So he didn't voice the idea to her, and she didn't suggest it or offer her place for him. That arrangement left them apart far more than they were together.

The communication between them dwindled to the necessary trickle of information keeping them linked together but not much more. He kept hoping she would volunteer some insight about her witchcraft. But she didn't. He wondered if he should confront her but felt the situation was already too volatile. The last thing he wanted was to alienate her and have her run off with his baby.

He considered pulling the altar pieces out of the garage and casting on her to make her tell him what he wanted. But aside from the wood he didn't have his supplies any more. Of course he knew where he could buy them, but purchasing what he needed from Delilah's brother just didn't seem wise. He was ashamed to say that it was the possibility of running into Tristan, and not the wrongness of the act, that really kept him from doing it.

He went through a brief phase when he wondered if maybe she wasn't really a witch. If maybe it was all merely coincidental. But he'd been alternating reading the pregnancy book and the witchcraft book at nights—it wasn't like Delilah was here to take up his time. He spent hours poring over them, and the more he read, the more the witchcraft explanation made sense.

He laughed out loud at the idea that 'the simplest explanation is usually the right one.' There was really nothing simple about this. There was nothing simple in her religion either. The idea at the very heart of the craft was that all beings were connected. Brandon had a hard time arguing that, in fact he was hard pressed to find a religion that didn't state that. But Wicca included the earth. Wounding or wronging the earth was as bad as wronging another.

There was a whole chapter on Pagan religions in general. While Brandon always thought 'pagan' meant sacrifices, naked moon dances, and multiple gods, he found out he'd been woefully undereducated in his bible classes. 'Pagan' also included earth religions that had been around before Judaism, and were earth-centered. A surprising quantity of the rituals sounded like his own catholic holidays. Ultimately he wasn't too shocked to see in print that the Christians took over a good number of pagan days in the effort to convert the 'heathens.' Rather than force an entire, new religion down their throats, the priests merely re-named a good number of the holidays and tweaked a few meanings. His Christmas tree sure looked a lot different after all that reading.

The thing was, he was getting caught up in it. He wanted to start this conversation with Delilah, ask her about all of it. He didn't know if he could convert, but it was beyond interesting. Fascinating really.

Sadly, Delilah wasn't talking to him. Not really. She didn't even know they could talk about this. He was grateful she was coming to lunch, and he managed several ways he could work the topic into conversation as casually as possible. He finally went to sleep, glad he had a little more of a plan.

But lunch wasn't very illuminating. Delilah spent most of it withdrawn and hardly talked at all. She'd picked at her food and done nothing but make him worry about her.

He asked every question he could think of, but he got only vague answers. Was she nervous about the appointment? Somewhat. Was her stomach feeling all right? Mostly. Had she thought about what to do up until the baby was born and after that? A little. How was work? All right.

He'd wanted to stand up in the middle of the café and scream that he was doing all he could, could she *please* give him something to work with here? He considered tearing his hair out, just to give them something definitive to talk about. Instead he stayed calm. He probed and got nowhere. He sent her home to bed and promised to pick her up the next day for the appointment.

At least she agreed to that.

So he was shocked to find Delilah a whirlwind of activity when he arrived at her apartment door. Again, he'd hit buttons until someone randomly let him in. That was going to have to change. Delilah and the baby weren't safe like that.

He'd knocked on her door and known the second she threw it wide that this was not the same woman who sat docilely across from him at lunch yesterday. And, even though she talked non-stop and made little sense, he liked her much better.

She ran frantically around the apartment, and it appeared to Brandon that she was throwing random things into her handbag. Of course they didn't all fit—the book, the pregnancy test, a small notepad, mints, and who knew what else? So she wound up searching for a larger bag and then having to transfer everything.

Once the bag was packed, she nodded—almost at him, Brandon wasn't sure. When he asked if she was ready, she smiled. Then said, "Oh, crap" before running off to the bedroom.

Brandon just waited patiently, grateful he was the kind of guy who regularly showed up early. She appeared again about ten minutes later.

"Okay, I think I'm ready." She stood with her right hand clutching the strap to her tote. Her feet planted apart, her lean legs showing beneath a swingy skirt where a few minutes before they had been encased in jeans. She'd also brushed her hair until it shone and redone her makeup after work, as though the baby needed to be impressed with its new mother.

He didn't even try to interfere with the whirlwind she was, but kept an eye on the time. He was pleased she had announced her readiness about five minutes before he was going to have to stop her insanity.

She chattered on the way to UCLA saying she expected to have to wait, and could he take the whole afternoon off? Obstetricians routinely ran very behind schedule because babies had no concept of their appointment times. He could drop her off if he needed, but she really wanted him to stay, especially if there was a long wait. Brandon didn't even want to picture a Delilah who'd been made to wait. Not if she was starting out like this. Still the thought brought a smile to his lips.

They parked in an underground lot, which seemed to make Delilah nervous. "I don't think they've ever gotten an accurate blood pressure reading on me in this building."

Before he could ask why, she forged ahead. "The parking structure makes me nervous. Earthquake Central should not have underground parking. Or a subway for that matter."

He didn't point out that no one was making her ride the subway.

She calmed down just a touch when the elevator passed above the ground floor. But they didn't speak as he followed her through the spider web of hallways to the door marked with a list of doctors' names. He stood back while she checked in at the desk, then sat silent beside her in the office lobby crowded by women with various stages of rounded bellies and punctuated with the occasional very tiny baby. He tried hard not to stare.

Both of them thumbed through the magazines piled high on the end tables while they waited to be called. It took him a few minutes to realize that the magazines were advertisements and not real journals. The articles were each geared in praise of a particular product that a new parent just couldn't live without. They seemed genuine enough, in spite of the matching coupon on the next page. But when he hit the second article, claiming that a different formula was the *only* formula clinically proven to be more easily digested, he caught on.

Time crawled. Especially once he gave up on reading the propaganda that was lying about. Then Delilah was called. The two of them jumped up like they'd just been announced the winners at bingo, and Brandon trailed Delilah to the wooden door that led into the mysterious beyond. Only the nurse refused him admittance, stating that they only needed Delilah.

With a placating smile, Lilah followed the round woman in the too-bright scrubs, and just left him standing there at the door.

Brandon blinked. He stood facing the closed door, dumbfounded. He'd come all this way, waited with her, tried to keep her calm, only to be shut out? Delilah hadn't stood up for him at all. Not even an 'oh, he's with me.'

He considered just leaving. She could call when she was finished. But just as he made that decision, the door opened, spitting Delilah back out. Her face told him nothing. While he waited impatiently for some little tidbit about how it had gone —other than *fast*—she walked over and sat back down in her seat leaving him to once again trail behind.

"Lilah?"

She looked up at him, only just then catching on that he had no idea what was happening. "Oh! They just weighed me and took my blood pressure, and made me pee in a cup. But we should get to go see the doctor in a little bit."

She went back to reading her advertisement-zine.

Brandon just sat and blinked for a moment. He was so out of his element here.

Luckily, he didn't get to dwell on it much further. The round little nurse popped her head out and called for Delilah again. This time Lilah grabbed his hand and pulled him along after her, through the heavy wooden door and into the inner sanctum of the obstetrician's office.

They were led into an office rather than an exam room, a fact that seemed to surprise Delilah, even though Brandon was pretty sure she'd said she liked this doctor and had seen her before. When the door closed behind them, leaving them alone on the guest side of the desk to wait again, he asked her about it.

"Well, I haven't been in here since my very first visit a few years ago. You know, the doctor likes to meet you face to face before they see you in a paper gown."

"Is this the first time you've seen her for pregnancy?"

Delilah nodded.

"Well, maybe that's it."

He wasn't afforded time to ponder that as the door opened behind them and the doctor breezed around to sit on the other side of the desk. "Good afternoon, Delilah."

It was almost as though the two women were friends.

Quickly, Delilah introduced them, "This is Brandon. He's the baby's father." She squeezed his hand, making him far happier than just that simple gesture should have.

"So," Dr. Bower leaned forward, her elbows on the desk. "If you don't mind my asking, was this pregnancy intentional?"

Quickly Delilah shook her head, and Brandon decided to let her do all the talking unless she specifically asked him for something. He had no clue what to do here. He was feeling more and more like a fish flopping on the shore gasping for oxygen.

The doctor nodded in return. "And how did you realize you were pregnant?"

"My stomach was bothering me."

"And that's all?" The black pen flew over the open page of the chart, but the writing looked more like Sanscrit to him.

"No, I took a pregnancy test."

The doctor asked what kind and when and Delilah explained that, too. At long last the doctor quit asking and started talking. "Your pregnancy test here didn't show a positive result."

Brandon perked up his ears at that. He frowned.

Dr. Bowen kept going. "The test you mentioned doesn't actually test for HCG like ours do . . ."

Brandon lost the thread there. She could have rattled off any three letters and he would have had to smile and nod. Eventually it came back around to the possibility that Delilah had caught the pregnancy very early. If that were true then an ultrasound would determine how far along Delilah was.

Then the doctor mentioned two other very disturbing possibilities. One, the baby had died. The office test was negative because the baby had stopped growing since Delilah took her home test a week ago. Two, Delilah had never been pregnant. The doctor didn't like the new tests because, although it was rare, they did sometimes yield false positives. The ultrasound should give them the answers.

Delilah gripped his hand a little tighter as they headed for the exam room. He was allowed in with her even though there was barely room after the bed, the tech's chair and the cart with all the wands and paddles.

They waited what seemed another eternity for the tech to show up. Then they watched the gray screen with avid interest although the tech would tell them nothing at all. Finally, they were escorted yet again back to the doctor's office for more waiting.

This wasn't turning out how he'd expected. He'd thought they'd go home with a picture of a little white blot that they would coo over and start thinking about naming. He'd wondered if he might get the chance to see the pulse of a tiny heartbeat on screen that online postings described as mesmerizing.

Delilah looked like she was in shock. He wanted to comfort her, but he was in a bit of shock, too. He told himself the doctor would come in and tell them that it was all good. She'd give them a due date and they could start planning.

But he hadn't seen a little white blot on the ultrasound. He'd seen lots of movies where the tech pointed and said, 'there's your baby' and the couple just stared, hopelessly in love with their child. But this tech hadn't said anything. She about refused to say anything, her manner very clear that she did not want to be bothered by their petty questions. He and Delilah shrugged at each other more than once. It didn't seem she had any better skill than he did at reading the patchy black and white screen. But still he searched for his little blot and came up empty.

He didn't question his commitment to this child. It *was*. And that was all he had needed. Until now. Now that confidence had been undermined and he needed confirmation.

The doctor breezed in again, planting herself behind the big mahogany desk. She looked at each of them and folded her hands. Brandon could see it coming and was grateful that she got right to the point. "I'm sorry." She shook her head. "There's no pregnancy."

Still, he was dumbfounded. Delilah wasn't pregnant? His world was shifting on its axis . . . again. He listened numbly to suggestions that Delilah start her birth control pills again. That they not try to get pregnant again until they'd thought about it for a few months. Then, if they decided to try in earnest, they should make an appointment.

The sounds of conversation were as distinguishable and as meaningful to him as the noise of a brook babbling by. With his head under the water.

Slowly, together, they gathered themselves and made their way silently and solemnly out of the office and down into the parking structure. This time Delilah was too preoccupied to be concerned about earthquakes. She seemed as shell-shocked as he was. For thirty minutes they fought traffic to his place, neither of them saying a word.

Brandon's brain turned over and over. He figured he should be happy. He was no longer having an unplanned kid with a woman who never confessed about why she tried to take his memories but not his wallet. But he *wasn't* happy about it.

He wondered if Delilah had faked the whole thing. He wondered if he even knew her well enough to know if she was the kind of woman who would do that. But he'd seen the test stick. It had read positive. There was no doubt about it, they checked the key three or four times each, because they were both so surprised. Besides, if she had faked it, then The Academy had been giving their Oscars to the wrong women for the past several years. Brandon just didn't see how Delilah could fake the catatonic stare that was on her face right now.

He took in a deep breath. If the baby had died and Delilah was miscarrying that might have made more sense, but the doctor was quite certain that Delilah had never been pregnant at all. It seemed to him the doctor was the only one who was certain of anything.

Brandon drove straight to his house—part of the 'not

thinking' thing. When he parked in his driveway, they climbed out, both on shaky legs. Numbly, Delilah followed him inside. No, there was no way she had faked this. Somewhere low in his gut Brandon began to feel really bad for her. She wanted this baby. This was a chance to fix what had gone so tragically wrong the first time. She looked to be in the early stages of grief. When she was standing in front of his couch, her legs buckled and she fell to where she was sitting on it. Her back was ramrod straight, her eyes wide and confused. Her voice was shallow. "I'm sorry. I thought I was pregnant."

Immediately, he was beside her, drawn by the intense gravitational pull he always felt when she was near. His arms draped her shoulders and he held her in a loose hug. "It's okay. I understand."

It seemed to be all he could say, even though it was nowhere near enough. Nowhere near what she needed, and he knew it.

Still Delilah shook her head. "I had morning sickness. That test was positive."

Again he whispered something to soothe her and himself.

She spoke disjointedly several more times. Things he didn't quite understand. Things meant to tell him she wasn't trying to trick him. Words that said she was sorry, when he didn't think she needed to be. Only he didn't know how to tell her that she didn't have to prove it to him. He believed her, even as he believed she lied to him repeatedly about other things.

Much later, with their arms still around each other, still in the same places on the couch, did he feel some of the rigid tension in her begin to ease. It seemed as her muscles let go of their need to hold everything in, so did her mouth. She expressed how much she wanted this baby in a river of painful and sometimes garbled phrases. The crazy thing was he understood every word.

"Me, too." He knew it was true.

"It's okay if you're relieved. I won't hold it against you." Her neck finally lost the last of its strength and her head rolled against his shoulder, and at last some of the cold they shared began to recede.

"I'm not really relieved. I was surprised about it, but I was excited. I was looking forward to this baby."

He could see in her eyes that she believed him. Her smile lasted a moment before it broke to accompany the tears that had started a slow trek down her face. "I just wanted a second chance. After I lost my last baby. I was so happy."

Her words again started coming out in fragments and phrases, thoughts and feelings that were sometimes discordant but needing to be released. He waited through all of it, cataloging the new information and re-playing the old as she told him more of the story about David and Juliet. How her sister held her own pregnancy over Delilah's head. How Delilah lost that same baby trying to save her sister. Her words all ran into and over each other. Brandon understood them all. Delilah made sense to him in a way he hadn't known before.

He rocked her back and forth as he would have soothed their baby, and talked to her until the words didn't come anymore. At last he carried her back to his bedroom, thinking that there was great irony in the fact that they couldn't make love. She'd been off her birth control pills for over a week because they'd thought she was pregnant. He didn't have any condoms because she'd been on the pill.

So, once again, he laid her on his bed with no thought of sex. She let him help pull off her shoes and skirt before sliding under the covers as though she could hide from the world there. Clearly, she couldn't. So Brandon stripped down to his underwear and climbed in beside her. Turning her to face him, and to maybe face some of what had happened, he wrapped his arms around her, enjoying the heat of her skin against his.

At last his brain stopped churning and he fell into a thankfully dreamless sleep.

CHAPTER 34

Delilah stood over her kitchen counter, bite by bite drowning her sorrows in bakery items. The baking—as well as the eating—was cathartic. There may be no baby, but there was plenty of flour smattered around and drips of chocolate smeared here and there.

For a moment, she thought this was what her kitchen *should* look like—like she'd been baking with a small child. She forced herself to take another bite.

"Delilah!" Tristan burst through her door, putting her about a millisecond away from needing a Heimlich maneuver. He scared her out of her wits and her depression. If only for a moment.

"What?" She turned to face him, her beer in one hand and a gooey brownie in the other.

Tristan came screeching to a stop, wildly eyeing the food she held. "You shouldn't be drinking!"

"I'm not pregnant." Her voice sounded monotone to her own ears. Brandon had gotten up and gone to work. He'd kissed her and said more than his usual good-bye, but still he was out the door and she was once again left at his place alone. She called a cab instead of her brother to get her home because she hadn't been ready to face Tristan yet. But clearly that had been a waste of money. In the end, all it had meant was that she'd managed to shower while the brownies baked and get halfway through her beer before he burst in.

"You're sure?" He blinked and frowned over her combination of foods, but Delilah stared back at him. Waiting.

"Yes, I'm sure. The doctor said." Like she'd be standing here drinking a *beer* if she wasn't one hundred percent certain.

"Oh." She saw now that he held slips of paper in his fist, yellow like the store receipts, but why he was once again bringing her receipts from Blessed Be was beyond her. She really didn't have the brain power for more than her brownies and beer.

So to keep him from thinking she'd miscarried again, she told him just the basics. "Actually, it was just a stomach flu. And a bad test. I was never pregnant at all."

"Oh, Li." His shoulders sagged, losing all the urgent energy he'd possessed when he entered. "I'm so sorry."

"Yeah, me too." She tipped her beer at him in a small salute then took a big drink. She didn't even have to work tonight. She would have welcomed a shift to help take her mind off things. It seemed there would be no such luck.

"Is that your first beer?" His shoulders took back some of the tension they'd lost at her announcement. His eyes revealed concern and she could practically see his brain working backwards and thinking about the cooking sherry.

"Yes, big brother, it is." She took another big swig.

"Lilah, this is important." He sat down at her table, practically pulling her into the hard wooden seat next to him. She wanted to say 'ouch' but he was talking before she had the chance. "This is the receipt for the birch bark sticks, that big order that we thought was Brandon . . ."

He pushed the paper towards her, but she refused to look at

it. Maybe it was the beer but her mind was on another issue. "You know, Yasmin has a thing for you."

Glory be, it worked. He was totally sidetracked. "What are you talking about?"

"Yasmin, your attractive assistant. She totally has the hots for you." Delilah smiled and took another drink of the beer.

Tristan grabbed the bottle out of her hand and set it out of reach. "Clearly, you're drunk."

"No!" Of course, at that moment she hiccupped just a little. But Tristan saw. Oh, well, the bottle had been nearly empty so she'd pretty much already drunk the whole thing. She hadn't lied, it was her first. But she was such a cheap date. "Look, that has nothing to do with now. Drunk or sober I can see that Yasmin's got it going on for you. That morning that Becky what's-her-face was in—"

"Becky Scarborough."

"Yeah, exactly." Delilah about laughed. "That look on your face, the fact that you know her last name, had Yasmin practically growling."

Tristan frowned, clearly totally clueless. But she could see he was piecing some memories into a bigger picture. *Good.*

Delilah got serious. "I'm just telling you because you work together and it seemed you were completely oblivious."

"Point noted. I'll just have to figure out how to deal with that later." He nodded then shoved the yellow receipt copy at her again. "But this is really important *right now*. This is the slip for the birch bark. Look what else is there."

Delilah saw the short list. It included a poppet. White ribbon. A few other things . . .

Her eyes widened.

"Yeah." Tristan's lips pressed together like he was trying to hold in his anger. "He wasn't *just* looking to see if there were spells on him. He's been messing around, too. Yasmin was pretty sure he was in her beginner class the other week. There's no telling what he's tried to do, or how he's messed it up."

She opened her mouth, but Tristan beat her to it. "Where does he live?"

"No! Tristan! *No*." She grabbed at his arm as he was already rising out of his seat, as though he was going to hunt down Brandon and throw the first punch. "You can't."

"Delilah, we don't know what he did to you!"

"And he doesn't know what I did to him." She hung her head. How had it all gotten so messed up? Still, she couldn't let Tristan get tangled in it, too. "You don't do *anything* to him. I'm not going to tell you where he lives or works, and I *will* hold it against you forever if you try to find him."

She was the last of his family. They were clearly all each other had. Since Brandon was aware and buying spell supplies, he wasn't what she had hoped he might be. Or might eventually become. So the threat to Tristan was a serious one. And one he would know she didn't make lightly.

"Why are you defending him, Li?"

"Because I love him!"

She sucked in air. Her spine pressed against the round rails that made up the back of the seat. Her eyes fought to contain the water threatening to overflow them. She couldn't look at Tristan.

"Are you serious? Delilah." Tristan sank to the seat next to her, looking defeated. But he didn't touch her.

All she could do was nod. Anything else was too much in the face of the wave that was crashing over her.

Oh shit. She was in love with him. The admission surprised her as much as it surprised Tristan. But how could she not be? Brandon had been excited about the baby. He'd been gentle and kind and held her while she cried when there was no baby.

She really wanted another beer, but she just couldn't get one out in front of Tristan. Which meant she shouldn't get one out at all. She was not going to become a shell of a person the way she did the last time she'd been turned over and found lacking.

After a few minutes of dead silence except for the living room clock ticking, Tristan stood. She thought he was going to excuse himself, but he didn't.

"Lilah, at least let me check you." He pulled a birch bark stick from his pocket. Apparently he'd planned ahead and figured they would need to see what Brandon might have done. "Maybe he hasn't been doing any of it to you. Maybe he's as good as you think he is and he's just been checking his house."

That was complete bull, but she nodded anyway. Delilah knew the things Brandon purchased weren't entirely used for checking his house. They weren't for seeing, they were for committing.

"Or," Tristan tried again, "maybe he was just protecting himself."

All Delilah could think was, *the only person Brandon had to protect himself from was me*. All in all, she only felt lower. Still, she agreed to let Tristan look for spells, as he seemed pretty immovable on that topic.

He went into her living area, dragging her behind. She kept a lighter on the bookshelf just in case someone was there when she needed a flame and neither of them was up for even the momentary focus needed for a spark. Also, neither was in the mood for the effort of a good clean ritual. A battery sparked propane flame wasn't really the way it should be done, but Delilah was beyond caring.

Tristan talked while he held the lighter to the bark and waited for the wood to catch. "The thing is, that receipt was paid in cash. Almost nobody pays in cash anymore. So I pulled up old cash receipts, since without a credit card number or an account I can't really trace his purchases."

Tristan let the stick burn until about half of it was engulfed in orange flames. The telltale greenish tinge at the center let you know it was real birch bark, properly culled. Then he blew out the fire, turning the stick into a billow of clean grey smoke. Still he waited. "There were a handful of other purchases in cash over the past week. Maybe he came in before the time Becky saw him, I really have no way of knowing, but there were several that showed basic set-up purchases. That would mean he's been in more than once."

She nodded. It all made sense. Really bad sense.

"I brought the receipts. I need them back, but I thought you might want to look at them, maybe you'll see something I didn't. Maybe you can scry and see if they are his purchases or not."

Delilah shook her head no. She didn't want to, it seemed she'd violated Brandon's privacy quite enough. Still, Tristan insisted that he leave them, and that she return them. Then he set about covering her in the smoke.

It didn't take three seconds to see that it was clinging. A fine sheen shrouded her everywhere with great globs clinging to her hair and legs. A mass swirled around her lower torso.

Tristan raised his eyes.

Delilah sighed. The fine sheen was from Tristan and herself —thin layers of safety spells and prayers for general health. A good witch did work like that. The globs were caused by beginners, by someone casting things they didn't quite understand or control.

Delilah avoided the real subject. There was a new spell on her, one of the clearer, cleaner layers of smoke. "What did you cast on me, Tristan?"

"A protection spell."

She snorted. "A day late and a candle short."

He shook his head. "No. I've been doing it every week since you were in the hospital."

A tear leaked from her eye. She hadn't been in the hospital since David and Jules died. All this time . . . They'd all been taught to do it themselves, keep themselves safe. Tristan would have known that she'd lapsed. "Thank you."

"For what it was worth." He indicated the blobs of birch bark smoke that were slowly sifting away.

She walked to the bookshelf and pulled down the incenser. She added sage and lavender and a sprinkling of poppy then lit the thing. It would help dissipate the birch bark smoke. While the smell of burnt black birch wasn't unpleasant, it wasn't exactly nice either.

Tristan said his good-byes and asked her again to check the receipts.

She smiled, having no intention of doing it. What was done was done. She'd have to talk to Brandon anyway, and she shouldn't go off half-cocked because of some receipt that may or may not be his.

Still she was drawn to the slips spread out on the table. She held tightly to the one she knew was his, the list Becky had identified as being bought by the man she'd said was named Brandon. One by one, Delilah went through each of them, first eyeing them analytically. Then, when that yielded nothing, she pulled out a pendulum and asked if the purchase had been made by Brandon, even though she'd sworn she wasn't going to do it. Each time the pendulum swung counterclockwise, indicating 'no.'

Delilah gave up. It had been a waste of time and she wasn't sure what Tristan thought she'd find anyway. She hopped in the shower again, to quickly rinse off the smoke she could still smell. It was likely all in her imagination, but she felt better after she did it.

She turned her face up to the spray while her scrubbie dangled from her fingers, and for some reason that yielded a thought. Tristan had that one purchase, just a while ago. The one he'd yelled at Yasmin about. The person who'd bought the set-up and the Almanac.

In her grasp, the scrubbie began to swing clockwise for 'yes.'

Crap.

CHAPTER 35

Brandon was surprised to see Delilah waiting on his front porch steps. She was perched on the top step with her feet tucked up under her and she was staring off into space. She looked sweet and fresh and was definitely a welcome sight.

Yesterday had been a shock. He'd gotten up and gone to work only because he had to. There was too much to do, too much to make up from missing yesterday afternoon entirely. He spent the day wishing Delilah had work tonight, so she could do something to take her mind off the missing baby. But now that she was here on his front porch steps, he was happy she didn't.

His brain told him he shouldn't be so glad she was here. Baby or not, there was still a lot to work out. But, as usual, he couldn't fight the rising tide of emotion in him.

Her clothes were different from what she'd worn the day before, and she was outside. So he guessed that she'd gone home, locking up behind herself, then when she came back she was locked out. He'd never given her a key. He thought about asking her to move in with him, but he didn't know who those thoughts belonged to, so he made a point never to act on them.

So here she was stuck on his front porch, untrustworthy, but somehow still welcome.

He parked his SUV in the back and trotted around to where she was. She seemed to be looking up for him, so she must have broken out of the spell she was in when he went right past her down the driveway. He smiled and sank down next to her, managing to keep his hands to himself. "Hey, Lilah. How are you holding up?"

She nodded, "Coming to grips with it."

She looked back out over the sky. The afternoon was late, just sliding into the bright early part of evening. He heard Delilah take a deep breath but she didn't say anything. Brandon joined her in her silence, just looking out across the street, at the cars going by. In the background were a few tall apartment complexes and large trees hid most of the city in the distance. While the view itself was enclosed, the sounds filtered in: the rumbling of tires on the beat up roads around the corner. Birds in the trees overhead. Front doors and car doors opening and closing. Brandon heard it all for maybe the first time.

Eventually Delilah smacked at her leg, clearly the little no-see-ums were coming out. Brandon broke the silence around them and suggested they go inside. He emptied his pockets just beyond the front door and started into the kitchen for a drink.

"Brandon."

The word hung behind him, her voice sounded sad. But that didn't take a genius. Turning, he saw her face matched the sound. She needed to be held, and he needed to hold her. He crossed the five feet to where she was, engulfing her in his arms, surprised when she stiffened. As though she didn't want, or hadn't intended to be hugged. After a moment she relaxed into him, making him feel better if not her.

She buried her face against him, but didn't cry. Her arms hugged him around the waist, tight. After a few moments he felt her take a deep breath. Then she looked up at him and stepped back.

"Brandon, I'm a witch."

He nodded. "I know." The words were too simple for the relief he felt. For the flood of hope that finally she was opening up. That maybe they were getting on the right track at last.

But his arms were still loosely around her. Because of that he could feel that her body didn't ease at the knowledge the way his did. Even so, her next words surprised him. "I know you know."

When he blinked, she sighed, then continued. "My brother owns Blessed Be. He and another regular saw you there. Buying birch bark sticks." She laughed a little, in a way that was almost, but not quite, natural. "You way overbought. You only needed one. The store was out of stock for almost a week."

He only nodded in return, still processing all of it.

Delilah gave him something he could work with though. "How did you know to go there in the first place? What tipped you off?"

"A school fair psychic, and some Indian man who wanted five bucks to tell me my fortune."

"Seriously? What did they say?"

Brandon took a deep breath. While he was glad it was all coming out, that didn't mean it was easy telling her everything. In fact, he'd expected a big confession on her part with little work needed from him. But he learned a long time ago with Delilah things often didn't go the way he predicted. "The Indian man said I had spells on me. Then I saw the store and just walked in, hoping to find something helpful. When I went in, they asked if I was there for the beginner's class. So I said yes."

He shrugged.

Delilah laughed. Again it was almost natural.

"That means you met Yasmin. And you met my brother."

Brandon nodded. "I wondered. It is LA, so there could be a million Tristans. But it made sense that it would be your Tristan running a witchcraft shop when already I knew his sister was a witch." Almost embarrassed to admit it, he added. "I didn't go back after I figured it out."

Turning away, Delilah paced the room for a moment. She looked to be winding up to something. Brandon figured he knew her at least that well. He wondered what she was going to throw at him next, but wasn't prepared for what she told him.

"I grew up as a witch. My folks were both Wiccan, us kids were raised that way. Juliet was the youngest and the most powerful. I'm so sorry about what I did to you. I know what it's like to be cast on. To wonder if your thoughts are your own."

She trailed her hand across the books that lined his shelf, over the few pictures he had framed. She looked small and sad and he was suddenly willing to forgive her anything. Her voice stopped him. Soft but strong, she continued her story, and Brandon became still, not wanting to do anything that would interrupt the telling. He needed to hear the whole thing.

"David and I got married when I was twenty-three. He died four years later. I just found out he and Juliet were having an affair when I decided to divorce him just a month before they died. I still have no idea how long the affair was going on."

She took a deep breath. "I found out about them the last time by walking in on them in bed together."

Brandon's heart broke at the way her shoulders caved and her head shook back and forth just a little, like she was calling herself all kinds of stupid. But he didn't interrupt.

"They acted upset. Juliet said she was sorry. While she was putting on her clothes she apologized, said it happened just the one time. David seemed shocked and a little confused, but Juliet waved her hand at him. I didn't recognize the communication for what it was, I was in such shock myself. My head was reeling and I kept seeing that image of them in bed together in my mind."

Her breath sucked in. "It never occurred to me that David would cheat. Or that Juliet would be the one he would do it with. But I kicked him out. Right there while he was still naked and Juliet was heading out the door. Just before she left, she told David she'd 'take care of it' and I can only guess now that meant me. But she couldn't take care of it, because I threw his clothes into a suitcase and called the locksmith the second I bolted the door behind him."

She sank down onto the couch now, as though there wasn't enough energy to hold her up. Brandon stood motionless, the way you did when you saw a deer and didn't want to scare it. He wanted this. Wanted to know all of this.

"I called Tristan. He intervened. He tried to make peace, but agreed Juliet was in the wrong and David was a snake. He tried to get me to forgive her since it was just the once. As the days went by, I did. I started to forgive her. I realized I was pregnant, and I began to think I could save my marriage. I thought it was the right thing to do. Tristan agreed to help me because it was what I wanted.

"Then I went to Juliet and found out she was pregnant, too. Which meant the time I caught them hadn't even been close to the first time. That she was five months along meant she'd flat out lied to me. Then she cast on me, tried to get me to come back and forgive her, but I fought it.

"I went home, got out the birch bark and looked around the house. She hadn't cast any spells on my house, and I thought everything was clean. But then I turned around and saw that the smoke was following *me,* in this big thick layer. Juliet had cast on me time and again. I still don't know exactly how many times I figured out they were sleeping together and she made me forget each time."

Delilah sunk her face into her hands, not quite in tears, but unable to deal with anything around her. Brandon was unable to deal with letting her sit there by herself. He sank down beside her, pulling her back against the cushions and cradling her in his arms. He was grateful she allowed the gesture. But he still didn't have any idea what to say. After a few moments, Delilah went on.

"I undid her work. It took a while, but I peeled the layers and started remembering. I caught them together on at least three different occasions. Each time Juliet cleaned up the mess, meaning me. She was good; she got through my protection spells and she made me forget.

"I have no real idea if David was in love with her, wanted her, or if she'd worked him over, too. But when I remembered, I found out that David had on several occasions pressed her to make me forget. So he wasn't innocent. And you can't pull people that far."

What? Brandon frowned down at her until she caught on and explained what she meant.

"You can't make them cluck like a chicken. The 'forget' spells were welcome to me because what I saw was so painful part of me wanted to forget. Because I didn't want it to be true. And if David truly wanted me and *only me* . . . well, Juliet wouldn't have been able to get very far. Then again, my parents had died, one right after the other the previous year and I'd been in a shell myself. So maybe David had a good reason to stray."

"Wait a minute." Brandon grabbed her arms and hauled her around to face him. "I thought he *married* you. Is there something different and non-binding about Wiccan marriages?"

Delilah blinked. Maybe he'd handled her a little too harshly, but he was upset. "No. If anything a Wiccan marriage is supposed to be more binding."

"Then what happened to 'in sickness and in health'? He's

supposed to stand by you when you need him, like, oh, say, your parents die." Brandon was surprised by the depths of feeling Delilah's self-doubt caused him. He wanted to write it off to his issues with cheating, but honestly thought more of it was due to his issues with Delilah.

She shook her head, making Brandon sick at the thought that she was going to defend David's behavior. "I wasn't there really. I was so sad I was lost. So how was he supposed to maintain a marriage to me?"

"That's the point. I don't know how. And he didn't have to either, but it was his job to figure it out."

"Well he didn't. And he paid for it."

Brandon remembered the school fair psychic, telling him that Delilah's past was dark. And something omniscient ran up his spine. "I don't understand." He wasn't sure he wanted to, but he was certain that he needed to.

"I told you, I saw David's car coming up the street." He could tell she was upset just at the telling. Her breathing had changed, but so had something else about her. She was going to get this off her chest. "I had just come out the front of the house. I needed fresh air to make up for all the work of undoing Juliet's spells on me. I saw the car and I got so angry. I pushed them off the road."

She got very quiet.

"Wait. You told me there was another car there. There wasn't?"

"There was. It sideswiped them."

"Then how did you push them off?" How could she possibly think she was responsible? Besides, a slip of a person like her couldn't push a car.

She didn't look at him. "Did you read that Almanac you bought? There's a lot of information in there."

He hadn't read the whole thing, it was huge.

She offered up some wisdom. "A spell works best when it can take time, when things can play into it."

"What do you mean?" he asked. She'd gone from being sad to making very little sense.

"Like if I wanted the remote to be on top of the TV." She pointed to where it rested on the arm of the chair. "Right now I would have to cast a spell that would lift it and *move* it there. Or teleport it. That's a *lot* of energy. But if I cast the spell even a few hours early, or if someone was walking around here, then the remote would have energy to it. It would have almost *wanted* to be on top of the TV and someone would have put it there. Almost unconsciously."

"That's not what most people think of when they think of witchcraft."

Delilah practically snorted. "Most people don't have a clue. It isn't moonlight dances and lightning from your fingertips. Hell, I never met anyone who rode a broom, and I know some damn fine witches."

He had to laugh at that. "But you didn't have time. I can't imagine that you would have set that up in advance to kill them."

"I didn't. It was snap. But there was a car there, and I saw in my mind David going over the side of the rail a moment before the other car swerved for no reason." She was getting more upset as she talked about it. "I did it."

"Honey. Are you really even that powerful?"

She cried, silent tears running down her cheeks as her head tilted to the side and he felt something go through him. A feeling, a wind, something. She held her hand out to the room, as though to say 'look.'

He'd kept a handful of the candles he'd bought, thinking they'd be good for light if the power went out. Every one of them flickered back at him. Even the little scent light for when he burned dinner, or when there'd been too much pizza and beer in the house the day before.

His brain went through it logically, since what he saw stunned him. He'd walked in with Delilah, he hadn't lit candles. They hadn't been burning all day either. There wasn't a wax drip in sight. And as he watched, still a little stunned, one by one they winked out.

His gaze came back, amazed, to rest on Delilah.

The tone in her voice was resigned. "I'm dangerous. It's why I didn't want to get involved with anyone. The first ideal of Wicca is 'harm none.'"

Brandon knew that, he'd read it in his witchcraft book. There was a sign with those words as you entered and exited Blessed Be. He'd told himself he wasn't harming her. More like teasing her.

"You're not dangerous, Li." His brain caught on something. "Besides, I thought Juliet was the most powerful of the three of you. So how did you, the less powerful one, get to her?"

Delilah shrugged. "Maybe she didn't see it coming. You can do all kinds of things with spells, but you have to *do* them. You have to think of it ahead of time and you have to remember. A lot of times I can't remember to get milk on the way home from work."

"Juliet made you forget you saw her in bed with your husband. More than once. Then she knew she'd screwed it up. She told you she was more pregnant with your husband's baby than you were. Then she cast another spell on you to get you to come back and forgive her. And you honestly believe she didn't see it coming?"

Delilah blinked.

"Baby, you didn't do it." His arms tightened around her, the feelings settling in. He'd been uptight, because you never knew where these big talks might lead. But they were going to be okay—even if they clearly had a long way to go. "You lost your baby trying to save her and hers. I read that you have to have pure emotion for a strong spell. Is that right?"

She managed a small nod in response, though she didn't look at him.

He leaned over, to where he was practically speaking into her hair. The feel and the smell of her next to him were almost overwhelming. "I doubt you had a single pure emotion about your sister or even your husband those days."

Delilah sank into him and his eyes closed as he held her. This was where he belonged. With his arms around Delilah. Here on his couch. Waiting for her to smile at him again.

She looked up. "I'm sorry for what I did to you. Really sorry. I was way out of line."

"Apology accepted. If you'll take mine." He grinned. "I'm sorry for what I did, too. Even though it didn't work at all."

She nodded, then laughed. "What were you trying to do anyway?"

Oh great. She wanted to know that! But he needed to confess. They were clearing the waters. Still, even though he told himself it was the right thing to do, he knew his face was beet red. He was simply grateful that the day had darkened into evening and maybe she didn't see. He worked to keep his voice steady. "I tried to cast a love spell on you."

"With Tansy? What did you—"

He jerked back. "How did you know what I bought? Are you spying on me?"

She looked at him like he was nuts. "My brother owns the store. We went through the receipts."

"I paid cash." How the hell had they gotten his shopping list? Was there a camera in the store? Oh, hell, it was a family of witches, he could just guess how they figured it out. "So it wasn't enough that you messed with my brain, you had to spy on me, too?"

"It wasn't like that. You know, if you were casting love spells with Tansy you were really off base."

No shit, he was off base. He felt violated all over again.

Delilah got up and paced. "You bought the ingredients for the equivalent of a spell bomb the first time. If you had Tansy and the black and green candles . . ."

He was so busy being upset at her again, he didn't register that her voice had trailed off. He didn't like where this was headed or the knot it made in the middle of his chest. He wanted to ask if she knew what he'd eaten for lunch or what searches he'd done on the internet at work today.

She turned and stared at him. "Your spells did work. Just not the way you wanted."

She was angry at him? Brandon stared back at her, wondering where the hell she thought she had the right and where she was going with this.

"You did it."

She looked like he'd killed her puppy.

Then she got mad and yelled. "Tansy is for female problems! You made that pregnancy! That's why there was never a baby. You put a spell on me and you *screwed it up!*"

Where did she get off getting upset at him about this? Who knew how many she'd put on him. He was opening his mouth to say so when she burst into angry tears.

"I *wanted* that baby! There is *nothing* I wanted as much as a baby." Her shoulders heaved and Brandon braced himself for whatever she might throw his way: harsh words, a spell, the lamp.

Instead she took a few deep breaths and sniffed twice, trying to get herself back together. "You couldn't have picked a better way to get revenge on me. You found the one thing I really wanted. Something I didn't even know I wanted that badly."

She gathered her purse from where she set it by the front

door. “I’m going home. I’m going to put a binding spell on you so you can’t mess with anyone else.”

“And who’s going to stop *you*, Delilah?”

She looked like he’d slapped her, but that was ridiculous. “Fine, promise me you won’t do anything else.”

“Delilah, with you gone there won’t be any need.”

She nodded, yanked her purse to her shoulder and headed out the door.

CHAPTER 36

Several days later, Delilah still didn't know quite how it had happened. One minute Brandon was holding her, telling her it wasn't her fault. The next she'd been yelling at him.

Looking back, she'd accused him of getting his revenge. That's what he'd been trying anyway. By accident, he'd succeeded far better than he planned. That idiot, using Tansy in a love spell. That Almanac was doubly dangerous because of the occasional error. Lilac was for love spells. Any decent witch would know better. Anyone with a rudimentary herbal knowledge would never put Tansy into a love spell. But an idiot with a book sure would.

She shouldn't have said those things.

But he hurt her. The fact that there was no baby was a very bitter pill to swallow. That *Brandon* had fabricated the whole thing was a knife in the back. Even though he hadn't intended to make her think she was pregnant, he had been trying to get back at her. She probably could have lived with one or the other, but that Brandon caused such great hurt, and that he'd been *trying* to hurt her was just too much.

She was better off without him, she knew. They were a

volatile match right from the first day. If only that first forget spell had worked.

Delilah went to work, she came home and slept, she went to work again. She put in extra shifts and stockpiled spare days because it seemed like a good thing to do. By the second week she began thinking about taking a vacation. A real vacation. She hadn't had one since she'd started the job almost a year and a half ago. She hadn't thought of anything beyond the next day. Until recently. But now . . . now she needed to get somewhere and find herself. The idea rolled around in her brain—five days off somewhere alone.

She swore off all spells that altered anyone but herself.

She didn't run into Brandon.

Tristan came over for dinner and breakfast a few times. When he was avoiding the subject of Brandon, he talked about Yasmin and how it appeared Delilah was right about his assistant. *Of course, she was.* When he was tackling things head on he told her she was better off without Brandon. Verbally she agreed. To herself she figured she'd completely messed it up.

Tuesday night, she made herself an apple and raspberry pie. Then she sat down with a steaming slice of it, doctored with caramel sauce and a scoop of really good French vanilla ice cream. She popped the top on a pale ale and—while she limited herself to just the one—got tipsy enough to let herself really think about Brandon.

She didn't hate him. She just ached whenever she thought about him. She finally opened her brain enough to ask herself how it was that Brandon managed to cast spells on her when she'd been protected from them. She and Tristan had seen the protection spells—the fine thin layers that the birch bark smoke showed. But she'd also seen the globs Brandon put there. They should have slid right off her with no effect. Yet he'd been able to make her think she was pregnant. He'd made her turn the test positive.

If she had done the protection spells herself, Delilah would have easily written the incidence off as something she messed up. She'd certainly not been meticulous girl this last year. But Tristan put those spells there—carefully, knowing full well she wasn't likely to take good care of herself. So how had Brandon gotten through that?

By the time her plate was empty and her beer was gone, Delilah didn't have any better answers. She wasn't about to drink another beer to find them. She also didn't think any decent answers would be found at the bottom of a second bottle.

So she cleaned up and pulled the shades against the light, before curling into a tiny ball in the middle of her bed and finding a little sleep.

The next morning after work she waited for Maggie to arrive. Told her about how she'd thought she was pregnant, but wasn't. Without admitting to any of the witchcraft, she told about how the fight had broken her and Brandon up. How she'd like to take six days in a row off.

Maggie obliged her.

Delilah worked the next night. She made last minute arrangements when she got home. For the first time she dug into David's large life insurance policy. The money covered the very expensive plane tickets and a nice hotel room. By Thursday evening, she was on the beach in South Carolina, watching the waves come in and trying to find some peace.

CHAPTER 37

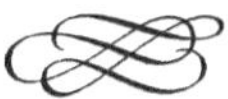

Delilah sat upright in bed, disoriented for a few moments. As her eyes adjusted, she realized she was in her hotel room and the strange sound like a slow heartbeat in the background was the waves crashing on the shore just beyond her patio door.

She'd left the heavy drapes open and the sheers allowed the light of a partial moon to filter in. The room was squarish, and nicely decorated with airy colors and beachy prints, but there was nothing in here to compare with what lay beyond the sliding glass door.

Though it was the middle of the night, Delilah quickly dressed in jeans and flip flops. She slid into a long sleeved t-shirt and quickly pulled her hair back into a ponytail. Her main goal was to get out onto the beach, but she didn't think it would be a good idea to just head out there in the oversized nightshirt she had slept in. In less than two minutes, she was hauling back the heavy glass door and slipping out to the sand.

The edge of the patio gave way to a beach that rolled right up and into her slip-on shoes. She stepped out of them, leaving them neatly aligned at the border of her territory and wandered off into the cool sand. There was always a breeze by the ocean, but tonight some mild alteration in the weather pattern kept it fairly warm. With her hands shoved deep in her pockets and her heart hanging out, Delilah made her way down to where the sea lapped at her feet.

Stopping at the water's edge, she stared out over the tips of the waves where moonlight bounced at every angle. Only for a moment did her mind absorb the beauty of it, enjoying the pleasure of being the lone person on the beach. Then her brain turned back to the dream that pulled her from sleep.

It had been simple, really. Jules hugged her and said good-bye. She walked away to her little car and drove off. Much the same way she had the day the whole family gathered to see her off for her first day of college. But in this dream it had just been the two girls.

Again, Jules' eyes had been blue. In life, her eyes had been a hazel blend of gold and green, just like Tristan's. But in all the dreams she'd had Delilah's shade of blue. Only now, as she stood on the beach, did Delilah get some understanding of that. Although whether it was Jules reaching from beyond her death, or merely her own mind showing her what she'd always known, Delilah was unsure. Finally she saw what she had missed when her little sister had been alive.

Jules had never truly been comfortable in her own skin. As powerful as she was, it had been hard for her to connect with others. Delilah had seen little of it—she'd been too wrapped up in her own teenage life—but the other kids were always a bit afraid of Juliet. And maybe with good cause. Her younger sister never set fire to anything or put a pox on anyone, but she could have. And with very little effort.

Delilah rolled her pants up above her knees and walked just a little further into the ocean, to where the waves washed up to her calves. Memories came flooding back, Jules at the dinner table, upset that she had no friends in LA. Not that she'd had many before they moved. Delilah brushed it off, not understanding. After all, she had no problem making friends—so why would her sister?

But as easy as the craft came to Jules, the rest had not. Only now, years later, did Delilah see. She had been jealous of Juliet's power more times than she could count. Even as an adult she'd harbored those feelings. But they came and went. Mostly she'd been good at seeing what she did have and being content with it.

But Jules had been jealous *of her* for years. There were things her sister said, times she'd commented on trading her power for Delilah's life. Delilah always laughed it off. Apparently her sister hadn't been able to. She'd wanted to be Delilah. She'd wanted the house and the husband, when in her own life Jules hadn't been able to maintain a serious relationship. Looking back, Delilah couldn't count a single time that Juliet managed to hold onto a real boyfriend.

No wonder she'd taken David. He was the focal point of Delilah's 'perfect' life. It was easier to admit, standing there on the beach over a year later, that Delilah rubbed it in a little. She hadn't intended to, but she had Jules involved up to her neck in the wedding planning. She'd talked incessantly about the house they were building, about how they were going to try for a baby. Would Jules like to help decorate the nursery? Her perfect life had once revolved around David, and she always praised her amazing husband for accepting her as she was. Witchcraft and all.

Yes, she had been very good at seeing what she had. And not so good at seeing what the people around her needed.

She'd been that way with David, too. He must have been easy pickings for her powerful little sister. Still, Delilah didn't miss him the way she ached for Juliet. She must not have loved him as much as she thought she did. Looking back, after loving Brandon, she wondered if she'd really loved David at all

—or if she had merely loved the life they shared. At least for a while.

She stood in the ocean for a little bit longer, her thoughts turning to her lost baby. The second one she couldn't even grieve for because it never existed.

Later, when she was getting cold and she needed to go inside, she raised both her hands to the sky, finally offering up a silent apology to the moon, since she could no longer offer one to her sister. Then, stuffing her hands back down into her pockets, she turned and went back to bed.

CHAPTER 38

Brandon drove home feeling restless. He'd been taking this class for three weeks now, but it was just another beginner's witchcraft class. At least he could catalog the things he'd improved in.

No longer bent on revenge, he paid far better attention in class. He now actually did what he was told to do and practiced tiny little spells. This time, it seemed he was getting things right on target. Then again, he wasn't using that cumbersome and possibly erroneous witchcraft Almanac either.

He got better parking spots. Well, everywhere except at the class. There were definitely better witches vying for those spaces. Every time he walked up to the front door, he would pass a space that was wide open, that he hadn't even seen when he'd driven by. That, it seemed, was the art to most witchcraft. Not that you could make a spot appear, the universe just finagled things in your favor. But at the mall, he watched car after car drive by an open space. Bethy would shout to him to take it, and he would just smile, still not telling her about any of it. Even though she could see he was nursing a serious wound.

Still, with Delilah gone, and his magick skills finally

improving, it didn't seem he was any closer to figuring out what he needed than he had been when he started.

He wanted to forget about Delilah, but as it was turning out that was practically impossible to do. Early on he thought about throwing out the books he'd been reading. It was easy to toss the pregnancy book. There was no pregnancy. There was no need for him to read it. But it had been much harder to toss out the witchcraft book. Although he was no longer looking up spells in it, it was still a Wiccan book of days. It told when the full moons were occurring and when the magicks would have the greatest power. When it was best to do protection spells and when to cast for self improvements.

Even before he started the class, Brandon found himself reassembling his altar. He'd used a kitchen knife this time, instead of returning to the store and buying another cheap athame. The kitchen blade worked remarkably well, especially when combined with the knowledge he gained from class.

Brandon was surprised by the simple things that were going right. Investors were frank up front, those who expressed an interest and took up a day of presentations routinely signed on the spot. He and Dan reached their capital level last week and were able to start hiring additional programmers.

Only later did Brandon realize that Delilah often used the kitchen knife he was casting with. Maybe that's why it was working so well. He wondered if she affected everything she touched. If maybe she wasn't aware of what she did.

In the evenings, he read about witches' holidays, the times of feast and prayer from long before the Jews walked the earth. The religion was as complex as any he'd heard of, and nowhere near what he imagined it would be. He always wondered what Delilah was doing when the moon was full or a feast was called for.

His skill still seemed limited, but while he would have liked to talk to the people at Blessed Be, he didn't dare set foot in

Tristan's store. He'd been going to Pan Pipes in Santa Monica every Thursday evening for their 'Beginning Spellwork' class. While he learned a few new neat spells, all it had really gotten him was a couple of dates.

A few *first* dates. The class was mostly female—big surprise there. The only other man in the class was gay. Brandon had been pretty certain about that until Frederick had asked if Brandon would like to go out on a date, then he knew for sure. He wished Frederick were straight, for no other reason than that would take some of the females off him—the only available guy in the class.

Most of his classmates were flighty and a few were downright frightening. One seemed to be convinced she was the main source of energy in the universe. Brandon couldn't figure out how she truly thought that when she was enrolled in a beginner class.

The first night he realized his view of witches was entirely skewed because all he knew was Delilah. This crowd more deserved the general reputation he'd been aware of before meeting a real witch. Most of these people were not real witches. Nor were they on their way.

After seeing a few of the batty women in his class swimming in the deep end without their floaties, a date with Jennifer seemed like a welcome relief. It turned out she was not only sane but a complete skeptic. She was writing her thesis at UCLA and wanted to know why he was in the class. She'd been shocked and appalled when he honestly replied.

"You actually believe there were spells cast on you?"

It had all gone downhill from there. Brandon hadn't been able to even finish his burger. "I'm leaving now. I know what I saw. And I know what happened to me. I'm not a specimen for your thesis."

He'd laid down some money and left her there at the table.

He didn't feel so bad about it. She'd been writing notes furiously even as she begged him to stay.

The next week he'd gone out with Millie, who only seemed sane. She was applying herself to witchcraft to get into Harvard Law. She was desperate to get a scholarship. So she was casting for it.

It seemed to Brandon that if she spent half the time studying as she did working on her spells she would be more likely to get in. Millie was utterly offended at this suggestion, even though he'd put it in the kindest frame he could. Still he gave her another chance and didn't walk out of the date like he had the week before.

That had been an error.

She talked the rest of the evening about the spells she was casting for herself and her friends in lieu of plastic surgery.

Brandon wound up extracting himself from that night, too. About a block away from the restaurant he swore off women all together.

The problem was, he missed Delilah.

In his brain, he'd replayed that last night. He remembered thinking they'd found their common ground and they'd worked everything out. Then, in less than a blink, she'd been accusing him of getting revenge. It was true—he'd done it. And she'd known about it even before she walked in the door.

She'd forgiven him easily, then reneged.

Logically, he was glad to have her out of his life. Delilah Goodman was trouble through and through. First the spells, then the pregnancy, then the fight. Okay, so ultimately the pregnancy had been his fault. But she'd stolen his memories and put that stupid love spell on him.

He still had all that leftover birch bark. Apparently he'd bought himself a lifetime supply. So he checked himself every couple of days. What else was he going to do with a bundle of black birch bark? As promised, the spells slowly faded away.

The smoke swirled and dissipated, no longer clinging to him the way it used to. But something was still wrong.

In a snap decision, he drove past his house and kept going toward LaBrea Avenue. His brain churned the whole time until he pulled up in front of Blessed Be. Parking was fairly clear this late on a Thursday night, and he slid into a spot up front.

Brandon ran up to the front and pulled at the door, only to have it nearly yank his arm out of the socket. Crap. Locked. They were closed. But the light was on.

Cupping his hands around his eyes, and leaning his face against the glass, he tried to see in. The light was on in the back office. He banged on the door.

Nothing.

He banged again. The second time it produced results. Of course it did. He sounded like a crazy man out here trying to get in.

The man came out of the back, pale brown hair cut short and combed. This time Brandon recognized Delilah's brother on sight. But Tristan couldn't see him. He was already making motions and Brandon could hear his voice saying 'we're closed,' but he didn't listen.

When Tristan got up to the door, he quit talking. His expression went flat. His hand twisted the lock and he opened the door only part way, keeping his body in the opening. His greeting was as cool as his face. "Brandon."

"Tristan."

Well great. Were they just going to stand here and have a pissing contest?

Tristan got the words out first. "What do you want?"

Brandon decided to play it nice. "I need your help."

When that didn't bring about the results he wanted, he changed his mind and didn't play it so nice. He shoved his way past Delilah's brother and into the store.

Tristan's eyes narrowed. "With?"

"Delilah." Not that the one word really explained anything.

Tristan just stood there with his arms crossed, waiting. Brandon knew he was the one at a loss. He was facing a witch, a powerful one, in a witchcraft store.

"Your damned sister put a spell on me."

"I'm aware. Apparently I sold you the means for revenge. I won't be doing that again." He didn't move.

"I'm done with her. So don't worry about that." Brandon ran a hand through his hair. "But she needs to be done with me."

"She is."

"No, she isn't!"

Finally, Tristan moved. But only the one eyebrow.

"I've been burning that stupid birch bark. And it doesn't cling anymore."

Tristan interrupted. "Then you're clean."

"But I'm not." He paced a few steps and turned. "She's still fucking with my head. I can feel it."

Calmly—too calmly for Brandon's taste—Tristan grabbed a birch bark stick and eyed Brandon for a moment before he cupped his hand around the end of the stick and blew a flame to life. Brandon had seen that trick before and didn't react. He couldn't tell if his lack of reaction impressed Tristan or not, but he didn't really care. Finally, Tristan waved the smoking stick at Brandon. "There. You're clean. Want to go home now, so I can close my shop?"

"It doesn't show, but she's still messing with me."

Tristan shook his head, for the first time displaying some emotion. Unfortunately, it was pity. "I don't think my sister is—as you so eloquently put it—fucking with your head. Besides, she's a witch. So anything she could do to you would show up here." He waved the still smoldering birch stick as though it were proof.

Again he invited Brandon to leave. "Sorry I can't help." His smile was fake but his hand motioning toward the door was sincere.

Brandon didn't take him up on it. He was only growing more frustrated. His hands clenched at his side. "Then why do I still want her? Why do I miss her so much?"

Tristan's face registered his shock. *Great.* For once, Tristan seemed human. The words registered awe. "You fell in love with her."

"No, I didn't. It was those stupid spells she cast on me." Brandon shook his head, finally ready to leave. This had been a bad idea, coming here. Tristan was no help whatsoever.

But Tristan sighed. "Brandon, sit." He motioned them behind the counter and pulled out a swivel chair.

"I'd rather stand."

"Please." Tristan took his own seat and waited. His hands pressed together and he rested them against his mouth as though looking for words.

Brandon sat.

Tristan took a deep breath, his face changing from the cold older brother to more of a concerned friend. "Delilah was really upset after Juliet and David."

Brandon interrupted. "I know."

"She didn't want a relationship. So, once in a long while, she would pick someone up in a bar and take him home, then cast a 'forget' on him."

Still Brandon waited for something new.

"She never put a love spell on you. She only ever tried to keep you away. She didn't think a relationship would work for her and she didn't want to get hurt. She did nothing to reel you in."

But Tristan was wrong. Brandon shook his head. "Sure she did. Why else would I feel this way?"

"Because you *do* feel that way. There are no spells on you. Anything you feel for Lilah is your own."

Brandon jerked back. "You're serious?"

Tristan nodded. "She only ever pushed you away. Well, she tried."

Was he really in love with her?

Tristan kept talking. "That would explain why the forget spell didn't work. Why you broke it. Oh crap. Delilah's out of town. Out of state, actually."

Brandon nodded. "Why are you telling me this?"

Tristan's head tilted as he took Brandon's measure, for this first time reading him instead of judging. "Because . . ."

He didn't finish, instead, he changed his tack. "You need to tell her."

"Why? What were you going to say?" Brandon was ready to grab the other man and shake some answers out. Had the whole family been this maddening?

After a sigh, Tristan answered. "I think she's in love with you, too. But it isn't my place to tell you that."

Brandon sat back, defeated. "She isn't in love with me."

Tristan raised that damnable eyebrow at him again.

"I cast a love spell on her."

Tristan had the balls to throw back his head and laugh at that. "I think you *tried*, but I don't think you actually *did*. Delilah said you used Tansy. So I think her feelings are her own."

"Yeah, yeah." He wouldn't have ever thought he'd see the day where level-headed Brandon Stewart got teased for a spell gone awry. "But I also did a binding on her. With a white ribbon and all that."

Tristan shook his head. "I don't think you were successful. But I did see some globs on her when we used the birch smoke." He leaned a little farther forward. "I've been trying to figure out why your spells even stuck to Delilah, I mean, she had protections all over her. But I'm beginning to think it's because I always tried to protect her against harm. And, even as mad as you were, you were never really trying to harm her. Still, I think it would be wise for you to take the poppet apart, just to be sure."

Brandon nodded, slowly forming an idea. He was going to go to Delilah and talk to her. For the first time his brain considered the possibility of them together. He liked the idea even more now that he was starting to believe he truly owned the feelings. The problem was Delilah might not feel the same way. He might have done that with the stupid binding spell. "When does she get back?"

"Monday night."

He blinked. He'd expected Tristan to say 'tomorrow' or some number of hours rather than days.

Then Tristan did something totally unexpected. He pulled out his phone and started copying information onto a message slip. He ripped the note from the pad and slid it to Brandon. "She's at Pawley's Island in the Carolinas. There's the hotel and her room number and the main phone line."

Brandon stared at it like it was a snake about to strike him. "Why are you giving me this?"

"Because I'm her big brother. And it's my job to protect her. Even from herself."

He didn't know what to say. Getting the blessing of the big brother was a big deal. He knew that experience from the other side. He stuck out his hand, "Thank you."

Tristan grasped his fingers in a firm handshake. But didn't let go. "If you cheat on her, I'll have to kill you. And it will hurt."

Brandon laughed. "Trust me, that isn't going to happen."

Tristan released his hand. "Then go. Unbind your poppet and have fun at Pawley's Island."

Brandon tipped his head. "You think I'm just going to go hop on a plane?"

"Aren't you?"

He laughed. "Hell, yeah."

~

Delilah sat at the bar with a martini in front of her. She'd made a promise to herself not to cast against anyone again. No more sex followed by 'forget' spells.

But that didn't mean she wouldn't do some of the rest. She was a witch after all.

"I have a booth back there. Sit with me and I'll buy you a drink?" The voice was smooth and Delilah turned, martini stem clutched in her hands.

A young man with a short haircut stood before her. His brown eyes were kind rather than leering and the fingers wrapped around the beer bottle looked like they didn't intend to hurt a fly. He was just what she should go for.

"Oh, thank you, but—"

She caught sight of the olive, twirling on its toothpick.

Clockwise.

Why would it go clockwise? Why would it say 'yes' for this man? She wasn't anywhere near over Brandon yet. If there was one thing she learned on this trip already it was that she likely wouldn't ever be.

The young man watched her decide, his eyes anxious. "Please?"

He was so polite. And he looked to be younger than her. Delilah stalled. She turned slightly away, and set the martini back on the bar. She stilled the olive. "Oh, I don't know."

She tapped the glass with her fingernail. That would do it. The clockwise circle had been a fluke. And when it didn't go the same way, she'd have her answer.

But the liquid sloshed and the olive twirled, and it did go the same way. Clearly clockwise.

That was odd. But who was she to argue with the olive? The olive was just a way to ask a question of the universe, and the universe was always right.

"All right." She smiled and followed him to a booth with a wide view of the ocean out the window.

He said his name was Sam. He said a few more things, but she only nodded a little and didn't listen much. She was having a revelation, even though she wasn't sure why she was having it now. If the universe was always right, then things happened for a reason. That was nothing new to her. She'd cut her teeth on that idea. But she'd had a hard time applying it these past few years. David and Juliet dying, even losing her baby . . . there was some higher purpose to it. There had to have been. Or her whole system of faith was off.

Delilah didn't know what that purpose was, but finally she believed in it again. The last weight of her sister's and husband's deaths lifted off her shoulders. Brandon leaving . . . well, she sure as hell didn't see the purpose in that one yet. But she was where she was supposed to be. Sitting here at this booth talking to Sam, with the people walking by outside the window.

For a moment she watched them run and jump and struggle with the sand, then she leaned forward and began to pay attention to the conversation. Sam was interesting. He'd done a lot; he was on leave from the National Guard. Delilah offered to buy his drink instead, but he laughed and waved her away.

She was on her third martini, several hours later, enjoying her evening with Sam. And maybe that had been the whole point, to not sit around and mope about Brandon. But she realized it had gone dark outside. "Sam, I've had a great time. It's getting late though, and I have to get back to my hotel room and get some sleep."

"Of course you do. I have to check back in tomorrow. Leave is over." He grinned and she couldn't help but smile back.

Until something bumped her hip hard enough to scoot her further into the booth.

She registered the shock on Sam's face first. He was standing to his full height with his fists clenched but held rigidly at his side. He wasn't going to use them, just yet. Delilah had a flash thought that she admired his restraint, when she registered the voice.

"Hey, Lilah, you out picking up men again?"

Brandon! What was he doing here? "Brandon?"

She looked at him in shock, but he only smiled at her. Somehow a real, genuine smile graced his face, and his cheeks nearly formed dimples.

Sam looked back and forth between the two of them. "You know him?"

She nodded. But Brandon spoke first. "Does he know what you are?"

Delilah blinked. And in that moment, Brandon turned to Sam. "Did you know that she's sixty? As in, sixty years old. She's a witch, that's how she keeps her looks."

"Sixty?" Sam squinched his eyes at them.

"Wait—" was the only word she got out.

Brandon was talking to her now. "You're not going to deny that you're a witch are you, baby?"

"No, but—" She practically sputtered it, but *sixty*?

Sam was giving them bizarre looks. "Delilah? Are you okay?"

She didn't get a chance to answer.

Brandon smiled and waved his hand indicating her form. "Of course she's fine. She's amazing for twenty, let alone sixty! Her secret is that she bathes in virgin's blood. It's how she stays so young looking."

Sam looked a little sick to his stomach, but he clearly wondered what was going on. Thing was, Delilah didn't have an answer for him.

Brandon did. He sighed in great theatrics. "And you just would not believe how hard it is to get virgin's blood these days."

Delilah laughed.

Sam asked if she was all right and she could only get out a

few words, "Thank you, Sam."

He nodded at her and pulled out a stack of bills to cover the drinks. Brandon waved him away. A look passed between the two men. Delilah could only decipher it as some weird passing of the baton, where she was the baton. Sam smiled at her as he left.

Brandon leaned toward her. "I just got into town. I got to the hotel and you weren't in your room. So I went out for a walk and I saw you in the window as I went by."

"Why are you here?"

"I was looking for you."

Delilah felt her heart swell. She was sure it showed in her eyes. But, if it did, Brandon ignored it. So she asked her burning question. "How did you find me on the other side of the country? Are you some great witch now? You pulled out a world map and cast a spell to locate me?"

"No. It was very mundane. Tristan gave me the address and your room number."

"He did!" That was as surprising as Brandon showing up here, on the other side of the continent.

"Look, Lilah, I thought you put a spell on me. I was convinced that was why I felt this way. But Tristan said you didn't put any kind of love spell on me. That these feelings were all mine. Was he right?"

"Yes." It fell from between her lips. Her eyes watered. Brandon was here. And he'd been worried that she'd altered his feelings. She leaned in to kiss him.

But he pushed her away.

She frowned at him, but he kept talking. "Lilah, I *did* put a love spell on you. I undid it last night, but there's every possibility that you don't really feel the same way about me."

So that was it. "When did you do it?"

She was pretty sure he was too late to have an effect even if his spell had worked.

"The same night I got the birch bark sticks."

Yes. Too late.

"Brandon, it didn't work." She reached for him.

"How do you know for sure?" He held her hands away, not letting her touch him.

"For the same reason I can't cast a spell to make your eyes green. You can't create what already is. I was in love with you before that."

The concern in his eyes vanished, replaced instantaneously with desire.

This time he let her kiss him. His mouth molded to hers, sparking a heat that was far too great for the little booth they were in. Quickly slapping cash onto the table, he grabbed her hand, pulling her along behind him until they were out under the moonlight, the sand of the beach sinking beneath their feet.

Halfway back to the hotel he stopped and turned her to face him. "Delilah. I love you."

She smiled up at him. "I love you, too."

His eyes searched hers for something more, something less. "That part was all real?"

"All of it."

His expression was serious, his gaze on hers. "Do you think you could keep doing it? That you could love me for the rest of your life?"

"I'm certain."

The moon was out. Brandon was at Pawley's Island with her. And he really loved her. He pressed his forehead to hers, and kissed her lightly. "Marry me?"

She didn't need an olive to figure out the answer. Even when she hadn't understood, this was where she'd been led. She needed to be in that window tonight, so Brandon would find her. So she could be right here. Because the universe was always right.

"Yes."

Thank you for reading! I love romances with real love and believable characters, and I hope you found all that in these pages. I want to fall in love right along with the characters, and I do, while I'm writing it.

About Savannah

I started writing when I was eight--I hand wrote an 80-page novella that I believed to be (adult) romantic suspense. I'm proud to say, I've gotten a lot better since then. I've grown up to be a nerd at heart! I love neuroscience and people watching, and if you look, you'll find some of that in each Savannah Kade book. Most days you'll find me in my office, looking out my window at a handful of the neighbor's cows, or watching my dogs or my cat roam the backyard.

Follow me, find me, ask me questions! I would love to hear from you.

www.SavannahKade.com
Savannah@SavannahKade.com

www.ingramcontent.com/pod-product-compliance
Lightning Source LLC
LaVergne TN
LVHW091023080826
845145LV00002B/337

* 9 7 8 1 9 3 7 9 9 6 3 1 4 *